ASHWATER

MELISSA KOBERLEIN

Parker West Books

Parker West Books
www.parkerwestbooks.com

ISBN- 978-0-9891425-9-5
Parker West Books
ISBN- 0-9891425-9-0

Printed in the United States of America

August 2019

Ashwater comes with a Spotify playlist!

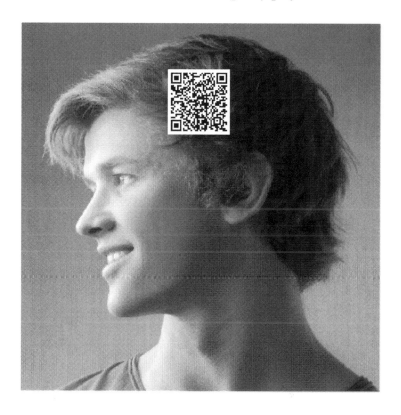

If you'd like to listen to the Ashwater soundtrack, simply scan the QR code with your device and enjoy the music Adam plays for you.

For my inaugural Publishing 101 class—thanks for your dedication to the publishing program at NCC and for creating an incredible writing community. You're my peeps.

PROLOGUE

Bio-Core facility located deep in the Rocky Mountains of the U.S., Present Day

Two men, one dressed in a black suit and the other in a white lab coat, exited the large service elevator. The suited man pushed a large cart as they walked side by side down a barren corridor. Fluorescent lights flickered overhead as the two made their way to the disposal area, where the facility discarded mistakes.

The cart pusher groaned, lowering his body and grip to gain more leverage. "Damn, these things are heavy."

His companion nodded, his eyes focused forward.

"What was wrong with this one?"

The man turned toward the cart-pusher and tapped two fingers to his temple.

"Oh, not much going on up there, huh?"

"Too much, actually."

He shrugged and heaved the cart forward. "You're the boss."

They reached the end of the hallway and entered a security

code to gain access to the double-doored room. Once inside, they deposited the cart next to another one in a long line of carts on a large conveyer belt. The disposal process was entirely automated. At the other end was a programmed door that opened and closed every minute or so, accepting the next cart on the belt.

After they left, something inside the cart stirred. A hand reached over the side. The man in the white lab coat was correct. Something was going on inside his head, and right now, it was telling him to *run*.

PART I

JACK'S ARCADE

Adam

Adam felt safe for the first time in his life. For an android posing as a human, it was a new concept.

He stretched his arms above his head and yawned. He slept like humans did, which made him wonder what percentage of his physical makeup was flesh. Since he also had a navel, he assumed quite a bit.

Adam switched on the power to the old-school arcade joint. Fluorescent lights flickered and steadied above his head. Games whirred to life in a concerto of tones, beeps, dings, and pings. There were about fifty or so cabinet, coin-op games lined up in rows and circles creating a labyrinth of amusements. At the back-right corner were pinball machines and interactive dance and musical instrument games. The walls were electric blue, and the black carpet had a red-and-blue geometric spider-web design. To his left was a snack bar, complete with popcorn machine, hotdog roller, and soft pretzel case.

He spied a glass carafe sitting on top of a counter next to a small sink. He blinked his right eye and a red laser shot from his eye to the bottom of the glass container, heating the water within. Tiny bubbles conjured from the heat burst the surface. As quickly as the laser emerged, so too did it retreat.

With a Styrofoam cup of instant coffee in hand, Adam used his built-in Bluetooth to turn on the jukebox he'd redesigned to play his choices on demand while still accepting coins from customers. It only played eighties' music, and his central processing unit lit up, sending tiny rushes of pleasure through his limbs. Music and dancing was his favorite part about being alive. While he enjoyed many different genres of music, eighties was his first love. His feet tapped to the rhythm of "Everybody Wants to Rule the World" by Tears for Fears as his sandy blond hair swooshed in front of his eyes, hindering his vision.

The sound of the front door opening and closing directed his attention to the front of the arcade, where an electric sign hung above the doors lit in neon blue—*Jack's*. Part of the *s* was no longer lit. Adam could fix the issues, but really, Jack should simply upgrade the sign for some new LED tech.

A tiny woman with short, hot pink hair, lips to match, wearing a short tube skirt and a tank top with four-inch plat-form shoes sashayed over to him. With the added height, she was still at least six inches shorter than him.

"Hey, Adam. How ya doin'?" Her lips smacked from the chewing gum in her mouth. She smelled like mint and flowers.

Adam smiled. He liked Daisy. She managed the snack bar. She was a native of Ashwater and started dating Jack almost ten years ago. She didn't ask too many questions and was always nice to him. And more to the point, she fed him. He didn't know much about what his insides looked like, but he ate like every other human he knew and hunger happened to him just like anyone else.

She was also the first person he didn't want to kill. He didn't know why, but he had a built-in killer defense mechanism that revved up anytime someone detected his true nature. Each time someone suspected that he wasn't human, warnings sounded in his head, and he was given options on how to best dispose of the person. Since he was new to the human population, it happened often. Although, his operating system was relatively new, and he hoped that he'd gain more control with time.

"I'm good. You look nice."

Daisy leaned in and kissed him, and he felt the sticky imprint of her pink lips on his cheek.

"Thanks, Shug. You're the best." She walked toward the snack bar and asked over her shoulder, "You hungry?"

He patted his perfectly formed middle. "Always."

"Well, you get to work opening this dinosaur up, and I'll fix you a snack."

"Thanks," he said.

Her idea of a snack was fine with him. She liked to get creative with the food she served at the snack bar. Last time, she cut up some hot dogs and soft pretzels and pumped some orange cheese sauce all over the both. She called it pretzel dog nachos. Adam computed the nutritional and caloric intake and concluded that the food she served him wasn't all that nutritious, but it sure tasted good.

Adam turned back and assessed his work for the day. The *Ms. Pac-Man* game was down, and *Dragon's Lair* was too. Kids loved *Dragon's Lair*. He didn't get it, since the game was overly focused on quick time events. After so many losses by players, the controls took a beating. Some of the pinball machines needed parts too.

He went to the register near the front of the store and prepared for opening. It was Saturday, so most kids were still sleeping. But in a town that offered little in the way of indoor entertainment, kids would stream in after twelve.

The front door blasted open, nearly shattering the glass as it ricocheted off the wall next to it. A man with dark shaggy hair, acid-washed jeans, and a Def Leppard T-shirt stood in the doorway. He reeked of something pungent and spicy, and his eyes were barely slits.

Jack.

Jack White, owner of the arcade, had lived in Ashwater his whole life, and while he aged as normal humans do, he was stuck in his favorite decade—the eighties. He had a passion for classic arcade games and eighties music. Daisy said it was "charming."

Jack raised his hands as if commanding a congregation at church. "If you please, maestro."

His eyes met Adam's in recognition. Adam nodded at the jukebox, using his internal Bluetooth. Jack didn't seem to care how Adam could play songs to his choosing, only that he could. The familiar riff of "Sweet Child of Mine" sounded in Adam's ultra-sensitive ears.

Jack swayed his hips to the music, tilting his head back, as he sauntered further into the arcade toward the cash register.

"It's going to be a good day," he said, matter-of-fact. He stopped, mid-sway and added, as if the universe was speaking to him directly, "I can feel it."

Adam smirked. Jack couldn't possibly predict the future. But if he thought so, Adam wasn't going to argue the point. He'd already wanted to kill Jack on seven separate occasions. That would be messy and leave him to find a new home. Besides, Adam had gotten used to him. Or, at least, as much as an android could get used to something. Not to mention, Jack was his boss and landlord.

He had done Adam a solid by allowing him to move into the apartment in the back of the arcade. When Adam stumbled into town, he was drawn to the mechanical chimes and whirs from the games and the notes floating into the air from the old jukebox that played eighties' music. Jack was working on a broken *Joust* game without much luck. Adam identified the problem and offered his assistance. After witnessing Adam's skills for video game repair, a bond formed between them instantly. Jack called their meeting kismet. After learning that Adam didn't have a home, Jack struck a bargain with him —room and board in return for Adam maintaining the games in the arcade.

Speaking of which, Adam had work to do.

"Hey, kid, come here." Jack pressed some keys on the cash register, awakening the ancient metal beast.

"Yes, sir?" He approached Jack, putting his hands on the counter between them.

Jack opened the register drawer and pulled out two fifty-dollar bills. He placed them in Adam's hand. "The part for your dancing game is in. It's at the post office, C.O.D."

Adam's eyes widened, squeezing the bills in his hand. Jack had entrusted him with some old scrapped dance games for parts and gave him free rein to create something new. Adam couldn't wait to finish the game, and the part he was going to pick up was the last he was waiting for. He grinned at Jack, excitement brimming from somewhere deep inside.

"Thanks, Jack. I won't be long," Adam replied, walking swiftly toward the door. *Ms. Pac-Man* would have to wait.

His first encounter with an old *Dance Dance* game awakened something in him that he couldn't quite define. He wanted more. So he accessed as many videos and movies as he could about dancing. He cast them on his wall with his eye projection tool and watched thousands upon thousands of human bodies moving in sync to booming rhythms and styles. He joined them on the dance floor. When his body was in motion, Adam felt something, something he later deciphered as emotion. From there on out, he was hooked.

Now, he had a chance to create his own small club, where the beats could rock his body for real. But Jack did have one condition—Adam could only play eighties' music on the system. Adam didn't mind. In fact, since he'd joined humanity, he had grown quite fond of that decade's music.

"Hey, wait a minute. I have a package to go out too." Jack lifted a poorly wrapped brown box with an address written on the side in black Sharpie. "You should have enough for both."

"Yes, sir." Adam went back to the counter and picked up the package. Remembering Daisy was making food for him, he yelled, "I'll be back in less than thirty minutes, Daisy."

She nodded. "No worries, baby."

Adam exhaled. He was still learning about the role of time in human interactions. Certain humans were more concerned about it than others.

"I love that woman." Jack glanced back at Daisy then turned back to Adam and frowned. "You've got to loosen up. No need to stress. It's just time, man."

"Yes, sir." Adam did his best to imitate Jack and relax his shoulders.

"Just Jack, Adam." Jack nodded, smirking. "Just Jack."

Adam's protocol warned him against a first name basis with a superior. That would be out of line. He obviously still had much to learn. "Jack, sir."

Jack groaned and waved at him dismissively. "Laters."

Adam breathed in fresh, mountain air and the smell of pine as he emerged from the darkened arcade to a bright Main Street, the August sun warming his skin. The town of Ashwater only had one streetlight on the main strip that ran through the center of town, and it was fifty feet from the arcade.

Not many people visited Ashwater unless it was ski season, and that suited Adam fine. But lots of wealthy folks retired to this area—some old and some young. They lived on the mountainside that towered over the town. The rest of the town's inhabitants lived closer to the earth, grounded by their means. With spring in his step, he made his way down the sidewalk past a few stores including Jameson Pharmacy, Tully's Gift Shop, Dalia's boutique clothing store, and Mac's Hardware Store. At the end of the row was the only post office within fifty miles.

Adam reached for the door handle to enter the post office and stopped, his breath catching. He sensed eyes on him from across the street. The telltale anxious strain seized his body, a prickling reaching from the tips of his toes to the top of his head. His heart pounded, his cheeks grew warm, and his hands felt clammy. Warning lights flashed before his eyes.

Don't kill. Don't kill. He was new to humanity, and his threat threshold was still difficult to control.

Slowly, he turned around to face the source of his concern.

Three boys were outside Dixon's Diner across the street. One, the largest and most muscular of the three, leaned against a lamp post, observing Adam. The other two, much smaller and leaner, sat on a bench talking to each other.

"Hey, Adam," yelled the boy standing.

Adam sighed in relief as his warning system quieted. He smiled as best he could and waved.

He'd learned about his approximate age from these boys, who'd assumed Adam was their peer when first meeting him at the arcade. That was good enough for Adam, who was desperately trying to fit into the town of Ashwater. When he'd arrived in town in June, he tried to minimize interactions with others besides Jack and Daisy. But working in a small-town arcade made that difficult, and they were dedicated gamers.

Together, all three boys slowly walked across the street toward him. Gage, the biggest of the three, lived atop the mountain in a beautiful home that overlooked the town. His light brown hair was cut short and gelled to perfection on top. Gage had a way of looking at Adam like he could see past the human exterior into the man-made core. He was the person Adam struggled the most with not to hurt.

Luke and Derrick, the two shorter boys, were twins. Their parents owned the diner, and Daisy was their aunt. The twins' appearances, dark brown hair and eyes, was where their similarities ended. Luke, the older of the two, was into sports. Derrick lived for science and technology. It was something he and Adam shared. Adam also liked the discount they gave him at their diner. They were all entering their senior year at Ashwater High, the small high school situated at the edge of town.

Be cool. Act human.

"Oh, hey," Adam said, his voice barely audible.

Luke and Derrick beamed at Adam, who stood a good six inches taller than them.

"What's up, bro?" Luke asked, clasping Adam's hand in a ritualistic handshake that Adam was still trying to understand.

Adam clenched back, causing Luke to wince.

"Yo, stop."

Too rough.

"Sorry." Adam dropped his hand.

"I have to get you on the team this year." Luke shook out his hand even though Adam didn't break any blood vessels or bones.

"I think I'll just stick with going to school."

Luke tapped Derrick on the chest. "Back me up. He'd be a beast on the field, right?"

Derrick nodded, pursing his lips in assessment. "I can't deny that. Probably a lineman, right?"

Gage interceded, staring at Adam in that way that made him uncomfortable. "Guys, I don't think he's interested."

On this one occasion, Adam was grateful for Gage's observant nature.

Changing the subject, Gage asked, "So what are you up to?"

Adam remembered his purpose, his smile returning. "I'm picking up a part for a game I'm working on."

This piqued the boys' interest, their eyes widening. True to form for committed gamers.

Derrick queried first, "What kind of a game? Did Jack finally get something new in?"

"Well, no, but I'm refurbishing a dance game in the back

room. It should be ready next week sometime. You guys can be the ones to test it out if you're interested."

They glanced at each other as if to say, *Who doesn't like testing out new video games?*

"Nice. How do you play?" Gage asked.

"You dance."

Luke and Gage scratched their stubble-forming chins, while Derrick's eyes grew large. Derrick loved music. He had a knack for mixing tracks too. He might be the perfect person to team up with to update some of the music.

"Like *Dance Spot* or something?" Derrick asked.

"Yes but better. It's probably best to wait until it's finished."

"I'd be willing to give it a try," Gage said.

"Is it competitive?" Luke shifted from side to side, his face scrunched up.

"Yeah."

Luke nodded, eyebrows raised with renewed interest.

Adam was sure they would have fun, except for one small detail, which he better share now. "There is this one thing though. The only way Jack let me do this was if I promised to stay in the motif of the arcade."

He glanced at the sidewalk. The twins did that a lot when they had to share something that made them uncomfortable. He hoped he was having the same impact. Gestures came naturally to people and were largely unconscious. This was not always a benefit because nonverbal behavior gave away the truth. It was a unique and beautiful quality of humanity. He, on the other hand, had to practice his actions to blend in.

The boys glanced at each other, smirking.

Gage spoke for the three. "Eighties' music only?"

"Yes," Adam replied, looking back.

Gage studied him. "That's tight. But, please, for the love of God, have some rock on there. Some Guns, Def Leppard, Van Halen…"

"But don't leave off the alternative stuff. Depeche Mode, Tears for Fears, New Order," Derrick added.

Luke shrugged. "I don't care what kind of music it is so long as I can wipe the floor with this guy."

Then he grabbed his brother around the neck and pulled him into a headlock, rubbing his knuckles vehemently across his dark head.

"Hey," Derrick said, pushing him away.

"All right, guys, I think we'd better let Adam get back to it. We'll probably stop by the arcade later this afternoon," Gage said.

Adam nodded. "Cool. See you later."

He was still working on teen jargon. *Cool* sounded great coming out of Gage's mouth, but Adam's inflection was still slightly off. He turned, mouthing the word over and over as he entered the post office. The more he practiced, the better he sounded. He slammed into something—or rather, someone—smack dab, chest-to-chest.

Adam dropped the package and backed up as a huge man with buzzed graying hair and biceps, the size of Adam's head, fell to the floor. Warnings resounded in his head and before his eyes.

Oh shit. He inhaled sharply and quieted the alarms as best he could.

"I'm sorry, sir." He reached out his hand to the man now studying him from the ground in disbelief.

The man looked shocked but smiled as he accepted the

sincerity on Adam's face. Well, at least that's what vibe Adam hoped he was putting out.

He took Adam's hand and pulled himself off the floor. "You're quite the strong young man, aren't you?"

"Clumsy too, obviously. Again, I'm very sorry."

The man studied Adam as if deciding what to do next. To make matters worse, he wore a tan uniform with a metal, star-shaped badge with the word "sheriff" inscribed, and he had a sidearm.

That was all it took to push Adam's nerves over the edge, and the tremors in his left hand started again as the threat warnings rose louder in his head once again.

Stop it. Get yourself under control.

Thinking fast, he put his shaking hand behind his back and ran his other hand through his hair.

After what felt like an eternity, the man finally replied, "I don't think I've seen you before. Are you visiting Ashwater? Staying nearby?"

"Yes—I mean no." Adam shifted his feet nervously.

The man stared, confused.

Adam tried his best to smile. "What I meant to say is, no, I'm not visiting. I work at the arcade. In fact—"

He glanced at the package he was meant to mail. A blue plastic tube with a metal stem protruding from one side lay on the floor next to a frail, sad brown box. Adam recognized what it was at the same time as the man in front of him did. Jack had them secretly scattered all over the arcade.

The man's eyes grew larger. "Is that a bong, son?"

Adam reached with shaky hands, scooped up the smoking device, and pushed it back into the box. He had a singular thought in his head—*kill him.*

He took a deep, cleansing breath. *Get control. He's not a threat. He's not a threat. Don't blow your cover.* "I'm mailing this for my boss. It's not mine."

The man narrowed his eyes in disbelief, eyeing Adam up and down. "How old are you?"

"I'm eighteen, sir. Just turned." Adam clenched the package in his shaking hands, his nails biting into the tender flesh of the already fragile cardboard. He had no way of knowing exactly how old he truly was, but he was perfectly aware of the laws for minors.

"I see. Perhaps watch where you're going?"

"Yes, sir, I will. Sorry again." Adam smiled as best he could and averted his eyes. With that, he moved past the man and headed toward the counter.

He sensed the man leave, but once he was outside, the man's gaze bored into his back. Adam held his breath, waiting for the man to move along. He fought against his killer instinct to discard of the man permanently even though images of the act continued to surface in his mind.

But he wouldn't let that part of him win. *He* was in control now, not them. His only hope for survival counted on him blending in with humans. He groaned inwardly.

This was *not* blending in.

2

SWEET DREAMS

Evie

Evie stared at the front of the old arcade on Main Street, her head tilted to the side, staring at the poorly lit neon sign that read Jack's. The apostrophe and *s* were the weakest.

Her hand twitched for a pencil. Ever since she moved here three years ago, she'd been sketching up a storm. Ashwater felt like home, and she couldn't imagine leaving. She swallowed hard. Once her parents found out that she wasn't planning on applying to college, shit would hit the fan and not in a good, artsy way.

She reached into her pocket, pulled out some iridescent lip gloss, and slid the slick wand around her lips once then twice for good measure. She turned to her best friend, Mazy, and rubbed her lips together, making a popping sound at the end. "How do I look?"

Mazy smiled at Evie, who was much shorter than her since her Doc Marten boots didn't add anything to her small stature.

"Like a rock star only you can pull off. What about me?" She wore a hint of mascara and light pink lipstick, the opposite of Evie's darkly lined eyes.

"Sketchable." Evie had drawn Mazy many times. She was an excellent subject—stayed still and her expressions were always thoughtful. She'd given Mazy her best work as a present for her seventeenth birthday.

"Great. Let's go." Mazy put her arm around Evie and steered her toward the arcade's entrance.

Evie pursed her lips at the dingy darkened glass door. It was in serious need of cleaning. As soon as she entered the building, her jaw dropped.

"Oh, shit, this place is ancient," she said.

They had been transported back to the eighties' era of arcades. Everything from the dated carpet to the jukebox playing a Billy Idol song to the smell of stale soft pretzels and Cheez Whiz hit her all at once. The place was dated and grungy. No wonder she never came in here. She didn't care much for video games, so why would she? She turned back around to look at the sign on the door to make sure that they were open for business.

"Hey, girls, welcome to Jack's," a squeaky voice said from a distance.

They looked around, trying to locate the owner of the voice. Walking toward them from the back of the arcade was a small woman with cotton candy-colored hair and the tallest platform shoes she'd ever seen. Evie liked her immediately.

Mazy beamed. "Hi, Daisy. We're supposed to meet some kids from school here."

The woman returned her smile, her hot pink mouth spreading across her small-featured face, a matching wad of pink bubble gum pinned between her upper teeth and cheek peeking out. She reminded Evie of a fairy—fun to sketch.

"Hi, Mazy, how are ya, hon?" She turned her attention to Evie.

"I don't think I've seen you in here before, but you look familiar. What's your name?"

Evie reached for Daisy's slender, hot pink manicured hand. "I'm Evelyn Grayson, but everyone calls me Evie. Your hair is amazing."

Daisy took her hand. "Well, thank you. You're sweet. So that means you're Sheriff Grayson's daughter?"

Evie nodded, gaze darting from Daisy to the neon lights depicted on the black carpeted floor. Being the sheriff's daughter sometimes felt like a dark cloud hanging over her head. It made people uncomfortable.

She pulled Evie closer and whispered, "Don't worry, I won't hold that against you."

Evie met Daisy's eyes and smiled. She liked her even more now.

"Well, you're as pretty as can be too, aren't you? You must get that from your mom. She runs that gallery down the street, right?" Daisy, still holding Evie's hand, spun her around. "Wow! Love your look, especially those boots. Did you paint them yourself?"

Evie looked at her flower-covered Docs and smiled shyly. "Thanks. I sure did."

Daisy let go of her hand. "Well, they're brilliant. Gage and my nephews are in the back with our newest employee, Adam. He's working on a new game, ya know."

Mazy glanced at Evie and raised her eyebrows. "Cool."

Evie was not what one would call a gamer, but she could hold her own if need be. Mazy, on the other hand—uh-uh.

Daisy turned toward the back of the arcade and yelled, "Boys, your girls are here."

She wasn't anyone's girl. "No, Daisy, I'm not—"

The jukebox changed mid-song to the synthesizing tune of, "Sweet Dreams (Are Made of This)" by Eurythmics.

Evie looked past Daisy as Gage, the Dixon twins, and another tall boy emerged from a hallway. She locked eyes with the boy she didn't recognize. Her lips parted as the better part of her body's temperature rose a few degrees.

She'd heard about moments like this, or maybe she had watched too many romantic comedies.

She felt an instant pull toward him, like a magnet causing every tiny hair on her body to stand on end. Her second thought after she reminded herself how to breath was that he was stupid hot. She arched her eyebrow as her hand itched for a pencil and sketchbook. He'd look gorgeous pinned up on her bedroom wall where she displayed all her work. She had the perfect place for him too.

Sweet dreams, indeed.

Gage smiled. "Hey."

Evie and Mazy walked over to the group of boys. Gage reached for Mazy, kissing her lightly on the lips. Gage and Mazy started dating that summer. They made a perfect couple—the richest boy in town dating the richest girl in town. Made sense.

New Boy continued to stare at Evie, his jaw slack and his light blue eyes unwavering. Evie tugged on her ponytail and glanced away. But each time she looked back at him, he watched her.

The moment had passed, hadn't it?

Evie cleared her throat and shifted from side to side nervously. This was bordering on weird.

Gage noticed and came to her rescue. "Hey, Adam."

"Oh, sorry." Adam looked down. But as soon as his eyes met Evie's a second time, he became entranced once again.

Evie squirmed some more, trying to look anywhere but at Adam. *Please, stop. Please?*

Gage and the twins glanced at Adam and laughed at his odd behavior.

Luke shook his shoulder. "This is Evie, Mazy's friend."

Evie peered at him as he moved forward. The closer he got, the warmer her cheeks felt.

God, you would be incredible to sketch. She made notes of his facial features so that she could draw something later from memory. Sweeping, dirty blond hair, thick, dark eyebrows framing almond-shaped baby blues, and light pink lips that seemed to pout without trying.

Then he opened his mouth.

"Here. For your eyes." He held out a small pack of tissues for her to take.

"Excuse me?"

"You have dark smudges under your eyes." He pulled out a tissue as if he was going to take care of the problem for her. Pointing, he said, "Just there."

A record scratching noise in Evie's head cut through the music and dizzying euphoria. Was he making fun of her makeup?

He reached toward her face with a tissue-wrapped finger.

Oh my God, he is. Evie's mouth formed an O as she narrowed her eyes at him. She batted his hand away, sending the tissue to the floor. "Are you freakin' kidding me?" She glanced at Mazy. "I'm outta here."

Mazy stared at Gage, who was still cringing from the awkward exchange. "I think we're going to go."

Gage nodded that he understood.

You think? Leave it to Mazy to be nice. Evie stared at Mazy and held up her hands.

"I'm coming." Mazy reciprocated Evie's disturbed gaze and sidestepped Adam but gave him a death stare before joining Evie.

Adam stood still, his head tilted slightly to the side, staring at Evie.

Evie shook her head in disgust and turned toward the door. Unbelievable. What a weirdo.

Before they made it to the door, the jukebox changed again, mid-song—to the opening lines of Bon Jovi's "You Give Love a Bad Name."

Evie stopped dead in her tracks and glanced at Mazy, who also came to a halt.

"Really?" Evie whispered.

Mazy shrugged her shoulders. "Coincidence?"

Evie turned back toward Adam, who hadn't moved an inch, and narrowed her eyes. There was something really strange about this place and that guy. She didn't know what it was about him, but he better keep his distance.

Adam

"I don't understand," Adam said, staring blankly at the door to the arcade.

Hadn't he nailed that exchange? Wasn't that the correct

protocol? He'd researched this extensively. When someone has tissue on the bottom of their shoe, you tell them. If someone's clothing isn't fastened correctly, point it out. The girl had dark smudges under her eyes. He simply offered her a tissue. He didn't want her to be embarrassed.

Next to him, Gage, Derick, and Luke all stared at him.

Finally, Derrick said, "Can you believe the jukebox changed to that song as they were leaving? It was like karma."

Luke nodded. "I know. So crazy."

The music was not karma. But Adam's internal Bluetooth was acting in ways he didn't fully understand. "She left."

Gage nodded. "Yeah, and she pretty much hates you now."

Adam eyed Gage. He wasn't exactly skilled in human conversation yet, but he was trying his best. He liked the look of that girl. She was different, almost ultra-human. Her eyes— she looked at him in a way that made his insides stir. He liked it.

"What do you mean? What did I do?" Adam asked.

Luke chimed in, "You made fun of her makeup. It's like the worst thing you could say to a girl."

Derrick added, "Or her clothes. That's off limits too."

Adam pushed his hand through his hair. Makeup? Those dark lines under her eyes were there on purpose? He filed that important piece of information. "Are all girls this complicated?"

The three other boys all exchanged glances with one another.

Lucky for them, Daisy approached. "What happened to the girls?"

"They left. Adam made fun of Evie," Luke said to his aunt.

Daisy's gaze honed in on Adam, her jaw dropping a hair. "Explain."

Adam shoved his hands in his jeans pockets. What was he supposed to say? He thought he was being helpful? No, Daisy wouldn't understand that. It would come across as odd.

So, instead, he lied, "She had too much makeup on."

"You don't get to decide that. No, no, no." Daisy pointed at Adam and waved her finger back and forth. "Adam, I swear, you must have grown up alone on a deserted island. Never, ever, make fun of a person's appearance. I don't care who it is. There are some things that you need to keep to yourself. Do ya hear me? You could do serious damage to a person's psyche."

Adam's shoulders dropped as he stared at the floor. He hated disappointing Daisy. She was his favorite human. She was partly right too. He did 'grow' in isolation. Sure, he was supplied with some basic programming about the world, but he hadn't lasted long enough to get any in-depth social skills. He was thrown in the trash long before he had a real chance.

He'd insulted Evie, and Daisy was upset with him. He glanced around. His new friends also avoided his eyes. Well, this was the opposite of fitting in, and he needed to make things right.

"I'm sorry," he said. "I promise that I will apologize to her."

Daisy sighed and put her small arm around his large frame. "Well, that's a good start. Sugar, I know you've had a rough go of it. So we'll work on your lady skills, okay? Let's forget about it for now. Jack said he's got some stuff for you to work on."

Adam leaned into Daisy as much as a normal human boy would so as not to hurt her. This was what compassion felt like. He liked it. He didn't have a mother, but if he had, he would want her to be like Daisy.

"Thanks," he said.

"Sure thing."

He turned to the boys. "If you see her before I do, tell her I want to apologize."

Gage nodded. "Will do."

3

GALLERY

Evie

E vie shuffled into her mom's gallery. She slung her backpack behind one of the desks. "Mom?"

Artwork hung on white walls around the small shop. A new shipment of paintings had arrived last week—mostly abstract stuff on canvas. At the back were a counter and two desks behind it. A passageway between the two desks led to the back where Evie's mom did most of her work.

"I'm back here. Give me a sec. I'm almost done." Her mother's voice was melodic, accentuating how much she loved her job and this gallery. She sold new art and was also a talented art restorer. People from all over the world sent her projects. That was part of the allure of moving to Ashwater. She could set up shop wherever she wanted. Truth be told, her mom preferred the cozy town just as much as Evie did.

"'Kay." Evie usually hung out in the front of the gallery to help customers when they came in. Most were people that bought vacation homes and needed art to decorate.

She relaxed into a high chair tucked behind the front counter and swiveled from side to side.

The front door opened, causing the hanging bells to jingle, and Sloan Simms walked in. "What's shakin', Evie?"

Evie liked Sloan, but she was by far the most intimidating girl she'd ever met. She didn't seem to have a filter for politeness—she said whatever she felt like. Evie didn't mind so much, but it drove Mazy crazy on a regular basis.

"Not much," Evie replied. "How are you?"

Sloan sidled up to the counter and spread her upper body on top of it, gripping the edge in front of Evie. "Just got back into town from visiting my aunt in California."

"That's cool."

"So..." Sloan's slanted doe eyes met Evie's, waiting for her to take the bait.

Evie leaned back in her chair and tightened her high ponytail. "Yes?"

Sucker.

Sloan massaged the top of the counter with long slender fingers seductively. "Luke tells me there's a new guy in town, Adam. Is he cute?"

Evie rolled her eyes, recalling the encounter from the other day. "I didn't really notice because when he opened his mouth, some bullshit came out."

"I heard you two had a weird first meeting." Sloan laughed.

"You could say that." Evie arched her eyebrow.

Before Sloan could reply, Evie's mom came out from the back room.

"Hi honey," she said, putting her hand on Evie's back. "Sloan."

"Hi, Serena." Sloan stood. Of course, she referred to everyone by their first name. She got away with it too. Even Evie's dad, the sheriff, didn't mind. "The new stuff looks great."

"Thanks, I'm happy with it. How's business at your parents?" Serena smiled, her green eyes striking against her creamy skin. She wore her hair in a messy bun at the nape of her neck. Evie shared her mother's features. It had been the longstanding family joke that Mac Grayson wasn't her biological father, but Evie knew better. While her appearance was all her mom, her edgy, stubborn personality came straight from her dad.

Sloan groaned and stretched like a cat in the morning. "It's good. I wish I could cut out of school to help out more."

"Well, school is certainly important. One last year, and you'll be free to do as you choose, right?" Serena asked.

"I guess." Sloan shrugged.

"So what brings you in here? Just visiting Evie?"

Sloan's devilish grin returned. "Yeah. Did Evie tell you about the new hottie in town? They've got all kinds of chemistry, from what I hear."

Hottie? Chemistry? Obnoxious, much? Fire reached Evie's cheeks as she kicked the underside of the counter with a Doc Marten thud. "WTF, Sloan!"

"Evie." Her mom's gaze bored into hers like lasers trained on their target. She was a free spirit and always allowed Evie to speak her mind, but rudeness wasn't tolerated.

Her mom's voice cut through her ire like a knife. She was being rude. Evie opened her mouth to say as much.

But Sloan beat her to the punch. "Hey, Evie, I'm sorry. I was joking around. I swear."

"No, I'm sorry. I'm really on edge lately." Evie sighed. She was still struggling with how to talk to her parents about not going to college. Time was running out, and her nerves were frayed.

Evie felt her mom's watchful eyes on her. *Not now.*

Sloan nodded. "Heard."

"Mom, I'm going to hang out with Mazy at the library for a while. See ya, Sloan." Evie got down from the chair and retrieved her backpack.

She opened the store's door as her mom said, "Say hi to Mazy for me."

Sloan added, "Me too."

Evie waved her hand in the air without turning back around.

***

Evie liked that her best friend worked at the public library. It was the oldest building in the small town, set back from the other buildings on Main Street. The quiet spots in the stacks were a great place for Evie to hide out and sketch. She hiked her backpack higher on her shoulder and entered the large doors that led into a small lobby, with the two-story library beyond.

Once inside, she spotted Mazy straight away and smiled.

Her best friend was typing on a computer at the circulation desk at the center of the large, tall room with a contented grin, her short blond hair tucked neatly behind her ears.

The circulation desk was in the shape of a square with cream-and-dark-gray swirling marble counters around the perimeter. At one end, there was a cut-out for people to duck under for access to the interior. Evie glanced at the high ceiling, which was framed with ornate molding abutting the walls to the ceiling, and fluorescent light panels alternated with ceiling tiles.

She walked over to Mazy and leaned on the counter. "Hey."

"One sec…" Mazy clicked the mouse a few times—she loved books like Evie loved to sketch—and turned to Evie. "Hey, what are you up to?"

Evie shrugged her shoulders. "Not much. I just came from my mom's shop where Sloan basically accosted me."

Mazy groaned and rolled her eyes. "Of course she did. What did she say?"

"Just some stuff about Adam."

Knowing Evie, sometimes better than she knew herself, Mazy added, "And you?"

Nailed it. "Yup."

Mazy moistened her lips and propped her forearms on the marble countertop. "And how are we feeling about that?"

Evie shrugged. "It doesn't matter. I came to chill out. Do you want to go eat when you're done?"

"I can't. My parents' anniversary is today. Dad likes to make Mom a special dinner, which means I'm helping."

Mrs. Gardner, the head librarian, tossed open the front door and rushed into the library. She strode over to the circulation desk in a tizzy, her gray hair wild and in disarray, her glasses falling too far down on her nose.

"Oh my gosh, Mrs. Gardner, are you okay?" Evie asked.

Mrs. Gardner flashed the girls a glance, her eyes widening as if just now realizing they were there.

"I—well, no, I'm afraid I'm not." She covered her mouth, her eyes glassy.

Mazy placed her hand on the older woman's arm. "What's happened?"

"It's that time of year, and no matter how much I try to keep busy, I still miss her." Mrs. Gardner paused, glancing between the two girls as if deciding about whether she should share any more.

"It's going to be okay." Mazy smiled at Mrs. Gardner and glanced at Evie knowingly.

Evie nodded and mouthed, *Oh.*

Sally Gardner was born in Ashwater eighty-some years ago along with her sister, Madeline. Sally was well-known in the town but not because of her cataloging skills. Although, according to Mazy, they *were* something to behold. No, she was famous because her sister disappeared forty years ago and was never seen or heard from again. Madeline Gardner was the first disappearance that started the alien abduction rumors. A few more followed, including Gage Strickland's mom, which was a touchy subject.

"I still miss her so much, even after all this time." A single tear streamed down the woman's crepe-lined cheeks, her steely gray eyes shimmering like two small pools.

Mazy drew the head librarian into her arms in the warm way that only Mazy could. "Oh, Mrs. Gardner, I'm sorry."

Mrs. Gardner hugged her back. The two were close, given their same affinity for books.

"Thank you, dear." Mrs. Gardner let go of Mazy and wiped her eyes with a tissue she pulled from the front pocket of her cardigan. She shook her head slightly as she attempted to tuck the memories of her sister away again. She glanced at

Evie, regaining her faculties. "I'm sorry, Evie. I'm a mess right now. How are you doing, honey?"

Right there with ya, Mrs. G. My wall is covered with drawings of a boy who insulted me, but I can't seem to get him out of my head.

Evie pressed her lips together and forced a closed-lip smile. "I'm okay, Mrs. G."

Mrs. Gardner smiled, the remnants of her anguish dissipating from her eyes and fine, wrinkled skin. "Well, that's good to hear. You're such a pretty one." She reached into her other cardigan pocket and pulled out another folded, crinkly tissue. "But you've got some smudges…"

OMFG. This can't be happening again. It's a smoky eye. Her cheeks heated as her mind searched for words.

Fortunately, Mazy came to her rescue, "Oh, Mrs. Gardener, that's a style now." She ducked under the counter to join Evie on the other side. "We've got to go. Will you be all right?"

"Hmm." Mrs. Gardner looked between them with her brows knitted together and tucked the tissue back in her knit pocket. "Yes. Yes, of course. You girls run along."

"Great." Mazy put her arm around Evie and turned her toward the door.

Evie allowed Mazy to lead her to the door, her mind still awhirl. Her friend faintly whispered words of encouragement. She couldn't believe it had happened twice in one week. She had been darkening her eyes like this for a while, and she was sure she had the right technique. She tilted her head to the side—maybe she *should* rethink her makeup choices.

4

ASHWATER HIGH

Evie

E vie shut her locker and turned to lean against the light blue row, the cool metal on the back of her dark head. Yup, summer was officially over. Senior year—tick tock.

Ashwater High was smaller than any other school Evie attended. But that wasn't necessarily a bad thing. Sure, everyone knew everyone else, and some kids had to travel for forty-five minutes by bus to get to the school, but small felt nice. No one fell into the background. The people here looked out for one another. Evie liked that about Ashwater.

And, yeah, Ashwater was quirky—supposed alien abductions and talk of odd experiments at the underground bio-tech facility, Bio-Core, was enough to fuel the rumor mill. But, what town didn't have urban legends? Or in this case, rural legends.

She looked to her left and right. The hallway was empty. Where was Mazy? Where was everyone for that matter? Where was the new year fanfare? The 'how was your summer'?

Evie huffed. The first bell would ring any minute, right? She checked her phone, to confirm her suspicion, when she heard a commotion coming from outside the front doors.

She headed to the front of the school and opened the door. Most of the kids were outside. They stood in rows on the front steps of the school, chatting and whispering as they checked out the new boy, flanked by Gage, Luke, and Derrick, walk the steps. Evie narrowed her eyes.

Adam.

He was wearing the same serious, pouty face she'd seen a few weeks ago at Jack's. His stride was measured, yet his hands trembled at his sides. Evie stared at the steps, her cheeks heating as her body betrayed her.

She didn't like him. He was a callous ass.

But she couldn't deny he was a hot ass. Her determination not to think about him failed miserably. She'd been sketching the hell out of him ever since they'd met.

When she looked back, Adam was staring at her. She glared back in the hopes he would look away.

He didn't.

Instead, he sprinted the steps two at a time toward her, not leaving her any room for escape as her classmates looked on.

Please don't embarrass me again. Please.

"Hey, Evie."

Her lips parted, surprised by how much she enjoyed hearing her name roll off his tongue.

"Adam."

"Your eyes are extra dark today."

Evie silently screamed so loud in her mind, it made her lightheaded. Feeling better for it, she smiled sweetly and rolled her eyes. "You noticed. I did that just for you."

Adam tilted his head to the side, eyebrows knitting together. Evie noticed a small oddly-shaped, white scar on his right temple. His features relaxed, as if coming to some resolution.

"Oh, thanks," he replied, a smile spreading across his lips.

All the kids surrounding them chuckled at his response.

Thanks? Evie frowned, heat rising on her cheeks. Enough. New boy or not, this was beyond annoying. "Look, I don't know what your deal is but leave me alone, okay?"

Before he could respond, she turned on her Doc heels and headed back into the school. As she walked, she listened to the chatter from the other kids.

"So awkward."

"Evie was so pissed. Did you see her face?"

"I can't believe he said that to her."

"Oh, shit…Adam and Evie."

Evie stopped dead in her tracks and cringed as laughter ensued all around her.

FML.

Adam

Gage grinned and patted Adam on the back. "Come on, dude. She'll get over it."

"I hope so." Adam frowned. He didn't even get a chance to apologize.

What was wrong with this girl? He was legitimately trying to be nice. Didn't she say that she wore her makeup for him? He even thanked her.

Adam followed Gage into the school. He was supposed to

report to the office for his schedule. Derrick and Luke saluted a goodbye to him and headed to their lockers.

Gage pointed to the end of the hall. "Last door on the right is the office. Good luck."

Adam nodded and walked toward the door. On his way, students at Ashwater High stared at him, some whispering, some smiling. He tried his best to smile and act friendly, but he couldn't help but be paranoid that they could see through him. His left hand trembled in the way it often did when he felt vulnerable as his internal hardware scanned the crowd for threats.

He reached the door to the office and stepped inside. At the counter was a tall girl with long, straight, dark brown hair that went past her shorts. She was facing a full-figured, older woman with short red hair sitting at a desk behind the counter.

"Mrs. Stimple, my parents want me to change my schedule. I have to cut out of school early to help out at the shop. Is Principal Kelly available?"

The woman shook her head. "No, Sloan, he's not available. You'll have to make do for now. You've only got one more year."

Sloan sighed loudly, her shoulders slumping as she laid her head on the counter. "Mrs. Stimple, I can't. Please…"

The woman tightened her lips. "Sloan Simms, your whining will get you nowhere with me. Buck up." Mrs. Stimple noticed Adam standing by the door. "Speaking of which, you're the new boy, Adam Williams, right?"

"Yes, ma'am." Adam stepped forward. He was still adjusting to his new last name. He'd borrowed it from a famous pinball manufacturer at the arcade when Jack put him on the spot for it.

Mrs. Stimple reached for some paperwork on her desk, brought it to the counter, and handed the papers to Sloan. "Miss Simms, please escort your new classmate to his home-room. I believe it's the same as yours."

Sloan groaned and took the papers, dragging her arms across the counter with extra effort. "Fine."

When she glanced at Adam, she smiled, her brown eyes twinkling. She reminded Adam of a doe he saw when he was traveling through the woods when he first escaped the facility.

"So you're the new guy, huh? Let me get a good look at you. I've only heard about you from Luke."

Adam held his breath as she walked around him. "You know Luke?"

"Yeah, he's my bestie." She swatted him on the chest with the papers in her hand and raised her eyebrows. "Well, you are lean, mean, and steamy. You must work out like crazy." She shrugged. "You're not my type, but I can see you being successful here."

Adam didn't know what she was talking about, but based on her affable grin, he assumed it was meant as a compliment. "Thanks."

Sloan tossed her hair over her shoulder and headed to the door. "Bye, Stimples. Come on, Adam, I'm about to educate you in the ways of Ashwater High."

***

By the time Adam was finished with his morning classes, he was mentally exhausted. Not from learning about subject matter—that was easy because he already knew all the material that the teachers were presenting. A positive effect of having a computer for a brain. No, it was talking with his new classmates that took his head for a spin, and it seemed like everyone in the school wanted to chat.

He walked into the cafeteria after depositing his textbooks into his assigned locker. His schedule indicated he was to eat lunch. He scanned the room looking for Gage, Luke, and Derrick. Before he could locate them, Mazy, Gage's girlfriend, approached him, her short blond hair grazing her shoulders. She wore a white collared shirt with a pink sweater. She reminded him of the research he had done on teenagers. He classified her appearance as straight-laced.

"Hey, Adam. How's your first day going?"

Adam smiled at her. He was worried that since she was close to Evie, she would be angry with him as well. But he read sincerity in her big blue eyes. "It's going well. I like my classes. But I've had to talk a lot."

"Yeah, one of the drawbacks of being the new student at a small school, I'm afraid." Mazy sighed and nodded as she watched at the rest of the kids in the cafeteria. She smiled, showing perfectly straight, white teeth. "It'll die down. Give it a year or so."

Adam stared at her. "A year?"

"No, I'm joking. Well, not really, I guess. Just go ask Evie. Oh—" Mazy pressed her lips together and looked at the floor.

But Adam didn't compute her nonverbal behavior. "Okay, where is she?"

Mazy looked around and pointed to a table by the windows. "We sit over there. But I don't think—"

Adam didn't wait for her to finish. He followed the path

indicated by Mazy's outstretched finger to Evie, who sat by herself with a sandwich in one hand and a pencil twirling through her fingers in the other, and headed straight for her.

She saw him coming. Her eyes grew large as she scrambled to gather her things and shove them into her backpack.

Before he could reach her table, Gage stood in front of him. "Hey, how's it going? We're sitting over here."

"I have to talk to Evie." Adam tried to understand what Gage was saying while his mind was on the small dark-haired girl that didn't like him.

"Give her some space. Not a good idea after this morning."

Adam looked past him at Evie's table. She was already bolting, backpack slung over her shoulder. Adam watched her go, walking right past Mazy, who turned and followed her.

He sighed and looked back at Gage. The last thing he needed was an enemy. Enemies looked for weaknesses, and Adam was all too aware of what his was—a secret of epic proportions. If he perceived Evie as a threat, he didn't know what his programming might do. He cringed as he remembered what he was capable of. He liked Ashwater. He couldn't let it come to that. He wouldn't.

5

DIXON'S DINER

Evie

Evie scrunched down in her seat on the bus. She had her driver's license but preferred the bus—it gave her more time to sketch and unwind after school. Today was no different.

She bit the eraser on the tip of her pencil, and buildings passed by as the bus roared its way toward Main Street. Over a month of school had gone by in a blink of an eye. The first snowfall had arrived early and covered roofs. This was good for Ashwater because it meant the resorts could open early for skiing. She glanced back at her sketch pad and groaned. She managed to avoid Adam at school, but her subconscious was still insisting on drawing him. She had gotten a good likeness, his stoic eyes watching her from the grainy, thick paper. She groaned and set to draw two horns emerging from his head and a tail from his behind.

"Hey, that's pretty good," a male voice said from the seat behind her.

Evie closed her sketchbook and turned in her seat to death stare at Derrick Dixon, who leaned on her seatback, his arms crossed. "Don't you know it's rude to look over someone's shoulder?"

"Sorry. I was complimenting you. You're really good." Derrick frowned and sat back in his seat next to Luke. They took the bus to their parents' diner after school to bus tables.

Evie liked Derrick—and Luke. Sometimes, when he wasn't being too macho. She sighed and looked over the seat at Derrick. "Thanks."

Derrick met her gaze. "You should lighten up on Adam. He's been through a lot in his life. He doesn't talk about it, but I think he's a runaway or something."

Luke nodded. "Yeah, bro's clearly had a rough time."

Evie glanced back and forth between the boys, whose eyes were also identical—dark and thoughtful. She should sketch them sometime.

"I'll take it under consideration," she said, turning around to settle back into her seat.

If Adam was a runaway, where did he run from? And why? Either way, if what they said was true, she should be nicer to him, shouldn't she?

Before she could give it too much thought, the bus slowed in front of her mom's art gallery. She tucked her sketchbook and pencil back into her backpack. "See you guys later. We're eating at the diner tonight."

The twins nodded and said in unison, "Later."

Adam

His new interactive dance game was finished and all the adjustments were complete. Adam stepped back from the game console, swiping his lengthy hair off his forehead, his eyes aglow. The enormous room situated at the back of the building that had been used to stow old games had been transformed. *Dance Paradise* in bubble-gum pink letters streamed across the massive screen aptly placed on the large back wall. The floor lit up in random patterns of blue, pink, green, and yellow like the disco floors he saw online. Everything exactly as he envisioned. The only thing left to do was test it out, and he knew just the crew. His chest clenched with anticipation and spread to his limbs as he made his way to the front of the arcade.

Jack stood behind the front counter with Daisy at his side. The two stared into each other's eyes, Jack's fingers entwined in Daisy's pink hair, smoothing it back behind her ear. Adam tilted his head, curious about what was transpiring between the two. Even though he was experienced in the anatomy of humans, a positive side effect of learning about physical vulnerabilities during his training sessions at Bio-Core, he knew next to nothing about human emotional connection. An electric current darted back and forth between their bodies. That wasn't physically possible, but there was a charge between them.

Fascinating...

Recalling his purpose, he snapped out of his trance and made a beeline for the door.

"Hey, where you off to, man?" Jack asked.

Adam stopped and turned toward them. They were watching him expectantly. "I finished the game. I was hoping to test it out with some of the guys. They're over at Dixon's."

Jack's droopy eyes sparkled. "Well, that's great. I can't wait to check it out."

Daisy smiled. "Yeah, cool, kid. You're a regular MacGyver, aren't ya?"

Jack tilted his head. His knowledge of eighties' television was as skillful as his awareness of the decade's music. "No, Daisy, that's not quite the same thing—"

But Daisy wasn't listening. She grabbed her purse and slung it over her shoulder. "Come on, Jack, you promised me dinner…out of town. Let's get going."

Jack sighed and opened the register to take out some bills. "Yes, I did."

Adam smiled. He felt more at ease around them. Calming, almost. But he couldn't let his guard down. At least, not yet.

Daisy grasped Jack's hand, leading him over to the front door where Adam stood.

"Lock up after you leave," Jack said, putting his arm around Daisy.

"I will. Have a nice evening. You two deserve it," Adam said.

Daisy replied, "We do, don't we? Thanks, sugar. You're so sweet."

Adam beamed. His skills at human conversation improved every day. In fact, he'd become quite good at it. Well, except for one person.

He followed the couple outside, and they headed toward Jack's car, a black and gold-trimmed 1980 Pontiac Firebird Trans Am. Jack loved his car almost as much as he loved his arcade. But as he opened the passenger side door for Daisy, it was apparent who was his number one love.

Adam's sighed with longing. Could anyone ever look at him like that?

His thoughts drifted to a dark-haired spritely-looking girl. Evie. He recalled the first time he'd seen her—his head swam, setting off his Bluetooth without consent, and his breath caught in his throat. Her eyes, large and jade-colored, were the most beautiful thing he'd seen in his short life. She hinted at having a beautiful smile too. What would it feel like to touch her? Was her skin as soft as it looked?

He sighed. What was the point? The girl hated him. Of that much, he was sure.

Adam waved goodbye to Jack and Daisy and headed across the street toward Dixon's Diner. Dixon's was owned by Daisy's brother and his wife. It sported red vinyl booths, a few tables, and counter seating complete with sparkling red, vinyl swivel stools. And the food? Excellent.

It was close to six, and the diner was packed as Adam pushed open the door. All the booths and tables were full, and only a few seats remained at the counter. Luke and Derrick were wearing white aprons marred by food stains, as they bused an empty booth. Gage and his grandfather sat opposite each other by the door. Mrs. Dixon took orders at the counter and served drinks. Adam spied Mr. Dixon at a grill top in the kitchen as the swinging doors between the front and back of the diner opened and closed. Servers bustled back and forth through the doors to retrieve trays piled high with piping hot food. The pleasant smell of freshly cooked burgers and french fries hung in the air, wafting toward Adam with each passing swing of the doors.

On the opposite side of the restaurant, Adam found a man with familiar eyes watching him. They were the same steely eyes that he saw last week in the post office. The man was sitting next to a woman that looked vaguely familiar, but he was sure he'd never met her. She glanced at her companion and then at Adam.

Tremors started in his fingers first and slowly made their way into his palm. He clenched his fists into balls. Warning signals exploded in his head.

He didn't understand what was inside him that detected threats or how to control it, but understood all too well what he was capable of. That much he did remember from his time at the facility.

His eye twitched. He had only a few seconds before his internal defenses took over.

Get out. Get out now.

Clinging to any sense of humanity he had and against his own programming, Adam turned and burst back outside, his chest heaving, every muscle in his body taut. Before he realized what was happening, he slammed straight into someone.

Everything around him moved in slow-motion.

Large green eyes stared at him. Her mouth formed an O as the wind left her lungs in a whoosh and she fell backward toward the pavement.

Evie.

He moved at lightning speed and grabbed her forearm before her body hit the ground. Utilizing his dance skills, he whipped her back toward his large frame, his other hand finding the small of her back.

She slammed into his chest, her feet and free arm unable

to keep up with the momentum change. Her legs gave out as she sagged against him, chest to chest.

An unfamiliar awareness tore through his body, like tiny sparks in his central nervous system. He liked how her soft breasts felt against his chest. Her ponytail, under his nose, smelled like Daisy's vanilla ice cream sandwiches. His metal brain swam, intoxicated by the new sensations.

Footsteps from inside the diner alerted him. His grip tightened on her arms possessively as the warnings in his head sounded again.

Let her go. You don't want to hurt her.

He came to his senses and set her away from him, making sure she could stand on her own. Without a second glance or thought, he took off running across the street.

From behind him, her voice grew loud. But he couldn't make out anything she said because his CPU blasted him with a threat containment plan.

6

FUNKY TOWN

Evie

"Are you kidding me? Seriously?" Evie yelled at Adam as he ran down the street.

Bewildered was an understatement for what was going on in her head. Everything had happened so fast. One minute she was flying through the air. Next, she was pressed against Adam's rock-solid body, and then, he was gone. All without a word. She looked down to make sure she was okay.

Good. All limbs accounted for.

"Hi, Evie. You coming in? Mom's already inside," Mac Greyson said from the open diner door.

Absently, Evie replied, "Uh, no."

She looked down Main Street to see where Adam was headed. No doubt the arcade. Her mind was still aflutter from the incident, trying to reconcile what happened. Did he knock into her on purpose? Or was it an accident?

"What are you talking about?" Mac asked reaching for Evie's arm to gain her attention.

When his hand grazed her, she turned and focused on her dad's face. She shook her head, snapping out of the trance. "I'm not hungry, and I just remembered that I left something at the library. Can I meet back up with you after you're done?"

"Okay. But you should eat, Eves. I'll get you a turkey sandwich for later."

"Kay, sounds good," Evie said, as she walked back toward the library and, more importantly, Jack's Arcade.

When she was confident her dad had gone back inside the diner, she picked up the pace. She would not let Adam off the hook this time.

Who even does that? Knock into someone and run off? Whatever happened to apologies? Don't people still say sorry when they bump into you?

Although, what happened could hardly be called a bump, more like face-meet-tank. Holy shit, he was strong, and he had a swimmer's body—tall, lean, and muscular. Her mind jolted to an intriguing idea for a drawing.

She inhaled sharply. Now was no time to fantasize about Adam wet in a pool.

Breaking into a jog, her legs carried her almost as fast as her mind raced, her arms swaying back and forth in stride. Breathing was harder with each step as her heart pounded. Making matters worse was the fact that she wasn't exactly out of shape, so the exertion couldn't solely be to blame.

Evie stopped outside the arcade and put her hands on her hips to catch her breath. She cursed his good-looking face and body as her mind betrayed her, trying to conjure up the fleeting seconds she spent pressed against him not long ago.

Knock it off. He's been nothing but a dick to you.

She took one last cleansing breath and opened the door to

the arcade with a fraction of the force she possessed a few minutes ago. She squinted in the darkened room, her eyes adjusting to the change in light. The arcade was empty, but that was no surprise since the closed sign was on the door. She glanced around, hoping Daisy would suddenly appear. She liked her quirky and non-judgmental personality.

Unlike Adam. Speaking of which…

Music coming from the back of the arcade directed her to where Adam must be. She made her way to a black door at the back of the arcade near some dimly lit pinball machines. She liked pinball. It was easy. Flick, flick.

She took a deep breath, readying herself to deal with this nuisance once and for all. She opened the door and stepped inside.

"Oh my God," she said, her gaze traveling the length of the room.

A large screen covering the back wall was lit with flashing lights and animated people dancing. The floor, from wall to wall, had a soft tile-like surface that lit up in geometric patterns. It reminded her of a seventies' disco dance floor. To the left of the screen was Adam, facing away from her, doing something at an arcade-like cabinet.

Evie moved forward on the floor, the lights moving in waves under her feet. For the moment, she forgot about their encounter. "What is this?"

He turned around, his hands resting on the cabinet behind him, his light blue eyes meeting hers. "It's my new interactive video game. I call it *Dance Paradise*."

She walked over to him, her eyes traveling the length of the cavernous room. "So it's like a dancing game?"

"Yeah." Adam leaned against the console behind him, his

hands firmly pressed between his body and the cabinet. A giddy smile crossed his lips, and his eyes twinkled.

Evie's instinct was to smile stupidly back at him, but she remembered why she was here and narrowed her eyes. "You knocked into me back there and took off without saying a word."

"Yes, I remember. I'm sorry." Adam looked down as he rocked back and forth, his hands behind him.

"Hey, I'm up here." She moved in closer, trying to force him to look her in the eye. He glanced at her, his intense eyes making her toes curl inside her Doc Martens. She parted her lips, her breath catching at the back of her throat. It was like he was trying to see right into her, to all her innermost thoughts.

"I see you," he said.

She stared back, mesmerized by his unwavering expression. Hell, he didn't even blink. Her cheeks heated, and she broke eye contact. She crossed her arms across her chest and thanked God for padded bras.

"Well, good," she said. "Apology accepted. Just, ya know, say something when you bump into someone. It's weird not to."

"You're not hurt, are you? You appeared fine when I left." Adam pushed away from the console and shoved his hands in his pockets.

Evie chuckled. "Well, I'm shocked that you were able to ascertain that in the two seconds after you slammed into me."

His eyebrows knitted together, working something out in his mind. As if having a huge epiphany, he parted his lips and nodded slowly. "Sarcasm. That's what you did at school this morning too."

Evie glanced side to side. Now, it was her turn to be confused. *What planet is this guy from?* "Um…yeah. So, you're saying you didn't know?"

He turned his head from side to side, his soft, loose blond hair brushing at the tips of his eyebrows. She made a mental note about the shape of his brows. They had more of an arch than she previously thought.

Knock it off, you sick art stalker.

She had to stop sketching him. Her bedroom wall was filling up with too much of him already. She hadn't obsessed over a model like this since she was a kid sketching her favorite blue pony from *Pony Tales.*

"No, I didn't. Clearly, I'm an idiot." He said the last word like he was trying it out for the first time. It almost sounded like a question instead of a statement.

But, the truth was etched in his face. He really hadn't known why she was angry with him. Okay, so he's not so perceptive when it comes to people. Granted, that also meant that he truly didn't like her makeup choices, and he obviously wasn't alone. But, still, he seemed remorseful for their awkward exchanges. She also tended to be sarcastic a bit too much.

"No, you're not an idiot. We had some very awkward first few meetings. I can be a little overly sensitive sometimes. How about we start over?"

Adam took his hands out of his pockets and smiled. "Really?"

Evie returned his smile and made another mental note about the whiteness and size of his teeth. She struggled drawing his smile because she had only seen him smile once before.

Stop it. You're demented. This isn't healthy.

"Yeah, sure. But, so we're clear, this—" She pointed toward her face in a circular motion. "Is on purpose."

Adam raised his hands in surrender. "I understand. I will never say another word about how you look."

She groaned as her cheeks warmed for round two. *Well, I wouldn't say never.* "You're hopeless, you know that? That's fine, I guess."

"Great. So, do you want to test her out with me?" He glanced at the large screen and back at Evie, hope and excitement setting up shop in his baby blues.

Evie followed his line of sight. She liked video games as much as the next person. Although, dancing wasn't exactly one of her strong suits. But how could she say no to those eyes?

She moved to stand in front of the screen. "What do you do? Follow what's up there?"

"For the most part. Hang on." Adam turned back toward the console.

To her right, two squares on the floor lit with footprints.

"Stand there so you can be scanned," he said. "Follow the directions on the screen."

Evie followed his directions and placed her floral Docs atop of the dress shoe shadows. A silhouette of her appeared on the screen. She followed the directions, mimicking her avatar, raising her arms and legs and bending.

Adam placed a black glove with lights on his left hand and joined her on the dance floor on his own set of footprints, following his avatar. Once they both finished calibrating, their images appeared on the screen, moving in sync with them.

She laughed and waved at her double, who waved right back. "Hey, we're on screen. That's awesome."

"Oh, that's nothing." Adam smiled. "You ready to play?"

Evie shifted from side to side, both excited and nervous. Dancing. She could follow some footsteps, right? Sure, she could. "Okay, but can you pick something easy?"

He nodded. "Sure. Jack limited me to eighties' music, but he didn't say I couldn't remix some of them to make them more modern."

"Cool. I love eighties' music." Evie swung her arms back and forth, looking at the screen.

"Hang on, I've got just the song." Adam double tapped on his footprint, and a menu appeared on the left side of the screen. The songs were categorized by difficulty level. He scrolled down using his gloved hand until he found the song he was looking for.

The next thing she knew, "Funkytown" by Lipps, Inc. album cover appeared on the screen. She could handle that. "I love that song."

"It's a good one to start with. Follow yourself on the screen."

Evie smiled and shifted from side to side as a timer counted down from ten to one on the display. "Okay, I'll try my best."

Together with Adam, her avatar moved, and she mimicked. Adam was right—it was easy. A few steps here and there, then the game added in arm movements once she got used to the rhythm. She kept up with the beat, swaying her hips in sync with her avatar. At the top of the screen were their respective points earned for correct moves. A quarter of the way into the song, she noticed a bar filling across the screen under their scores. Adam's was filling faster than hers.

Feeling confident about the moves, she glanced sideways at

him. He was dancing without looking at the screen. It caught her off guard, and she miss-stepped, sending her filling bar back to zero.

"Ah, darn it. What's that bar for anyway?" she asked, hoping her voice carried over the music blaring all around them.

Adam's bar finished filling and blinked wildly, asking for release. He leaped, and when he landed, the bar exploded across the screen, lighting his avatar with fluorescent sparks.

"Freestyle!" He left his footprints and glided over the floor with moves she never would have guessed he knew. He was all around her, and he could dance. Like, really dance.

She slowed, no longer caring about her own game, until she stopped completely. Her eyes on him, mouth agape, as he moved his body to the rhythm like he was born to do it. Up, down, side to side, he moved around the floor, circling her. She didn't know the names to his style of dancing, but she thought some of it was called pop locking. He was fantastic— like seeing a new collection of paintings at her mom's shop. He moved fluidly, like the music was in every fiber of his being, his soul, even. His freestyling came to an end as he reached his original footprints and his bar of light was depleted.

He glanced over at her, smiling bigger than humanly possible. He nodded at her unmoving feet.

Startled back to reality, Evie looked back at the screen and got her feet moving again to the rhythm. The game wasn't that hard to follow. At least, this song wasn't. But she didn't think she'd ever get her freestyle bar to explode like Adam's did.

The song ended, and their scores displayed on the screen. No surprise, Adam demolished her.

She put her hands on her knees and took a deep breath. "Damn, Adam, look at your score. You did awesome."

Adam flipped his hair off his forehead, his eyes glistening, and grinned. "Thanks. It's fun, right?"

Evie laughed. "Yeah, but I don't think I'll ever have a chance to beat you. I'm not much competition, I'm afraid. So, where did you learn to dance like that?"

"YouTube."

Her eyes grew to saucers. "Are you serious? You learned how to dance like that from *YouTube*?"

He shrugged, seeming nervous. "Yeah."

She chuckled in disbelief. "Wow. You must have watched a lot of videos."

"I did."

"I never was much of a dancer. My mom put me in classes when I was little, but it didn't stick. What made you want to learn how to dance?"

"Dancing makes me feel."

Evie waited for him to finish his thought, but he didn't.

Instead, he moved closer, the warmth from his body transferring through the space between them to her. "We could try co-op sometime if you want."

Her heart pounded, and her scalp prickled. What she wouldn't do for a pencil and paper right now. His brow had tiny little beads of sweat, and the tips of his hair were moist and spikey across his forehead. His eyes were ice blue, brilliant and watchful. And his lips, parted, waiting for her to respond, looked so soft, she wished she could run her fingers across them.

She cleared her very dry throat. "Co-op?"

Before he could respond, the door to the back of the room

opened, and Gage, Derrick, and Luke burst inside. All three hollered at once as they stormed the dance floor.

"I'm up first," Luke yelled.

"Second," Derrick added.

Gage approached Adam and Evie and put his arms around them, as they continued to stare at each other, oblivious to the newcomers. "Hey, guys. So, I'm guessing the two of you are on better terms now?"

Evie snapped out of the trance and tried her best to smile. Her face must be bright red. She glanced at Gage and back at Adam, who was still watching her. "Yeah, we're all good now."

Gage smiled. "Great. So you guys won't be awkward skiing together next weekend."

Both Evie and Adam stared at Gage with blank stares.

Adam asked, "Skiing?"

Gage nodded, his smile widening. "Yes. For my birthday. With the first snowfall and the cooler temps headed our way, my granddad will be able to make some snow to add to what we already got. He's opening some trails next Saturday, and the two of you are invited."

Gage's family owned the mountain that overlooked Ashwater, including the ski slopes, and his grandfather doted on him. Evie wasn't exactly fond of skiing, but she could hold her own. She'd much rather perch herself on a cozy sofa in the lodge and sketch. But Mazy would never allow that.

"Okay, sure." Evie glanced at Adam, whose eyes were still on her.

"Yes, I'd like that." Adam smiled at her, and butterflies took flight in her stomach.

"Cool," Gage said.

Stop smiling like an idiot.

"I gotta go." Slowly, she backed away from the boys toward the door—she had a date with charcoal and her sketch pad. She turned to leave and whipped back around. "Um, thanks, Adam. It was fun."

Adam stared at her, opening and closing his mouth, words seeming to escape him.

Feeling awkward, Evie smiled. "Well, see ya, I guess."

She turned and bolted to the front of the arcade. Before she could get out the front door, the jukebox started playing. Evie jumped, as music poured from its speakers like it was possessed.

"Shit," she whispered, covering her heart.

This was the second time this had happened when she was in here. She wasn't one to believe in the paranormal, but if she ever needed proof, this would certainly be it. She crept over to the jukebox to make sure it was plugged in. Wasn't that the creepy bit in all scary movies? Some machine working, but not plugged in?

She peered behind the jukebox. Sure enough, it was receiving power from an outlet against the wall. She patted the Plexiglas on the front. "Well, maybe you just like playing music for me."

As she turned to walk out of the arcade, she recognized the song playing and paused—it was from some eighties' movie her dad made her watch about a girl, whose family forgot her birthday, and the boy she was crushing on.

Huh.

7

DOWNHILL

Adam

The crisp, cool air coming off the powdery snow made the others' teeth chatter. Adam's lip quivered too but for a very different reason. Hundreds of feet beneath him was his old prison—the Bio-Core facility. He hadn't connected the dots between the ski slopes and the location of the facility, but now that he was standing on top of the mountain, surrounded by his friends, he was fighting hard not to let his fear show.

He took a deep breath to calm his nerves.

They don't know you're here. You're safe.

Gage tapped his arm. "Hey, you okay? First time?"

Adam smiled nervously. He'd done his research about skiing and practiced ahead of time. He had a good sense of balance even though he didn't like how the boots felt on his feet. But, Gage had provided a perfect cover. "Uh, yeah."

Gage nodded. "Okay, so, there are three paths you can take from here. The left and right are blue squares, and the straightaway is a black diamond. Since this is your first time, I'd recommend one of the blue squares."

"I'll go blue square with you," Evie said.

Evie. He'd barely paid her any attention because of his anxiety about the proximity of the facility beneath them. She was dressed in black ski pants and jacket. Her hair pulled in a ponytail with a band wrapped around her head to keep her ears warm. He couldn't see her eyes behind the dark sunglasses, but her smile was hopeful.

He smiled back at her. "Great."

Sloan pulled down the goggles from her forehead and pushed off toward the center. She, along with Luke, had decided to snowboard. "Laters."

Luke followed, waving.

"Show offs," Derrick yelled after them but followed them in his skis.

Gage laughed and said to Adam, "Sloan could be a professional snowboarder if she put her mind to it. But, well, who knows what goes through her mind." He looked over at Mazy. "Blue?"

"Sure." Mazy nodded at Evie. "Have fun."

She turned to her left and pushed off.

Gage followed. "See you guys at the bottom."

Evie slid over to Adam in her skis and reached for his arm. "Gage probably should have let you start with a green circle."

Adam's skin tingled where she touched him and distracted him from what lay within the mountain. "It's okay. I think I can handle it."

She chuckled. "I don't know why, but I believe you." She pointed to the right. "Want to do that one?"

"Sure."

Evie took off first, and Adam pursued. The trail mean-dered among the trees, sloping steeply at various points and leveling off. Even though the temperature was teetering just above thirty degrees, the sun warmed his face. Evie was quite a good skier. She swooshed back and forth, side to side, with little hesitation. He followed her lead, mimicking her, flying down the mountain.

A smile crept up on his face. Skiing was exhilarating. It couldn't take the place of dancing, but it was fun. He used his internal Bluetooth to play some music on his phone, his hips finding a rhythm.

Evie came to a stop by the tree line after a few minutes, plowing snow into the air. He stopped next to her.

"How are you doing?" she asked.

Adam turned down his music and smiled. "Amazing. I like skiing."

"Cool." Evie took off her glasses and wiped her forehead with the back of her gloved hand. Her cheeks were rosy. "Just want to catch my breath for a minute. I bet Sloan and the twins are already headed back up the ski lift for another run."

Adam turned his head back the other way, listening for them with his audio sensor. She was right. "Yeah, they are."

"And how do you know?"

Oh shit. He'd done it again. Evie was staring at him, her eyes narrowed, adorable nose wrinkled up. "Sorry. I meant to say I bet they are too."

Evie gave him one last curious look and seemed to accept his excuse. "It's nice that Gage's grandfather does this for him, and for us, I guess."

"How do you mean?"

"Well, most people think Gage has this perfect life—his

grandfather owns all this land, he's the captain of the football team, and he's got a great girlfriend. But he lost his mom and never met his dad. That has to be hard."

"How did he lose his mother?" Adam asked. Gage didn't talk much about himself with Adam beyond gaming and football. He lived with his grandfather but hadn't given much thought beyond that.

Evie tilted her head to the side. "Oh, you don't know about the alien abductions? It's kind of a thing here."

He laughed. Androids posing as humans? Yes. Aliens stealing humans? Highly improbable. "Come on."

She punched his arm. "I'm serious. Gage's mom wasn't the first either. Mrs. Gardner, the head librarian, lost her sister too."

Adam stopped laughing. "You're serious."

"Yes, I'm being serious. No one knows what happened to them. One night they went to bed, and the next morning, they were gone. How do you explain that?"

Adam opened his mouth to say, "Where should I start?" but thought better of it. He was open to the idea of other lifeforms beyond Earth, considering how vast the universe was. But alien abductions in the here and now seemed unlikely. His best guess was that the missing people simply left for reasons unknown to their loved ones. Occam's razor—the simplest solution was usually the right one.

"I guess anything is possible," he said.

Evie shrugged and put her glasses back on. "I'm not saying it's true either. But that's the rumor. You ready?"

"Sure."

He pushed off first this time and headed down the hill. Every so often he looked behind him to make sure Evie was following. Along the way, he contemplated the new information Evie had shared about Gage's grandfather. He owned this mountain. Did he also own everything beneath it?

Evie

Adam was a natural. He could probably handle some of the more challenging runs, but she was pleased that he didn't request it. Her skis felt comfortable under her feet but only on the blue square trails. They'd finished another run, and she was toast. All she wanted now was something warm to drink and eat.

"I'm done." She stabbed her ski poles into the snow and took off her gloves.

Adam followed suit. "That was fun."

"Yeah. Want to grab something to eat and drink?"

"Okay."

Evie used her poles to unlock her skis from her boots.

Before she could pick them up, someone yelled, "Watch out!"

A boy was flying down one of the black diamond runs headed straight for her, and he was out of control.

No time.

She closed her eyes and braced for impact as the yelling grew louder. Strong arms encircled her, and her face pressed against a familiar chest. A slight bump pushed her backward, and she lost her balance, bringing them both down. The snow was cold on her neck and face, but the body on top of her was warm and rock solid.

When she opened her eyes, Adam was above her. "Are you okay?"

Okay?

Evie had no idea if she was okay. She couldn't get past him lying on top of her. She opened her mouth, but nothing came out.

He propped himself up on his elbow and smoothed some hair away from her eyes. "Are you hurt?"

"No."

"Good." He rolled off her and gently pulled her back to her feet.

The boy who had come down the slope was on the ground behind Adam, moaning.

Adam bent next to him. "Don't move. You might be injured."

"Anthony," a woman yelled, running toward them from the lodge. Once she reached them, she knelt next to the boy.

Evie didn't know him very well. He was a junior and played football with Gage and Luke. She assumed the woman was his mother. Others gathered around the scene including Sloan, Derrick, and Luke.

Sloan said, "I knew it was too much for him to handle."

Anthony sat up. "How did you—"

The woman next to him scolded, "I'm taking you to the ER just in case. Let's go."

"I'm okay. I think I got the wind knocked out of me." With the help of Adam and the woman, Anthony stood. "See? All my limbs are still intact."

The woman groaned. "What am I going to do with you? Can you walk?"

"Yeah."

She put her arm around him just in case.

"Thank you for your help," she said to Adam.

"You're welcome."

She turned and led Anthony away toward the parking lot, leaving the others standing around.

Derrick asked, "What the heck happened?"

Good question. Evie had caught her breath and was watching Adam. He had somehow put himself between her and Anthony and stopped the boy's forward momentum. She had only fallen because she lost her balance.

But before she could ask, Adam replied, "He was headed straight for us and fell before impact. Lucky, I guess."

Evie eyed Adam. That wasn't even remotely what she could piece together, but now, she didn't care. Now, the only thing in her head was his baby blues looking down at her. Her hand twitched for a pencil. "Yeah, lucky."

8

CRUSH

Adam

Adam lay awake in his bed at the back of the arcade as the sun inched its way up on the horizon, light dancing at the corner of the back window. He'd reached a new milestone in his quest to be human. He'd saved Evie from being plowed by a runaway skier. He'd taken a risk using his built-in laser to pop the kid out of his skis, but he'd determined that the injuries would be drastically minimized by doing so. As far as he could tell, no one had noticed what he'd done. Well, perhaps the boy did, but he was in no shape to recollect.

His heart swelled—he chose to put himself in danger to save another. That was progress.

And then there was Evie.

He used his built-in ocular projector to display images he'd captured of her on his ceiling. The smile etched on his face was hard to conceal. Evie Grayson was wonderful. Like Daisy's orange cheese-covered french fries, confusing and divine in one beautiful package. He loved the warmth he saw in her bright green eyes when she looked at him…like he was normal. She was a passionate human, of that much he was sure. She wasn't much for dancing, or gaming for that matter, but he read passion in her eyes and couldn't wait to find out what truly made her feel.

Adam had spent the better part of the last two weeks searching dating rituals and speed-watching romantic movies that weren't too dated. Daisy had provided him with a list. He had no experience in this area at all and, even though he had more CPU power than any human, he was an inexperienced neophyte when it came to interpersonal relationships. Not that he hadn't researched human behavior—he'd been doing so ever since he left the facility—but he'd focused mainly on how to fit in and stay under the radar. He'd paid little attention to romantic love, dating, and attraction. Why would he? But given his incredibly fast processor, he made short work of his studies into love and had come to a glaring conclusion.

He had something called a crush.

Or at least, that's what he wanted to believe. He didn't actually know if what he felt was the same for humans. But the way his body reacted to the thought of her… His heart beat faster when she was near and the breath in his lungs stuck in his throat. Not to mention other things happening in his lower half.

But deep inside the recesses of his high-functioning brain, he knew his feelings could never be acted on. There were two reasons he could think of off the top of his head and made a note to add more as they came to him.

One, he was designed to be a killing machine. Plain and simple. This was why he ran every time his hands shook, his brain sending messages to his limbs to obliterate anything that posed a threat to his wellbeing. His innate drive was to conceal his identity at all costs, and it made him wonder why the facility that created him thought that important.

Two, he was an android. Or at least some kind of freakish mashup of human flesh and metal. Truth be told, he didn't know what parts of him were flesh and which were not. But if Evie knew what he was, she would be revolted. And why wouldn't she? He was disgusted about his nature too.

Squashing those thoughts and moving back to thinking about Evie as sexy cheese fries, he got out of bed. Today he had some exams to take. They would be simple, but he didn't want to arouse suspicion so he would answer some of the questions wrong. He liked going to Ashwater High, especially seeing Evie, and his teachers all seemed genuinely interested in the subjects that they taught. His favorite teacher was Mr. Garcia. He was new to Ashwater High this year, like Adam, and taught Adam's best subject—information technology. He felt at ease talking to him, like he'd known him a long time. But that wasn't possible because Adam had recorded every second of his life.

After a quick shower, he slipped his favorite black, V-neck T-shirt over his head and pulled on some jeans. He had finally made enough money to purchase new clothes. When he first got to Ashwater he had only what he was wearing—stolen clothes from a camper in the woods. He didn't like stealing because it drew attention, but after the facility had stripped him for disposal, he'd learned quickly that humans didn't walk around naked. Daisy gave him some of Jack's old clothes, some of which were ill-fitting considering their size difference. Jack was a good five inches shorter and much rounder around the middle. But she retrieved some clothes from the back of his closet that fit well enough. Jack said they were from a time when he was "the bomb."

Adam pushed his newly purchased phone in his front pocket and headed out the back of the arcade, locking the door behind him. He had plans for this phone, and it involved getting a certain girl's digits. He stopped in the alley between the arcade and the shop next door. Someone was talking on the street out front, and he recognized the voice.

It was the man he'd run into at the post office. "Yes, sir. I know. I'm working on it. This isn't my first dance with Bio-Core. Besides, I've got a lead."

Adam froze and held his breath as his hands shook violently. Was he talking about him? Was the facility aware that he'd escaped?

The man spoke again. "Will do."

After a few seconds, the man groaned.

"Calm down, Mac. Isn't this the very reason you moved back?" another voice said.

Adam pressed his hands on the brick side of the arcade and closed his eyes, blocking their voices out.

A war broke out in his mind, and he jettisoned back to his time at the facility. *Lifeless, mangled bodies strewn everywhere. His hands trembling. His skin glistening in low lights, soaked with perspiration.*

Adam inhaled deeply as he got control of the voice inside his head that only seemed to want to kill. He had to control the paranoia and the urges.

He crept out of the alley onto Main Street. A few blocks away was a patrol car. The sheriff leaned against the side, arms crossed, talking to another officer. Before they saw him, Adam turned the opposite way and took off in a slow jog. He'd deal with this new problem later. Right now, he had a bus to catch.

***

Adam slid into his seat for the first period. Behind him and to his left were Gage and Derrick. Info Tech wasn't a required course for seniors, but it sure was considered an easy A for anyone that knew their way around an operating system.

Gage tapped Adam on the shoulder. "Hey, can we play some DP after school?"

He was referring to Adam's new video game, *Dance Paradise*. Since Adam had first introduced his Ashwater friends to the game, they'd played until ten every night. Adam didn't mind since he didn't require much recharge time.

"Sure."

"Cool," Gage replied. "I'm ready for a rematch."

Adam had played against Gage, Derrick, and Luke. He won every time. But Gage gave him a run for his CPU. He found it interesting that Gage had the same anticipatory reaction to the notes that he had. Gage wasn't a natural dancer though, and Adam typically beat him through his bonus freestyles. Although, Gage was near perfect outside that box and improving each time.

But most of all, Adam was having fun. Real fun. They were his friends, something he never dreamed he could have, and it made him smile.

"Bring it," Adam said.

"Yeah, and I need a rematch against Luke. We're tied up now," Derrick added, rolling his eyes.

It was clear that Derrick was annoyed that his brother,

who wasn't nearly as interested in video games, was holding his own in DP. Luke was more physically agile than Derrick and had an edge in freestyle, but Derrick was technically perfect during the regular part of the game.

Adam chuckled. He loved watching them play against each other. He wondered what it would be like to have a twin or a brother for that matter.

Gage laughed. "You guys *are* twins. No surprise there."

"Do you think we could invite some other people?" Adam asked.

Gage and Derrick exchanged glances.

"By other people, do you mean Evie Grayson?" Gage replied.

Adam's chest lurched and expanded as warmth spread through his limbs at the mention of her name. "Yes."

"I'll say something to Mazy. That is, unless you want to ask Evie yourself?" Gage smiled knowingly.

"I do." Adam sat up in his seat, his senses on high alert. He wanted more than anything to talk to Evie. "I have a phone now. Do either of you have Evie's number?"

"I don't, but Mazy does. Give me your number, and I'll text you between classes."

Before Adam could reply, the bell rang, and Mr. Garcia walked into the classroom. He nodded at Adam and smiled.

Mr. Garcia reached into a draw in his desk and pulled out a stack of papers. "Test time. Clear everything off your desks. Computers off. All other electronic devices stowed under your chairs."

Adam did as Mr. Garcia asked and readied himself to get a perfect seventy-two percent on the test.

***

Gage held up his end of the bargain and texted Adam Evie's digits. Adam sent her a message as soon as he created a profile for her during study hall, his last period of the day.

ADAM: *Hi Evie, It's Adam. How are you?*

He clicked send and waited for the three bubbles to appear, indicating her response.

"Adam, may I speak with you?"

When Adam glanced up, Mr. Garcia stood in front of him, and he didn't look pleased.

Adam glanced around nervously and tucked his phone in his front jeans pocket. "Sure."

"Good. Come with me." Mr. Garcia said and nodded at Mrs. Thompson, his study hall teacher. "I'm borrowing Adam."

Mrs. Thompson looked up from a worn paperback book, smiled, and nodded.

Adam followed Mr. Garcia into the hallway, growing nervous. He hoped his teacher would address what he wanted with him as soon as they hit the hallway, but that was obviously not the case. Adam walked alongside Mr. Garcia back to his computer lab classroom.

After entering the room, Mr. Garcia turned and pointed to a chair next to his desk at the front of the room. "Take a seat."

Adam acquiesced, his left hand acting up again in the bothersome way it often did when he sensed exposure. "What's this about, sir?"

Mr. Garcia shuffled through some papers on his desk. "Well, I have something I want to talk to you about." As if something else occurred to him, he switched gears abruptly.

"Say, do you know what language would be best for database management?"

"SQL would be best."

Mr. Garcia smiled triumphantly. "That's right."

Adam was confused. Why was he asking him about this? He tucked his troubled hand under his thigh. "Mr. Garcia, if I've done something wrong…"

The teacher studied him. "You're such an intelligent young man, Adam. You know that, right?"

Adam swallowed hard. He didn't like where this was going. "I guess so."

Mr. Garcia held up Adam's Scantron sheet from the test he had taken earlier. "You should have aimed for at least an A- on your test. A C was a dead giveaway."

Now, both of Adam's hands were shaking. He didn't like where this conversation was headed. He didn't want to hurt Mr. Garcia, but he wasn't sure he would be able to control himself.

"Um…" he stammered, his pulse pounding in his ears, and his mind raced for the right words to get him out of the situation.

Mr. Garcia put the test back on his desk. "Hey, Adam, you're not in any trouble. It's not about that. I only wanted to understand why you would purposely do poorly on a test that is clearly easy for you."

Adam didn't know how to answer. What could he say? *Well, I'm an escaped android from Bio-Core, and the material on your test is beyond simplistic for me? Nope. Not going to go there.*

"I'm new here, and yes, I like computer programming. But no one likes a show-off, right?"

"That's what I thought. But, Adam, you shouldn't shirk

your academics to fit in. I'm okay with keeping your skills on the down-low if you're that worried about it. But promise me that in the future you will take all my exams to the best of your ability, okay?"

Adam sighed as relief washed over him. Mr. Garcia didn't suspect anything remotely close to the truth, and why would he? Adam looked like any other human.

He sat up in his seat. "Yes, sir. I won't let it happen again."

Mr. Garcia leaned forward, a smile spreading across his face. "That's good to hear. You'd be surprised about how accepting the folks around here are. We do have a reputation for being a quirky town. What's wrong with a kid who's got a knack for programming?"

Knack? Well, that was one way to put it. In any event, his mind eased as the threat passed. Mr. Garcia was just concerned about the test. Before Adam could give it much more thought, his phone buzzed against his thigh.

Evie. His cheeks flushed.

Mr. Garcia also noticed. "You aren't supposed to have your phone turned on during school hours."

"Oh. Right. I'm sorry. I'll turn it off." Adam reached to pull it out of his pocket.

"That's okay. The day is almost over, and by the look of you, you can't wait to text him or her back."

Adam's cheeks warmed even more as he stood. Every time he had a physical response to a thought about Evie, he felt more human. He silently thanked whoever made him this way, even if the facility thought him a reject. "Again, I'm very sorry, Mr. Garcia. I promise I won't let it happen again."

Mr. Garcia stood as well. "Be sure that you don't. Maybe I'll head downtown to check out your new game at Jack's. The other boys have said great things about it. I'm not much of a dancer, but I can admire great programming."

"Sure, sounds great. Thanks." Adam walked to the door of the classroom, waved goodbye, and stepped into the hall. He pulled out his phone to read the text message he received.

EVIE: *Hey. Ur not supposed to have ur phone on during school.*

He smiled.

ADAM: *But urs is on.*

EVIE: *You are not me.*

She followed it up with a winking emoji.

Adam laughed.

ADAM: *What are you doing after school?*

EVIE: *Homework. Why?*

ADAM: *Gage, Derrick, and Luke are going to Jack's to play DP. Thought you might want to come.*

EVIE: *What's DP?*

He exhaled slowly.

ADAM: *Dance Paradise. The game I showed you.*

EVIE: *Oh. IDK. I have a lot of homework.*

His heart sank. While it took him less than ten minutes to churn out all his schoolwork, most humans took much longer. He couldn't fault her for doing homework though. Adam started typing his response, but she interrupted him.

EVIE: *JK, What time?*

Adam smiled at his phone.

ADAM: *Four?*

EVIE: *Kay. I'll take ur bus into town. See you after school.*

Adam stared at his phone. The dismissal bell would ring in twenty-five minutes. Suddenly, he felt unkempt and self-conscious.

ADAM: *OK. See you then.*

He shoved his phone into his pocket and rushed his fingers through his hair. He'd started wearing body spray on the recommendation of Daisy, and he had the bottle in his locker. Grooming, per Daisy, was very important to girls, and he didn't want to disappoint.

He lowered his head and sniffed under his arms as he walked down the hall toward his locker. He didn't know if androids perspired the same as humans. He thought he smelled fine, but he wasn't going to take any chances.

When he looked up, Luke and Sloan, with her long dark hair swaying back and forth to the beat of her hips, were walking toward him. The two of them were always together, but in a strictly platonic way as far as Adam could tell. They both had a thing for snowboarding, and Luke liked Sloan's parents' head shop too. Adam had never taken a drug, but marijuana was legal in Colorado and people partook, especially Jack.

Luke frowned at Adam. "Bro, do that shit in the locker room. This is a public hallway. No one needs to see that."

Sloan chuckled. "Hot date?"

"No," Adam said. "I mean, well, kind of. I don't know, actually."

Luke grinned. "He invited Evie to play DP after school." He held out his hand for Adam to grasp, which Adam did. "Well done, dude."

Sloan raised her eyebrows seductively and pursed her lips. "Agreed."

Adam shook Luke's hand and pushed past them. "Yeah, so I gotta go. See you at Jack's?"

"Yep. See ya there." Luke nodded at Sloan. "You coming too?"

Sloan beamed. "Are you kidding? Of course, I'm coming. I have yet to see this infamous game." She turned and glanced at Adam, who was hurrying off. "Hey."

Adam stopped and turned back.

"Stoke the flames, Adam. Stoke the flames." She turned around and headed the opposite direction with Luke.

Adam didn't know what she meant, but his arms and legs were on fire and his chest was tight like he couldn't get enough oxygen to his lungs. He blew out a breath and placed a hand over his heart, his fingertips caressing each beat as if corralling his heart's desire to leap out of his chest. Is this what would happen every time he anticipated seeing the dark-haired beauty that sent his internal Bluetooth on the fritz? He didn't know, but he couldn't wait to see what would happen when he saw her.

9

BUS RIDE

Evie

Evie checked her face one last time in the bathroom mirror. She'd been waiting for Adam to make a move. After the truce, she was left to wonder if he would try to text or talk to her. For a while, she thought that her attraction to him might be one-sided. Now, today, he finally pulled the trigger. She smiled at her reflection and pulled her thick, dark tresses from their high ponytail perch and ran a small brush she kept in her backpack through her hair so it framed her face. Luckily, she had worn one of her favorite outfits today— an argyle pink-and-black top with her favorite black skinny jeans and Doc Mary Janes.

Mazy stood next to her, studying her own reflection in the mirror. Her long blond bob kissed the tops of her shoulders, tucking under neatly. Her blue eyes sparkled without even a hint of liner or shadow. She only wore a bit of mascara, a stark contrast to Evie's makeup sense.

She frowned at herself and turned her head side to side as if the new perspective would reveal some deep secret. "I don't think Gage is really interested in me."

"Are you serious?"

Mazy shrugged her shoulders. "Yeah, I don't know. There's no…spark. Maybe it's me. Am I too plain?"

Evie stared at Mazy. Plain would be the last thing Evie would use to describe her best friend's perfect features. Wholesome? Maybe. "Are you kidding me? You're like the prettiest girl in school. How could you even think such a thing?"

"If you say so." Mazy sighed and rolled her eyes. She tucked her hair neatly behind her ear and turned her attention to Evie. "Don't take this the wrong way, but I've never seen you without makeup. What are you like under there?"

Mazy leaned in close, her eyes crossing intentionally.

Evie pushed her away, narrowing her eyes playfully. She hadn't forgone her heavy, dark shadow and liner since eighth grade. To forgo it now would be like going to school naked.

"A monster. Like the most horrid, gross disgustingness. And I eat human flesh." Evie raised her hands as if she were going to attack her friend.

Mazy grabbed her hands and laughed. "I'm kidding. You know that, right? You're super pretty, and I'm sure that's true with or without makeup. I'm sure Adam thinks so too."

Evie turned back to the mirror and smiled at their reflections. "Thanks, Maze."

***

Adam's bus was the first in line at school. Evie usually took

Bus Ten downtown because it stopped right in front of her mom's art shop. But Adam's bus dropped closer to the arcade.

Evie shaded her eyes with her hand, the sunlight bouncing off the windows of the yellow school bus. Her heart pounded softly. The time she spent sketching Adam was taking its toll. She drew lots of people, but he stirred something in her. She couldn't seem to stop putting pencil to paper with his image firmly planted in her mind. She took a deep breath as she reached the door of Bus Thirteen, hoisted her backpack on her shoulder, and climbed the steps. The bus driver smiled at her and asked for her pass. She handed it to him and glanced down the aisle at the half-full bus to locate Adam.

Their eyes met and he waved at her. He was seated in the middle of the bus, by the window.

Her breath caught at the back of her throat as butterflies swarmed in her middle. She smiled. Music started playing somewhere in the front of the bus. She recognized it immediately.

"Sweet Dreams (Are Made of This)"

"Hey, since when do you like eighties' stuff?" a girl asked, laughing.

"I don't. I didn't do that." The boy sitting across from her with his laptop scratched his head. He stared at his laptop, sizing it up for its betrayal.

"Leave it. I like this song," the girl replied.

He shrugged. "Okay."

Evie looked back at Adam and narrowed her eyes playfully. There was definitely something kismet about him and their encounters. She approached his seat, and he stood, hunched because of his height and the sloping side of the bus.

"Do you want the window?" he asked.

"No, I'll sit on the outside." Her skin tingled at the antici-pation of her thigh next to his. She pulled her backpack off her shoulder and sat, putting her backpack on the floor between her legs. Sadly, her thigh was a good six inches from his. *Bummer.*

Adam smiled at her as the bus shut its doors and pulled away from the school. "How was your day?"

She stared back at him, entranced, half-smile. *Damn, I could swim in those ice blue pools you call eyes.* They were more oval-shaped than she had been drawing. Her fingers twitched on the top of her backpack as if able to conjure her sketchpad and pencil with magic.

His eyes shifted from hers to her hand on her backpack, causing her to respond.

"Oh, sorry," she said. "It was okay. How about you?"

"Your hand." Adam glanced at her backpack again, his eyes grew serious. "Are you okay?"

Evie clasped her hands together and set them on her lap. She was obsessed with drawing but actual physical twitches? What was this, withdrawal symptoms? *Sooo embarrassing.*

"Um, it's nothing. Sorry." Her cheeks heated as she squeezed her hands together so tightly that her knuckles turned white.

"Oh." Adam put his hand over hers causing Evie to jump. Instead of pulling away, he stroked the top of her hand with his thumb. Back and forth in a rhythm while his foot tapped the floor of the bus to the beat of music in the air. "I get twitches sometimes too."

Evie's lips parted as every fiber of her being stood on end like static electricity. Slowly, she separated her hands as he pulled the one closest to him into both of his, stroking her now moist palm.

"Better?" he asked.

She swallowed, her mouth dry as the Sahara, and her heart pounding so hard she could hear it in her ears. "Um..."

"Um?"

"You're holding my hand."

What was she saying? She didn't know. This was the most sensual thing that had ever happened to her. Sparks shot up her arm and into places that had her fighting the urge to hop into his lap.

"Oh, sorry. Too forward?" he asked.

Evie looked at her hand in his as he continued to lightly rub his fingers over the soft part of her hand between index finger and thumb. *God, if he can make me feel like this by touching my hand, imagine what else he could do?*

She couldn't let this go on. She would lose her mind if he continued. They were on a school bus for God's sake. She pulled her hand away from him.

"It's okay." She held up her hands which were now shaking for a different reason. Realizing her mistake, she slapped them on her thighs, pressing them into her jeans. "I'm good."

Adam stared at her, unmoving, his eyes unreadable. Finally, he said, "Good."

The awkward tension between them was so thick she could cut it with a knife.

He put his hand on the seat in front of them and leaned against the window to face her. "So this isn't your normal bus. Which bus is yours?"

Evie drew in a deep breath and relaxed against the seat, glad for the change of subject. "When I'm going to my mom's shop, I take Bus Ten. But when I go home, I'm on Bus Four. I get dropped off at the edge of town. I live in the Canyon Ridge development." She turned and glanced at him. "Why? You planning on stalking me?"

Adam nodded, his eyes as serious as a heart attack. "Yes."

"Ha-ha. So funny." She covered her mouth and laughed.

He hung his head and looked out the window, his leg shaking nervously. "Yeah, I was kidding."

She tilted her head to the side to study him. "Hey…"

Adam wouldn't look at her.

"You were serious, weren't you?" The hair at the back of her neck stood on end.

"What? No, of course not." He glanced between the window and her with a smile that didn't quite have the authenticity to convince her.

What a minute. Hang on. She didn't know anything about him. Where did he live before he came to Ashwater? Where was his family? Did he even have one? Why did he move here? Did something bad happen to him to make him run away? She didn't want to be intrusive, but he did have an odd social sense, and she wasn't up for being murdered in her sleep any time soon.

"I just realized we don't know each other that well," she started. "What's your story? Where did you move from, and do you have any family?"

Adam put his hands underneath his thighs on the seat and exhaled slowly. "Sorry, it's hard to talk about it."

"Oh, I'm sorry. I shouldn't—"

"No, it's okay. I don't have a family. At least none that I know about. The people I lived with before here didn't care if I lived or died.

Evie frowned. "Oh my God. That's terrible. Was it like a foster situation?"

His eyes darted back and forth before replying, "Yes."

"I didn't mean to bring up any bad memories." Now it was Evie's turn to reach for Adam's hand. She pulled it out from under him and entwined her fingers with his. He felt cold.

Adam smiled. "It's okay. I'm much better off on my own. Besides, I'm eighteen now."

"I know, but I shouldn't have pried."

"I understand why you'd ask."

She sighed, letting go of his hand and allowing her shoulders to relax against the seat. "It's my dad. He's always telling me to keep my guard up."

He nodded. "Well, that's actually good advice. Maybe I'll meet him sometime?"

Evie hadn't considered that encounter. Her dad was the sheriff of Ashwater. Huge negative for a love life. Luckily, up until now, her prospects had been nonexistent. Now, there was Adam—she didn't know how her dad would react to him. He lived by himself at the back of an arcade and had no family to speak of besides Jack and Daisy. Evie knew all too well how much her dad disliked Jack. They'd had some kind of falling out when they were kids. Evie's dad moved away, but Jack stayed and opened the arcade. Whatever animosity Mac Grayson had for Jack White was still palpable, and he would likely hold that same angst against Adam. No, for now, she preferred to keep whatever she had with Adam to herself.

"Yeah, sometime," she said noncommittally.

Evie and Adam spent the rest of the bus ride chatting about school and mutual friends. In the back of her mind, she wondered if Adam was in Ashwater long-term. She was afraid to ask. Most of her friends would head off to college after their senior year and come back to visit. Evie wouldn't be one of them, and she was okay with that. She had her art and plenty of open space to capture with pen and pencil. But for the first time, she felt sad about being left behind, and it had everything to do with the blond Adonis at her side.

10

PLANS

Adam

Every time he thought he was doing a good job pretending to be human, he screwed it up. Making matters worse was that he kept saying odd things to Evie, the one person he wanted to appear human with the most.

Of course, girls don't want to be stalked.

Unfortunately, quite a few of the romantic movies Daisy suggested depicted men covertly spying on women. In the end, the women in the films saw the behavior as flattering. This, among other things, was confusing. But now was no time to reconcile the odd, social constructs of humanity.

The bus stopped outside of Jack's. Evie, Adam, and some others got off and walked toward the arcade. Adam opened the front door and scanned, detecting that the others meeting them were already there, along with sixteen other patrons.

Jack, wearing a black Bon Jovi T-shirt stood behind the counter, grinning. Daisy was behind the snack counter toward the back of the arcade with a line of at least eight waiting. She was busy popping some popcorn, her hips swaying to the music floating in the air from the jukebox. Adam closed his eyes and inhaled the heavenly scents of roller hotdogs, popcorn kernels frying in oil, and cheese.

This was home.

Jack waved them over to the counter. "There's my star employee."

Business had picked up ever since word about the impending release of Adam's new game had gotten out. Derrick, Luke, and Gage were excellent advertisers. Although, no one was allowed into the back game room yet.

Adam and Evie walked over to Jack.

"I'm your only employee, right?" Adam asked.

"Yeah, I guess that's true." Jack smiled and swayed back and forth to the music, pleasure radiating from his hips. "But you're drawing in the crowds now. People are talking about your new game. When can we open it to the public, man?"

Adam nodded. "I've got a few more tweaks, but I think it should be ready by the end of the month."

"I've only played it once, and I thought it was really fun. Adam did a great job. You'll be a huge hit." Evie glanced at Adam with her large, round eyes framed with charcoal.

The circuits in his man-made brain lit up. A few short weeks ago, she couldn't stand the sight of him. Now, she was his advocate. He wanted to pull her close to him like he did in front of Dixon's Diner. His heart, or whatever it was he had in his chest, soared.

"I like her, Adam." Addressing Evie, Jack asked, "Do you have a job? I could use someone like you to bring people in."

"While I appreciate the offer, I do kinda have a job. It

doesn't currently pay. I work at my mom's shop down the street. Grayson's Art?"

Jack nodded, slowly, as some sort of underlying recognition happened in his mind. Adam wasn't sure what it was, but something clicked. "Oh, yeah, I know it. You're Mac's kid, and your mother restores and sells art, right? Does that mean you're an artist as well?"

Evie beamed. "I am. Sketches, mostly."

"Groovy. Have you always enjoyed drawing?"

"Yeah. Even when I was little, I drew on whatever paper or napkin I could find. Paper diner menus were my favorite. It's like a calling. Hard to explain, I guess."

"Not at all. I get it. That's how I feel about this place." He raised his hand and waved it around as if signaling a curtain call for the arcade games. "I've always loved video games. I was actually a finalist in a video game competition back in the eighties. But that's a story for another day. Now, this is my mecca. I've acquired every game I love plus some. If only I could make customers feel what I do about these games."

Adam watched the interchange, mesmerized by the instant connection between Evie and Jack—two very different devotions but the same passion. He recorded the exchange and snapped a few pics with his ocular lens to store away for reference. Each time he observed people interact, he learned a bit more about how to be human. These real-life experiences were certainly more valuable than the rapid speed at which he could search the internet.

Evie grinned. "I'm telling you, if everyone plays Adam's game, you will have a steady stream of customers." She glanced at Adam. "Isn't that right?"

Adam swallowed. He loved the game he created, but he

also loved to dance. He didn't know how much others would like it if they didn't like dancing. Although, if Evie, who just proclaimed that she enjoyed his game, liked it, maybe others would too.

"Yeah," Adam finally agreed. "DP could be popular, especially since I have a setting for group play."

"Oh my God. I know what you should do." Evie slapped her hands on the glass countertop. "Did you program in any Michael Jackson stuff?"

"Of course."

"'Thriller'?"

"Yes. That's one of the most popular songs."

"Perfect. You should have the Ashwater Halloween party here."

Adam had no idea what Evie was talking about, but Jack seemed intrigued by her suggestion.

"What's Halloween?" Adam asked.

Evie and Jack exchanged wide-eyed glances.

"Are you serious?" Evie asked.

Oh shit. Warnings flashed in front of his eyes. He'd done it again. His impulse was to do a quick search for the term, but whenever he searched his database, his eyes darted back and forth at such a rapid pace, he'd be a dead giveaway. His hand shook.

"Oh. Your foster family was probably religious, huh?" Jack asked.

Adam glanced between Jack and Evie, holding his breath. He didn't know what religion and Halloween had to do with one another, but he sensed Jack had cast him an unexpected lifeline. He nodded, praying he was doing the right thing.

Jack nodded, pursing his lips, eyes narrowed. "That's cool,

man. Everyone's got a right to their beliefs. Not that I have many."

Adam let out the breath he was holding as the threat warnings subsided.

Evie's mouth formed a small O. "Wow. So you never celebrated Halloween before?"

For the first time, Adam didn't have to lie. "No, I've never celebrated Halloween."

"Do you want to?"

"Sure?" Adam shrugged.

She grabbed his forearm and smiled. "Well, get ready to be corrupted because I freakin' love Halloween."

Adam arched an eyebrow, his breath catching. He was definitely going to research Halloween if it made Evie want to touch him like this.

"Okay, so we have a Halloween party at Ashwater High every year as part of the Fall Festival." Evie beamed, her mind in overdrive. "It's like a week-long celebration. The whole town gets involved. It's a pretty big deal here. Mazy and I are in charge of planning this year. We planned for it to be at the school, but we could move the party here. That would bring in a ton of business. Not to mention an opening for Adam's game. Guys, this could be epic." She looked between Adam and Jack, who didn't quite seem to share her enthusiasm. "Mazy, come here."

Mazy was playing a hunting game with Gage not far behind them. Her legs were in an open stance as she followed something on the screen with a plastic rifle in her arms.

"Hang on." She shot a few more times and put the rifle back in its holster.

Gage frowned and put his rifle back in its place. "Mazy, you're a ringer. You won again."

"What can I say? I'm a mystery." She shrugged and walked toward them.

He muttered under his breath behind her, "She can't get past level one of Pac-Man, but put a rifle in her hands and she's a world-class gamer."

"What's up?" Mazy raised her eyebrows at Evie.

"I know we don't have much time, but we should move the Halloween bash here this year. Adam's game could be a fun focal point. He has 'Thriller.' Don't you think that could be fun?"

Mazy nodded slowly as the idea sank in. "Yes. This is the perfect place. It's dark and spooky."

Jack opened his mouth and Adam thought he was going to say something, but he closed it instead.

"I can see everyone here in costume too. Yes, it's a fantastic idea." Mazy glanced at Jack and tucked her hair behind her ear. "Mr. White, would that be all right? Could we have a school event here?"

"Call me Jack, and I'm game for anything that brings business in. Adam, will your game be ready for the end of the month?"

"Yes, I'm sure it will be ready by then."

"Can you be our point man for this since you go to Ashwater High?" Jack asked. "This could be huge for the arcade."

"I don't know much about advertising." Adam nodded at Evie. "Could you help with that?"

Evie glanced at Mazy and back at Adam. "You focus on

making sure your game works. Leave the rest to me and Mazy."

Mazy nodded. "Yeah, we'll take care of the advertising. What will you charge for the new game, Jack?"

Jack shrugged his shoulders. "Good question. I haven't a clue. I know about coin-operated games. What do you say, Adam? What's the charge to play your game?"

Adam looked at the counter. He had no clue about monetizing his game. He only knew how to program and make it fun. Plus, he had some adjustments to make to some of the eighties' songs Jack required him to play. Derrick was helping him to alter and update some of them. He hoped Jack wouldn't mind, but those would take a few more weeks to work out.

Slowly, Adam said, "I would recommend that you charge for entrance to the whole arcade. Allow playing on my game as part of an entrance fee."

Jack smiled. "Smart. A flat fee for the evening. Great idea. You girls will handle planning?"

Evie and Mazy smiled and nodded.

"Great" Evie replied. "I suddenly have an urge to play DP."

Adam offered his arm to her. "Me too. Let's go."

11

BEAT IT

Evie

E vie loved the feel of Adam's arm under her fingertips—strong and solid. She'd only played *Dance Paradise* once, but now that they were going to have Ashwater High's latest shindig here, she'd better practice. Spending more time with Adam was a bonus.

Adam led Evie into the cavernous back room where his game resided, their friends behind them. Evie let go of Adam's arm as he went to the game console, joined by Gage, Luke, and Derrick. Mazy and Sloan joined Evie at the center of the room.

"This is badass, right?" Sloan swung her long, straight hair from side to side as she scanned the room.

Mazy followed suit, spinning around, her gaze traveling the length of the room and ceiling. "Yeah. I can't wait to see what it does. Evie's already played with Adam, but this is my first time."

"Mine too. Maybe we could test it out together?" asked Sloan.

Mazy raised her eyebrows, smiling. "Sure."

Derrick and Luke walked over to them, and Evie couldn't help but notice that, while their appearance was identical, their demeanors were distinct. Derrick, a hair shorter, kept his hands tucked in his jeans pockets, while Luke folded his across his muscular chest.

"Hey guys, you want to see Adam's skills?" Derrick asked.

"I already have," Evie replied. "He's a really good dancer."

Derrick and Luke exchanged glances.

Luke responded, "Um, are you talking about when you and Adam danced to 'Funkytown'? Because that song is easy."

Evie wrinkled her nose up. "Haha. Yeah, so what?"

"Go see for yourself." Derrick pointed to the gaming console where Adam and Gage were.

"Okay, I will." Evie walked up behind Adam and Gage and peered between them.

There, on the large monitor mounted in the console, were categories and song titles. Adam scrolled through them, using his fingertips on the touchscreen.

"So, Derrick and Luke said I need to see your skills. Can I pick a song for you?" she asked.

Adam and Gage moved aside to give her access to the console. Adam said, "Sure, pick a song."

Evie eyed Adam and Gage, who grinned from ear to ear. She looked at the console. Sure enough, at the top of the list was 'Funkytown' under Easy. She sighed. She wasn't exactly light on her feet, but the song was plenty hard for her to keep up with. She couldn't imagine what a difficult song might be like.

"Okay, let's see what we have." She drummed her finger-nails against the console and scrolled through the list.

Quite a few songs were in the Difficult category. Further down, she saw a category listed as Insane. Two songs were listed—one eighties' rock and the other pop. She recognized both. But which to choose?

"Can I pick any song for you?" she asked, eyeing the insane category mischievously.

Gage laughed. "Go for it, Evie."

"Whatever song you want," Adam said.

"Done." Evie tapped on the song at the very bottom.

Adam raised his eyebrows at Gage.

"No, bro." Gage laughed. "You're on your own."

Adam unbuttoned his short-sleeved shirt, revealing a snug-fitting, ribbed, white tank.

Evie tried her hardest not to stare, but it was a losing battle. *Damn, he's got a great body.*

He laid his shirt across the side of the game console and picked up the glove he used the last time they'd played together. He smiled at Evie.

She arched her eyebrow and smiled back, her eyes wandering to his chest and arms. His skin was smooth and taut, with not even a hint of a freckle or mole—perfect. God, what she wouldn't do to have him sit for her to sketch properly.

"Hey, I'm up here," he said.

Evie inhaled sharply, snapping her eyes back to his, her cheeks aflame. "What? Sorry."

"See, I'm learning."

She laughed nervously. *Touché.*

Adam walked to the middle of the dance floor. He

followed the simple steps on the screen, so the game could recognize his body movements.

Evie joined the others at the back of the room for a better view. Gage and Luke were making a bet about Adam's score, while Derrick explained to Mazy and Sloan how the game worked.

"I helped Adam modify some of the songs to make them more current." Derrick grinned at the others, his pride showing. "Jack said that they had to be eighties' songs, but he didn't say anything about us remixing them. This is one of them, not that it needed it though."

"Yeah, I have to admit you guys did a good job," Luke added.

Mazy linked her arm with Evie's. "So what song did you pick?"

Before Evie could respond, the telltale synthesized gongs started, and the mounted, colored spotlights in the room all directed toward Adam. The screen lit with an image of Michael Jackson as the sound of "Beat It" filled the room.

"Nice," Mazy said.

Adam started moving, side to side, slowly at first. Different pathways around the dancefloor lit up as if foreshadowing what was to come. When the guitar kicked in, Adam was moving, traveling the length of the room at lightning speed, his entire body in sync with the beat. His score was off the charts as his freestyle bar filled. He flew through the air like he did when he played with her, slamming his feet down hard as his freestyle bar exploded. The entire floor lit in different colors, as a new beat started.

He changed his dancing style, moving around the room to

a new rhythm in freestyle mode. Evie didn't know much about dance moves, but he was using every part of his body. One second he was on his feet, the next he was on his knees sliding, and then he was on his hands to launch himself back onto his feet. It was like music flowed directly into his body like electricity through a conductor. When the bar on the screen was empty, he followed the dance moves on the screen again.

Evie's breath caught in the back of her throat. While the others clapped and hollered his name around her, she stood still, mesmerized by his beauty and skill. Thankfully, Mazy nudged her shoulder, jolting her mind back to those around her. She joined the others in clapping to the rhythm while Adam continued to rack up points, hitting every note to perfection. When his freestyle bar filled again, he took advantage. How he'd learned this from watching YouTube was beyond her.

The song faded out, and Adam came to a halt, chest heaving. His score lit the board, almost perfect. The others joined him on the dance floor.

"That was amazing," Mazy said.

Sloan added, "Yeah, sick."

Luke and Derrick patted Adam on the back.

"Nice one. You tried out some new stuff in freestyle," Luke said, nodding in Gage's direction.

"Yeah, it was." Gage frowned and handed a folded twenty from his front pocket to Luke.

Adam pushed his hair off his forehead, beads of perspiration dotting his hairline, a smile firmly planted on his face. He licked his lips, his blue eyes sparkling as his gaze found Evie's. He pulled the glove off his hand. "Thanks, guys."

"All right, I'm next. Luke, you want to challenge?" Derrick reached for the glove.

"Mazy and I are after that," Sloan said.

The others walked over to the game console, leaving Adam and Evie alone. Evie didn't care about playing DP anymore. She was too busy capturing the expression on Adam's face in her mind. There was tenderness there, a look of contentment. But also heat and passion. It was the same for her when she had a pencil in her hand and a subject in her mind. Her heart clenched.

"That was incredible," she said, beaming at him.

Adam closed the distance between them, the heat from his exertion radiating from his body to hers. "Thanks."

Now, it was her turn to wet her lips as she stared at his.

God, his mouth is kissable.

She wanted to know what those lips would feel like pressed against hers. Would he be soft and gentle or strong and forceful? She'd had her share of kisses, but she was no expert. Perhaps a bit of both would be nice. Her stomach did some flip-flops, and she instinctively licked her lips. But as the tension mounted, she snapped out of her trance.

What am I doing? Quit staring at him like he's a piece of meat. Get a freakin' grip, girl.

She chuckled anxiously and looked away.

"Um, I guess I should go check out some of the other songs you have." She turned to walk toward the others, who were crowded around the game console.

Adam said nothing but reached for her hand. He slipped his arm around her shoulder, sending sparks up and down her arm and back. As they walked over to the others together, Evie held her breath, afraid to let go of the moment. She could stay nestled to his side like this for hours, and the thought sent her over the edge.

She wouldn't stop drawing him. Not now, or any time soon.

Even worse, there was no getting around a very important fact—she had it bad for Adam Williams.

12

EVENING INTERLUDE

Adam

Adam sat on his bed, tapping his toes to music in his room. He was still working on remixes for *Dance Paradise*. Not every eighties' song worked, but many did. He was adding a new option for the songs so that players could select classic or remixed versions when they played. Derrick was helping when he didn't have to work at Dixon's. Adam was happy for his help—he had an aptitude for arrangement.

Jack peeked his head inside the door after a quick knock. His brown hair was pulled back in a low ponytail, his graying sideburns showing his age. But he had a youthful sparkle in his blue eyes. The pungent scent that followed Jack everywhere rolled into the small room. Daisy called it patchouli.

Adam turned down his music.

"Hey, kid," Jack started. "Daisy and I are going to take off for a few days. You know, get away from it all. Can you run the joint after school tomorrow and this weekend?"

Adam stood. "Sure thing."

Jack smiled. "Groovy. I'll pay you extra." He turned to leave but hesitated. "Hey, if you ever need anything or, like, someone to talk to, Daisy and I are here. Well, not this weekend, but you get my drift, right?"

Adam nodded and smiled. He had grown very fond of Jack and Daisy. They were as close as he would probably ever get to having a family. But they would likely feel differently if they knew what was humming inside his head. He didn't know what he would do if he told them the truth and they reacted negatively. Yeah, best to keep that secret from them—and everyone, for that matter.

"Thanks, Jack," Adam said.

"You're a good kid. Later." He shut the door, leaving Adam to his music and thoughts.

The phone buzzed next to him on the bed. He picked it up and read:

EVIE: *What r u up to?*

Adam's heart, or whatever resided in his chest, sped up. He had been wanting to text with Evie all day, but the arcade was busy and he didn't have time. It was past ten when he finished and thought it might be too late for her.

ADAM: *Listening to music in my room. What r u doing?*

EVIE: *:) Homework. I hate math.*

Adam smiled. Math was beyond easy for him. A benefit of having a computer for a brain.

ADAM: *I could help you if you want. Math is my strength.*

EVIE: *Seriously?*

ADAM: *Sure, why not?*

EVIE: *Okay.*

"Yes," Adam said, fist pumping.

He glanced in the mirror above the sink, checking his

teeth and running his fingers through his hair. He slipped on his converse and pulled a hoodie over his head. It was getting cooler, and while he had trouble sensing hot and cold, his skin reacted to both temperatures—perspiration in heat and goose-bumps in cold. He put his phone in his pocket and headed out the door. He had Evie's address filed in a permanent folder in his memory.

Evie

Evie stared at her phone, waiting for him to respond. But no little bubbles appeared. She drew her knees to her chest, sitting on her bed, her sketch pad and pencils strewn around her. Her parents were out at the movies tonight, and she had the house to herself. She told Adam that she was working on her math homework, but really, she was procrastinating and sketching instead.

She stared even more impatiently at her phone.

Why won't you respond?

Her phone stared back at her, unmoving. She groaned and tossed her phone on the bed. She got up and headed to the bathroom to get ready for bed. Math homework would have to wait until tomorrow, just like Adam's response apparently.

***

Evie emerged from the bathroom with a clean face and teeth, wearing fluffy shorts, slippers, and her favorite tank top sans bra. She had piled her mass of dark hair on top of her head in a messy bun. She counted her blessings where her complexion was concerned. For all the makeup she liked to wear, her skin tolerated it well. Sure, she got a zit or two before her period but nothing like some of the other kids at school.

The doorbell rang.

Evie jumped and covered her mouth. Who would be at her house this late? Suddenly, she wanted her parents to be home pronto. She crept back to her room and peered out her window where she had a view of the front door from the second story. She gasped.

Adam!

She lifted her window open, leaned her head out, and whisper-yelled to him, "What are you doing here?"

Adam moved back off the porch and looked up, beaming. "Oh, hey, Evie. I'm here to help you with math."

"What?" Evie gripped her windowsill, her nerves fraying. "Oh my God, I didn't mean *now*."

"Oh. Sorry." Adam frowned, his head dropping. He turned and walked back down her walkway.

He was just going to leave, after coming all this way? She should invite him in, shouldn't she? Besides, her parents wouldn't be home for at least another hour or so. Her chest clenched as she made her decision.

"Hey, hang on," she said. "You're already here. Give me a minute, okay? Then you can come up."

Adam turned back around and smiled. "Really?"

"Yeah, sure. Just give me a minute."

"You got it."

Evie turned around, her mind awhirl about what to do first. Makeup? Get changed? Put a bra on? She looked at her wall.

Oh, holy Jesus.

One side of her room to the other was covered in sketches of him. *Covered.*

Some of them depicted him shirtless. A bra and makeup could wait.

She launched on top of her bed and carefully pulled them down. She didn't want to ruin them, but she couldn't let him see either.

"Hey," Adam said behind her.

Evie jumped, a scream catching in her throat. Slowly, she peered over her shoulder to confirm that Adam was, in fact, now seated in her windowsill.

Damn everything to hell. He was.

She cringed and took the sketches she was holding and shoved them down her tank top. She looked up. There were plenty more still pinned on the wall in plain sight. She was caught. Dead to rights. Full exposure. Her cheeks burned, and her heartbeat pounded in her ears. She didn't want to face him.

"I said I needed a minute," she said.

"I know. I waited a minute."

Evie turned, holding her breath. She wanted to die and have it be a quick one. Nothing too drawn out. A split second and have it be done. A lightning strike. Yes, that would work. But, it wasn't likely since she was inside, and the storm predicted wasn't due until after midnight.

He was inside her room, her window pushed all the way up. Fortunately, or maybe unfortunately, he wasn't looking at her. His eyes traveled the wall behind her, his mouth set. Evie stepped off her bed, her arms crossed over her chest, staring at her dark blue carpet. Would he notice if she quietly ducked out of her room?

You coward. Of course, he would.

Adam moved forward and pressed his fingertips on one of the pictures. It was one she drew of him when they first met. "I don't have hair on my chest there."

Oh yeah, he was shirtless in that one too.

Why is this my life? Why God?

"I don't know what to say. Um—"

Adam turned to face her. "This is how you feel."

How I feel?

She wasn't sure what he meant by that, but she was certainly feeling something right now. Her cheeks burned, and her head swam at an Olympics pace. If only she could crawl under her bed and die with the dust bunnies. But that wasn't an option, now was it? She peered at him, not sure what to expect.

To her surprise, his eyes were soft and appreciative. He wasn't freaked out or angry that she had drawn him to the extent that he saw. But he also didn't see the dozen or so more she had shoved down the front of her tank top.

As if following her train of thought, he glanced at her clumpy chest and back at her face. He shifted side to side, glancing everywhere but at her. He opened his mouth a few times and shut it.

"What? Just say it," she said.

"I promised you I wouldn't."

"What? When?"

"At the arcade. I said I would never say anything about your appearance again."

"Oh. Yeah, that's right." Evie looked down at her large frumpy chest and smiled. "Maybe in this case, that's a wise choice?"

She turned her back to him, pulled the sketches of her shirt, and set them on her desk face down. When she turned back around, he was looking at more of her sketches, some of him and some of other kids from school.

"You've got a great eye for the human form," he said. "This one is Gage and Mazy, right?"

Evie walked over to stand by his side. "Yep. They sat for me last winter, I think?"

"Sat?"

"Modeled. You know, they stayed still, so I could draw them."

Adam glimpsed at her and back at the sketches of him. "But I've never sat for you."

Her chest rose and fell like ocean tides, making the fact that she was not wearing a bra more obvious. She stared at the drawings. If a rock bottom for embarrassing moments existed, she had descended past that mark straight into humiliation hell itself.

"I know," she said. "Sometimes, I capture things in my mind and draw them later from memory."

His eyes lit up. "I can help you."

"Oh, I'm not up for math homework anymore."

Adam pulled his hoodie and T-shirt over his head. He placed both on her bed.

Oh shit. Adam Williams just took his shirt off in my bedroom.

He was right too—no hair at the center of his chest like she had imagined and drawn. But all the cuts and lines of muscle were exactly as she pictured. Her heart rate whipped up a furious beat. She couldn't look away, and at the same time, she tried to look everywhere but at him.

"Um, what are you doing?" she asked.

Adam pointed at the sketches. "Sitting for you."

She glanced around her room, butterflies taking flight in the pit of her stomach, her mind on fire. He wanted to sit for her. Shirtless. Here. In her bedroom. Home alone? She looked back at his clean, formed chest and abs. *So, six packs do exist.*

Her fingers twitched for her pencils, but she was having trouble focusing. "I can't…I mean, I don't think I could."

Adam reached for her hand. "Sure, you can."

13

ARTIST AND MODEL

Adam

His CPU was on fire, igniting the rest of his organic body along with it. Evie was the most beautiful thing he'd ever seen. She'd forgone her usual dark eye makeup, her cheeks were a lovely shade of pink, and she wore a light blue tank top that no longer looked crumpled but accentuated the fullness of her breasts. Her dark hair, piled atop her head, bounced around, threatening to come undone. Her short fluffy shorts had clouds on them, appropriate for the angel that stood before him, and her bare feet wiggled into the carpet, her toes colored fluorescent pink. He glanced at his outstretched hand she had yet to take.

Evie tilted her head to the side, glancing between his hand and his eyes, weighing her decision. She inhaled sharply through her nose and placed her hand in his. An electric current shot from his central processor to his extremities. He'd done his research on sexual attraction, but experiencing it for real—remarkable. He squeezed her hand gently and smiled.

"Okay." Her cheeks flushed a deeper pink. She led him over to her desk chair. "Why don't you sit here?"

He let go of her hand and sat in the chair she indicated.

Evie picked up a large sketchbook from her bed and a pencil case. When she looked back at Adam, she narrowed her eyes. "Um, is that comfortable for you?"

Adam didn't know what she was talking about. He felt perfectly comfortable. His legs were firmly planted on the floor, his hands resting on his thighs, back straight. "Yes. Should I do something different?"

She chuckled, putting her things back down. She approached him and placed her hands on his bare shoulders. "Let's start by loosening you up."

He stiffened. She nudged his legs apart with her thighs so she could straddle one leg to access his shoulders more easily. He had never been this close to someone before. Her body heat permeated through space and denim onto his thighs.

Slowly, she massaged his shoulders. He leaned into her touch and closed his eyes. He had a folder in his brain called human emotions. In his short life, his dancing experiences were the only files in the folder.

Now, he'd add this moment.

"There, that's better." But she wasn't done. Her hands moved to his knees, and he opened his eyes. Her heart-shaped face was right in front of his, and she was smiling. She shook his knees side to side. "Loosen your bottom half."

He smiled back and tried his best to relax. *Loosen up. Stop acting like a robot. Be human.*

She stood and crossed her arms, narrowing her eyes at him, assessing. "Try leaning back and to the side for me and rest your arm on the top of the chair."

He followed her instructions. "Like this?"

"Yeah. Now, maybe straighten your legs out toward me or cross them casually."

Casually? Adam had no idea what she wanted him to do. So he straightened his legs out and crossed his ankles. "How about this?"

Evie moved back, eyeing him from head to toe. She nodded. "Yeah, that works. Now stay in that position if you can."

He smiled. He was an android. He could remain stationary for inordinate amounts of time. Of that, he was sure. "I can do that."

"Great." She went back to her bed and plopped, crossing her legs and pulling her sketch pad into her lap, pencil in hand.

Adam watched her work as she glanced at him and back to her sketch pad. Time stood still. Her large eyes stood out like emeralds, dedicated and serious about the task at hand. Her hair jostled on top of her head as her pencil raced across her sketchpad. Every now and then, the tip of the pencil found its way to her lips as she considered something she had drawn. Occasionally she reached for an eraser, her lips pursed, insistent on getting the drawing right. Sometimes she would smile at her work and then at him.

He recognized what was going on in her head because he experienced the same thing when he danced. But this was much more intimate than that. Dancing, for him, had only ever been a solo act. Art was her passion and purpose, and right now, he was her muse.

After thirty-eight minutes and some change in seconds,

she set her pencil down. She took one last look at her sketchpad.

"Okay, I think I'm done." She glanced back at Adam, smiling. "You were a great model too. I've never seen someone sit so still. Maybe I should check you for a pulse. Were you even breathing?"

He chuckled and stood.

Please don't.

He had biological parts, but he didn't think they worked the same as a human's.

"I'm okay. So can I see?" he asked, changing the subject.

She climbed off her bed and waved her hand at the sketches of him that were still on the wall. "Well, it's not like I've got anything left to hide, right?"

Evie turned her sketch pad around to show her work.

Adam's eyes widened in wonder. She had captured his likeness perfectly. He reached for the sketchpad.

She handed it to him. "What do you think?"

He held the image she created of him in his hands. His eyes focused on his drawn face. She had captured his short, angular chin, his mouth, and his high cheekbones. He'd never seen such likeness in a drawing before. But it wasn't just that. She had seized on something else in his eyes, peering at him knowingly.

There it was—her talent. Somehow her gift allowed her to see his true nature and capture it: his desire to be something he wasn't, his desire to fit in, his desire for control, and most of all, his desire for her.

Evie tilted her head so he'd look at her. "Don't leave me in suspense. If you don't like it, say so."

No. It's perfect."

He was so entranced with the drawing that he decided to take a photograph. He blinked his right eye, snapping a picture for his files.

"Did you just wink at yourself?"

Adam glanced at Evie, whose eyes read confused and wary. *You idiot. Why did you do that?*

He handed back the sketchpad and smiled as best he could. "Oh, no. That's silly. I get dry eyes sometimes."

Evie narrowed her eyes at him. "In one eye?"

Fair enough. "Um, yeah. I guess."

Before she could say anything else, a door slammed shut somewhere below them. A male voice yelled, "Evelyn, we're home."

Evie's eyes grew large. "You have to go."

She picked up his shirt and hoodie and shoved it into his chest then pushed him back over to the window.

"But I want to meet your parents."

"Not now and definitely not with you half naked in my bedroom." She pushed him against the window sill.

She was very anxious, and he didn't understand why. But he didn't want her to worry. He stepped out onto the roof but sat on the edge of her windowsill. "Okay, don't worry. I'll go."

The sound of footsteps on creaky stairs caused Evie to turn to her door once again. When she turned back around, she smiled wickedly. She grasped Adam's cheeks and leaned toward him.

Threat warnings blasted his vision as she startled him. The music playing in the background abruptly changed songs. As she was about to press her lips to his, his eye twitched, and his hand formed a fist.

His defense system was moving into attack mode.

No. I won't hurt her.

With every fiber of his manmade being, he forced himself back, causing him to fall out the window away from her. He rolled down the sloping roof, catching himself before he fell from the second story.

"Oh shit, I'm so sorry," she whispered loudly, leaning out her window. "You okay?"

Adam shook his head, trying to find a clear space. Everything was out of focus.

What happened?

He identified the faint outline of Evie above him, framed in the window he took a dive out of.

"I'm…okay," he said, waving.

"Okay, good. You have to go."

"Okay," he said, looking around, hoping his vision returned to its former state. He rolled over the edge of the second story roof and dropped back to the ground. Once there, he shuddered, glancing back at Evie's empty window. His mind was one big foggy mess. He pressed his fingers to his lips.

You idiot. The girl of your dreams tried to kiss you and instead of kissing her back, you almost killed her.

He groaned, his processor returning to normal. Adam pulled on his shirt and hoodie, waiting for his vision to clear. Once it did, he took off in a slow jog back to the arcade. Along the way, he accessed the image he took of Evie's drawing. He liked how she saw him, and he wanted to see more of her.

14

FALL FESTIVAL

Evie

The fall festival was almost here, and Mazy had put Evie to work. Not that she minded, but Mazy was an organizational force to be reckoned with. Yesterday, she snapped at Evie for copying flyers on the wrong color orange. Granted, colors were important aesthetically, but for a flyer? Seriously?

Despite dealing with a stressed-out best friend, this was Evie's favorite time of the year. Sweaters, jackets, and her assortment of Docs were comfier. The festival was a week-long event that culminated with a Halloween dance that was now being held at Jack's arcade. Technically, Evie guessed it still was a dance because of DP. The high school's clubs ran booths up and down Main Street, along with the shop owners. Dixon's had their own food stand set up outside the diner.

Mazy sat across from Evie at their lunch table, tapping a pencil on the table. She wore a red headband in her sandy blond hair that matched her red-and-black argyle cardigan. She always looked pretty, but today was extra.

"Red's a good color for you," Evie said, reaching for her backpack where she always had a mini sketch pad on hand.

"Oh, no you don't. This is an organizational lunch. Not Evie-draws-Mazy-again." Mazy smirked. "Besides, I might start getting a big head if you keep that up."

Evie shrugged and went back to picking at her salad. She didn't know why she had packed it. She didn't like salad. "Fine, what's on the agenda, Maze?"

Mazy smiled like the Cheshire Cat. She reached into her bag and pulled out her planner and a stack of flyers printed on the *right* color orange. "We need to distribute these flyers to all the shops on Main to get more participation. Do you think you and Adam might be able to handle that?"

Adam. Evie groaned and slouched in her seat. She'd been avoiding him like the plague. The last time they were face to face, she tried to lay one on him, knocking him almost clear off her roof. And that was only after he saw that she was sketch-stalking him. He'd texted her a few times, but she engaged minimally. She didn't know what to say about what she was now referring to as The Incident.

"Oh, it couldn't have been that bad. I've had awkward kisses too. One time a boyfriend kissed my nose, open mouthed."

"Yeah, I guess. But that wasn't your first kiss, was it?" Evie shifted in her seat. "The Incident was, or I guess, *wasn't* our first kiss? I mean, technically, we didn't, right?"

Mazy nodded behind her. "Maybe now isn't the time to consider whether you and Adam had a meeting of the lips?"

"Why's that?"

"Because he's coming this way."

Evie grabbed her bag. Did she have time to escape? He was

within ten feet and closing in fast. She turned back around, frowned at Mazy, and mouthed, "Help me."

Mazy narrowed her eyes and whispered, "Buck up, buttercup."

"I hate when you call me that." Evie scowled.

"Hey, Evie," Adam said.

Time to face the music. Evie twisted her torso around to look up. Yep, there he was, looking fine as hell in his form-fitting heather gray t-shirt, worn jeans, and black Converse.

"Hey, Adam."

"Can I sit, or are you guys busy?"

"Actually—" Evie started.

"Of course. Sit. We were just discussing the fall festival. Evie is in charge of handing out flyers to the shops on Main. She could really use your help."

Evie glared at Mazy. *Payback will be a bitch, my friend.*

Adam slid onto the bench next to Evie and smiled at Mazy. "Sure, I'll help out." He glanced at Evie. "If that's all right with you?"

"Yeah, sure." Evie shrugged, fingering the flyers, avoiding his eyes.

"Okay, great. After school? How about I ride your bus to your mother's shop?"

He wanted to meet her mom? Evie's breath caught in her throat, causing her to cough.

"That's a great idea." Mazy nodded slowly in approval. "Evie's mom is amazing. You'll love her."

Evie opened her mouth again, and still, nothing came out.

"Cool. I'll meet you on your bus," Adam said. "See you after school."

Evie stared at her salad again. Now she had full-blown lost

her appetite. Her stomach was tied in knots, something that happened often when Adam was around. She managed a nod and stared at Mazy, who watched Adam depart.

After a minute, Mazy said, "He's gone."

"Why did you do that?"

"Because I knew you wouldn't. Stop being such a coward. He obviously likes you."

Evie sat up and leaned forward. "You could tell all that from the one minute he was here?"

Mazy split the distance between them, crossing her arms on the table. "Evie, anyone with eyes within thirty feet of this table could see that he likes you."

Evie smiled and glanced around at the rest of the cafeteria. Most of the other kids were focused on their own conversations, but a few tables of girls whispered and glanced back over at her and Mazy. On the other side of the cafeteria, Adam sat with Gage, Luke, and Derrick. The group of boys smiled in her direction.

She met Adam's gaze, and she understood. She parted her lips, as the distance between them shrank. It was like they were the only two people in the cafeteria. Her heart skipped a beat, and the nervous knots in her stomach turned into beautiful butterflies.

Mazy was right. Adam liked her despite The Incident. She smiled and nodded back at him.

***

Evie wasted no time getting to her bus, hopefully before Adam. She wanted to collect herself before she saw him. Her heart beat so hard it was deafening. Her palms were sweaty, and her breath caught with each step down the sidewalk in front of the school. She reached the entrance to the bus and climbed the stairs, smiling at Midge, the bus driver.

Midge was an older woman, probably in her late sixties. She had lived in Ashwater her whole life. She came into Evie's mom's shop often and always seemed to buy a piece. Evie often imagined what her house must look like, with all the artwork she had purchased. Her kinky gray hair was worn wild, and she let the open windows swirl it even more out of control. Evie had grown close to her in the last three years, like a gran.

Midge whistled. "Hello, Evelyn. Well, you certainly look pretty this afternoon."

Evie's cheeks warmed. She perused the bus, which was close to empty and didn't include Adam. "Thanks, Midge." She leaned closer and whispered, "I kinda have a date."

Midge's mouth formed an O. "Well, it's about time you found interest in someone. I was beginning to wonder if you were in love with your drawings."

"Haha," Evie said, rolling her eyes.

"Well, go find a good seat, girl."

Evie nodded and headed to the middle of the bus by the window. The sun peeked out from behind the clouds that covered it for most of the day, warming her face through the glass. She closed her eyes and took a long cleansing breath.

Calm down. It's a bus ride and handing out flyers. Don't try to kiss him again. Let him make the first move.

She wrinkled up her nose and stretched her hands out to her knees. *What if he doesn't?*

Quit. Stop thinking about it so much.

"Hey."

Evie's eyes flew open. Adam was leaning on her seat in front of her.

"Oh my God." She covered her heart with her hand. "You almost gave me a heart attack."

"I'm sorry. You were in another world there with your eyes closed. I'm afraid I was going to startle you no matter what I did." He sat next to her.

"Oh. Yeah, I do that sometimes—zone out." She detected a fresh coating of body spray—notes of cedar and leather. She fought the urge to lean into him to get a better whiff.

He looked her up and down and smirked. "Well, I'd tell you that you look beautiful, but I promised you I wouldn't."

Evie's stomach flip-flopped, her breath catching. No one— well, except for her mom and dad—had ever referred to her as beautiful. Cute? Sure. But beautiful?

She nodded approvingly and nudged his shoulder with hers. "Well, wonders never cease. You're catching on, Williams."

"Does this mean I have permission to remark on your appearance?" He arched an eyebrow, and Evie melted. She'd add that sexy expression to her next sketch. She'd started some water coloring too. She didn't have nearly as much experience with paint, but she needed to get out of her comfort zone. Sketching was like breathing now, and she liked a challenge.

Evie put up a hand. "Well, let's not get ahead of ourselves here. Per my tally, your record is one compliment to two insults."

"Okay, fair enough. But this one was good, right?"

The honesty in his eyes told Evie something she wasn't quite comfortable with—he really *didn't* know the insults he had flung at her previously were rude. It reminded her of the last time she rode a bus with him. She didn't know much about him and his background. She needed to work on that.

"Yes," she said. "Telling me that I look beautiful is always going to be welcome."

Adam glanced around at the rest of the kids on the bus, grinning like a teacher's pet. A song started playing, coming from the person seated in front of them. It sounded like an eighties' rock song. She wasn't exactly up on the rock music from that decade, but she had some working knowledge. Adam started drumming his hands on the seat in front of them and tapping his toes on the floor.

"What's going on? Is that my phone?" the boy sitting in front of them asked.

Adam popped his head around the seat. "I like it. Leave it."

"Okay?" the boy said.

Evie couldn't see the boy, but his tone sounded confused.

Adam looked back at Evie, his hands and feet still in motion. "Hey, after we hand out those flyers, do you wanna DP?"

Evie's parents didn't have a dinner planned, so she could go home later if she wanted. Adam made pouty faces at her, not that his lips had to do much work.

"You really love that game, don't you?"

"Yeeeessss," he said, bobbing his head to the music.

"Okay, sure."

He kept his drumming up for another two or three songs. The boy in front of them occasionally muttered that he didn't understand what was going on with his phone. Somehow, music seemed to play wherever Adam went. Evie smiled at Adam as he occasionally tapped on her thigh with his fingertips as if she were a cymbal, sending electric currents running up and down her leg. His smile was contagious, his love for the music so evident. Her skin prickled and warmed.

Stop staring at his mouth.

She forced herself to look out the window and take a deep breath.

Calm down. You are not going to attack him again. You can handle this.

Evie turned to face him. *Oh, God. I'm screwed.*

15

GROOVY

Adam

His hand swayed back and forth inches from Evie's as they walked to her mother's art shop. He hadn't been able to shut down properly since the fall from her roof a week ago. Every time he texted her, she responded with only a "k" or "yep."

Had she seen something? Did she suspect what he was?

So far today, he was in the clear. But there had to be a reason that she wasn't bringing up the incident. His instinct was to leave it alone. Although, the next time an opportunity for a kiss arose, he'd be prepared.

Evie scrunched up her face. Her gaze darted from the door of the shop to the sidewalk and back again.

Why was she nervous about him meeting her parents? Based on his research, this was an essential step in courtship for humans.

He tapped her hand with his. "Hey, we don't have to go in, if you don't want to."

She peered up at him. He held his breath, hoping she didn't take him up on his offer.

"No, it's fine. My mom's okay." She walked over to the door, Adam in tow.

As soon as they stepped inside, he cringed, covering his nose.

The scent of acetone hit him hard. Granted, his smell detection was much keener and more accurate than most humans.

"Sorry. It's the varnish remover. My mom does restorative work. You get used to it."

Adam nodded and dropped his hand, even though he didn't want to. He glanced around at the paintings adorning the walls. Most were landscapes, oil on canvas.

Evie leaned over the counter. "Mom!" She turned to Adam. "She's usually in the back, and she doesn't always hear the bells on the door."

Adam joined her at the counter. Despite the smell, he liked the look of the shop. While the walls were painted white, the furniture was homey. Two coffee tables with price sheets and comfy armchairs were situated at the front of the store on either side of the door. He couldn't help but envision Evie curled up in one of the chairs, sketching while she waited for her mom to finish.

An older version of Evie emerged from the doorway behind the counter. She smiled at Evie then at Adam. He could tell by the tiny lines around her mouth that she did it often.

"Evie, I didn't know you were coming into town today. Who's your friend?"

"This is Adam Williams. He's new this year."

"Please to meet you, Mrs. Grayson." Adam extended his hand, hoping she would take it before noticing that he was trembling. This was something he couldn't control. Something about his nature forced him to see anyone new as a potential threat. Although, he was slowly getting better at it.

"Serena," she said, placing her hand in his.

He relaxed, detecting her normal pulse. "Serena."

"Well, I must say, it's nice to finally meet you in person."

Evie stared at her mom and shook her head in slow motion. "Adam and I are handing these out." She slid a flyer across the counter. "Are you going to put some art out front?"

Serena nodded abruptly and picked up the flyer. "Yes, I think I will. Do you want to add anything to sell?"

Evie shrugged. "I don't think so."

Adam turned to Evie. "You should sell your drawings. They're really good."

"He's right, honey. If you want to be a professional artist, you're going to have to start putting your work out there."

"I don't know." Evie scratched at a crack in the countertop, her eyes cast down. "I'll think about it." She glanced at Adam. "We should get going."

Serena nodded. "Okay, well, it was nice meeting you, Adam. I hope to see you again?"

Adam smiled. "I hope so too."

"Bye, Mom." Evie walked to the door.

"Bye."

Adam held the door for Evie, and they walked back outside. "Your mom seems really nice."

"Yeah, she's cool."

"Now, I need to meet your father."

Evie's shoulders tensed, and she glanced everywhere but at him. "Uh, yeah. Sometime. We'd better get going."

Adam tilted his head, his CPU awhirl. This wasn't the first time she'd skirted the issue of him meeting her father. If he was anything like Serena, they would get along fine. But he didn't want to ruin their afternoon by pushing her to talk about it.

Instead, he took half the flyers from her hand. "Okay, after you."

Adam and Evie canvased most of Main and had a few more shops before they ended back at Jack's.

"So, tell me something about you that I'd be shocked by," Evie said. "And, you can't say that you're a professional dancer or gamer because that wouldn't be a shock."

Adam took a deep breath. "Did you know that Jack was a competitive gamer back in the eighties? He competed in world tournaments and everything."

"Really? I guess that shouldn't surprise me because he owns an eighties-themed arcade. But he's so chill. I can't see it."

"It's true."

Evie took the remaining flyers from Adam. "You, sir, are dodging my question. I'm going into the dress shop while you think of an answer to my question."

Warning. Warning. Possible exposure.

Adam silenced the message and rubbed his trembling hand up and down his thigh. "'Kay."

After she disappeared into the shop, he paced back and forth on the sidewalk.

Think. What can you tell her that will shock her?

His hand shook violently at the thought of revealing his true nature. Nope, not that. He'd never hurt her.

Oh, that she was the first. *That's it. That's what I can tell her.*

The door to the dress shop opened, and Evie's eyebrows were raised as she sauntered over to him. "Well? What did you come up with?"

"You're the first girl I've ever liked."

Her jaw fell, eyes wide.

Did he say something wrong? Was it odd that he hadn't dated before? Well, of course, he hadn't. As far as he knew, he'd only been alive for a year.

"Too forward?" he asked.

"No. Just, I can't believe you've never had a girlfriend."

"Why's that?"

She smiled the same way she did right before she tried to kiss him. His heart clenched. "Because you're stupid hot."

Adam had made huge gains in learning how to talk like a guy his age should, but stupid seemed odd in front of hot. He was far from stupid, and he didn't think she thought he was either. So, he filed stupid as a complimentary statement.

He smiled. "So does that mean my answer suffices?"

"Yep. Sure does."

Adam reached for her hand, which she placed in his. "Come on, then."

Together, they walked to Jack's. As soon as they opened the door to the arcade, they were greeted by Jack and Daisy in a heated exchange.

Daisy's hair was red today, like the ire in her tone. While she was tiny, she held her own with Jack, pointing her polished fingertip at him. "You never want to spend any money on this place. The snack bar needs to be redone. My brother knows people in the biz. I can get a good deal, you know?"

Jack tried to put his arms around her waist. "Babe—"

She moved away from him. "Don't you 'babe' me. I mean it, Jack. You have to start updating this place if you want to keep up in business." Daisy noticed Adam and Evie. "Good, the kid's here. Even he's doing stuff to this dump. He took that huge storage room and turned it into a kickass game that kids want to play."

Jack glanced at Adam and Evie. "Hey, guys. We're having one of those old couple tiffs."

"Tiff?" Daisy groaned and stomped off back to the snack bar and proceeded to bang things.

Adam and Evie approached Jack. "*Dance Paradise* is ready. We should be able to make some good money. Maybe that would help?"

Jack grabbed Adam and Evie by the shoulder and turned them away from Daisy's view. He whispered, "It's okay. I ordered all new equipment for the snack bar. I want to surprise her. They're going to install everything before the festival on her day off."

Evie replied quietly, "Oh, that's awesome. She'll die."

Adam stared at Evie. Die? He hoped not.

Jack smiled. "Yeah, she'll be blown away, for sure."

That term, Adam understood. They were using words to describe how surprised she would be. Now, it was his turn. "Yeah, she'll go straight to hell."

They stared at him, mouths agape.

Evie asked, "Are you okay?"

Jack squeezed his shoulder. "That's okay, Adam." To Evie, he added, "He's had a sheltered life. Sometimes he gets stuff mixed up. No one's perfect, right?"

"Uh, yeah. Sorry." Adam cringed and documented his

blunder. The phrase he used was popular, but obviously not in this instance. Luckily, Jack covered for him like he always seemed to do.

"Okay, well, you guys keep this on the down low," Jack said. "I don't want my girl to know any of this."

Evie twisted her index finger and thumb in front of her lips and tossed an imaginary key away. Brilliant! Adam understood her meaning perfectly. He mimicked her, although he must not have had quite the same impact because both Evie and Jack were staring at him again.

"Just go." Jack chuckled. "Thanks, guys."

As Adam and Evie walked to the back room, Adam smiled at Daisy, but she was busy staring at the sparkly countertop, her eyes troubled. He cued "Faithfully" by Journey on the jukebox and turned around and nodded at Jack, who saluted him in kind.

There. Maybe that would help them make up.

As they entered the hallway to the back room, he heard "A View to a Kill" by Duran Duran coming from DP. Adam smiled. Something about the song resonated within him. He'd given the guys permission to play whenever they wanted. The more they played, the more data he acquired for wanted adjustments.

Derrick was playing against Luke and winning. Gage and Sloan were standing at the back of the room, clapping along to the beat. Adam and Evie joined them as Derrick and Luke battled on. Derrick was good at pop and alternative songs, while Luke had a better feel for some of the more physically challenging rock songs.

But today they were neck and neck. This one would probably come down to freestyle, and they both had one more.

Derrick hit his freestyle first as the chorus started. Luke hit his a few beats behind. They danced, hitting as many squares on the floor as they could while staying with the beat. Once the freestyle ended, they returned to their spots and finished following the prescribed moves to the end. Their scores lit up.

Derrick won and had no problem rubbing it in his brother's face. "Not good enough, Luke."

"Yeah, well, let's see how you do when we're playing a real song."

"Don't hate on my music. Let me guess, you want to dance to some Whitesnake."

Luke stepped closer. "Absolutely."

The brothers were all talk. They'd never gotten physical with one another.

Sloan stepped in between them. "Oh please, I'll wipe the floor with both of you guys. Besides, it's not your turn." She dipped her head to the back of the room. "Look who's here."

Derrick and Luke nodded at Adam and Evie, their grimaces turning into smiles. "Adam, Evie, sup?" Derrick said.

Adam smiled. "Not much. We were handing out flyers and getting people to sign up for the festival. Thought we'd take DP for a spin." He glanced at Gage and Sloan. "You guys have next?"

Gage nodded, but Sloan smiled at Evie. "No, you guys go ahead."

"Okay, we're after you two," Gage said.

"Hey, you guys want to try out group mode? We can play up to eight people." Adam raised his eyebrows.

"For real?" Gage cracked his knuckles.

Sloan nodded slowly. "Hell yeah. I'm in."

"Absolutely," the twins said in unison, eyeing one another.

The competitive vibe in the room was palpable. Adam smiled. He could take all of them. But how would they place behind him? His best guess was Gage in second, followed by Derrick, then…

Evie swatted Adam's chest, snapping his attention to her. "Okay, I'm in, but pick something easy. I'm not competitive like you guys."

The others nodded and responded.

"Oh, yeah, sure."

"No worries."

"Easy-peasy."

Adam smiled. "Don't worry, I've got just the song. We can take the back row."

"Back row, huh?" Evie replied, arching her eyebrow.

He opened his mouth to reply, but Sloan beat him to it, "Don't worry, we won't watch. God knows you've had a panty fire blazing since Adam blew into town."

Evie inhaled sharply, and the room fell silent.

Gage intervened first, "Jesus, Sloan. What the hell?"

Sloan shrugged.

Luke recovered and came to Sloan's defense, "Hey, she speaks Sloan truth."

Adam watched Evie. Her creamy, soft cheeks were stained red and her eyes cast down. He didn't know what Sloan meant by what she said, but it was obviously upsetting to Evie and for a girl who had a retort for everything, to be speechless was significant. His instinct was to come to her defense, but he wasn't sure how. Plus, he'd been screwing up a lot lately. His "straight to hell? comment was still fresh in both his and Evie's minds. He should lay low. Not say anything else that could draw attention.

Evie glanced at him.

Screw it. He said, "If you think her panties are on fire, you should see mine."

Now everyone stared at him, and he didn't know which way it would go. He held his breath as warnings sounded in his head. Keeping his secret was tantamount to him not killing all his new friends. But since he met Evie, he was doing all kinds of stupid shit.

Evie covered her mouth first, her eyes mirthful. Everyone erupted in laughter.

"Bro, I can't believe you said that," Derrick said, his eyes filling with tears.

Sloan chuckled. "Touché." To Evie, she said, "Sorry I blurted that out. I lack a filter."

Evie shrugged her shoulders. "It's okay." She blinked up at Adam and raised her eyebrows. "You wear panties?"

Everyone erupted in laughter again.

Adam exhaled and smiled. He'd finally said the right thing, and his new friends thought he was funny. Maybe he should press his luck. He leaned over and whispered in Evie's ear, "Name the time and place, and I'll show you."

He leaned back and raised his eyebrows.

Evie smirked and swatted his chest with the back of her hand. "Let's not get ahead of ourselves. How about that song?"

"Oh, right." Adam took the controller glove from Derrick and went over to the console. He entered group mode and number of players. Six separate footprints lit up on the dance floor. "Everyone, stand on a spot."

The group followed suit, Evie standing on the one in the back next to an empty set of footprints. Adam walked over to his spot, and everyone calibrated. He used his glove to cue the song he wanted. "Come On Eileen" started, and the rest of the group cheered.

Luke laughed, swaying. "I even like this song."

Adam looked over at Evie.

She smiled. "Cool."

Soon the beat started, and everyone followed the directions on the screen. But Adam didn't need them. He hit all the correct moves along with the notes and was well on his way to filling his freestyle bar. The others did the same. He glanced over at Evie, who was concentrating on the screen. She parted her lips, glancing between the screen and her feet. She was still getting used to the system, but her hips had a feel for the rhythm.

Abandoning gameplay, once his freestyle was full, Adam jumped to ignite it right as the chorus started. He reached Evie in two seconds, grabbing her hands and rocking back and forth, twirling her around the floor. She smiled and followed his lead. He kept it simple, enjoying how she felt in his arms. When his freestyle came to an end, and he didn't want to let her go, she pushed him away.

"Get back to your spot." She laughed.

He smiled, acquiesced, and continued to dance, wanting to fill his freestyle again. The others were doing the same. Evie was getting close too. He calculated that he would finish filling his again before she did. He couldn't wait to see what she did with her freestyle.

Evie followed the steps exactly, and her freestyle bar filled. "What do I do?"

Adam replied, "Jump!"

She jumped, and as she landed, she turned toward him, her hips swaying seductively. Adam's heart pounded. She reached for him and stomped his foot, igniting his freestyle. He pulled her into his arms and moved her around the floor, their eyes locked. She fit against him perfectly, his hand on the small of her back. She wasn't a natural dancer, but she followed his movements like his CPU executed code.

After their bars depleted, she went back to her spot to finish the song. He followed suit, but he didn't care about the game anymore, his body betraying any inclination to win. Instead, he focused on Evie. Her bright eyes shifted from the screen to her feet as she kept up with the rhythm, a perfect smile on her lips. He was glad he selected an easy song for her.

The song came to an end. The others were talking, but he wasn't listening.

"Shut up. I placed third?" Evie swayed her hips in a victory dance and smirked at Adam.

Snapping out of his trance, Adam looked at the screen. Gage had come in first, followed by Derrick, then Evie. Sloan and Luke followed, with Adam at the bottom.

Derrick approached Adam, the concern in his dark brown eyes was palpable. "Dude, are you feeling okay?"

"Of course he is. He's just got his mind on other things." Luke replied for Adam and nodded to Evie, who was still doing her proud-of-herself dancing.

Adam didn't care about his score or the game. He danced with a girl for the very first time in his life. And this wasn't any girl. This was Evelyn Grayson, a girl that made his CPU run wild. He couldn't help but reflect on the gravity of the moment and how far he'd come. Before Ashwater, he'd only known a locked white cell, unkind guards, and the training room at the facility where he'd learned how to kill.

Now, he was dancing. Now, he had friends—real, live ones

too. He also had Jack and Daisy, who treated him more like a son than an employee. Now, he wanted Evie. His heart swelled, his eyes softening. He wanted a life here, and he wanted her to be a part of it.

He caught Evie's eye and smiled.

She danced over to him and extended her hand for a high five. "Nailed it."

Adam slapped her hand. "Yeah, you did."

16

COSTUME DILEMMA

Evie

Last year, Evie and Mazy had dressed up together as an angel and a devil. Mazy already had the makings of a perfect angel—cherubic blond hair, freckles dotting her nose, and pale blue eyes. All she needed was the halo and white dress. Evie, on the other hand, was born to be a devil, and she had the boots to match. She'd hand-painted a pair of tall black Docs with red flames. She loved them, but they didn't exactly work with anything else she owned except the devil costume. She'd been trying to come up with something else she could dress as to match the boots, but nothing was surfacing. Besides, why waste all that brainpower when she could repeat what she did last year?

Mazy, on the other hand, was having a fit. "No. I won't allow you to wear the same costume two years in a row. It's like a rule or something. You can't do it."

It was the day before the Halloween party at Jack's, and

Mazy rode the bus home with her so they could hash out costumes once and for all. Mazy and Evie had been going nonstop all week with the fall festival activities. So far, it had been a great success. Locals and tourists visited vendors and shops on Main Street and bought, bought, bought. Ashwater, being a quaint town set in the Rockies, attracted adventure seekers, skiers, and anyone looking for a peaceful getaway from city life. Many came from Denver, but Evie had met people from all over the world. The tourists did tons for business owners, including her family's art shop, which was why Evie was always happy to help out with the festival.

Now, it was time to celebrate the culmination of the week —Halloween night. Or rather, the first Friday before the thirty-first, which happened to fall on the thirtieth this year. The younger kids would be out trick-or-treating on Main Street, while the high schoolers went to the annual Halloween party, held this year at Jack's Arcade. Dixon's agreed to provide a discounted menu for students as well since it was basically across the street. A few teachers had signed up as chaperones to stand guard at both locations.

Evie sat on her bed with her legs crisscrossed and stared her best friend, who leaned against the same window sill Adam climbed in. She lifted her boots as if Mazy was having trouble seeing them.

"Do you understand how amazing these are?" Evie said. "I hand painted them myself. They're gorgeous, and they go with nothing but my devil costume."

Mazy blew her long bangs off her forehead in a huff. "This is why you've been avoiding the costume conversation with me for the last two weeks?" She slid off the ledge and onto the floor. "Eeeevieeee…"

Evie had a flashback of Adam falling out the window and was glad Mazy landed on the floor. "If you can think of something else that would go with these boots, I'm all ears. But they are being worn."

Mazy sat straight up, eyes aglow, exhaling loudly. "Give them to me."

Evie tossed her the boots.

Mazy kicked off her ballerina flats and stuck her foot in one of the boots. She tried on the other, stood and walked around. "Maybe a smidge tight but doable."

"What are you—"

"I'm going as the devil this year, and you, lovey, are going to be the angel."

"I don't do angel."

"That's what Halloween is all about. You get to dress up and be something you aren't. Think about it. You can't wear stuff like you always do. It's like you aren't even dressed up."

"Watch it." Evie scowled. "You're on dangerous ground."

"No offense or anything." Mazy held out her hands.

Evie stood and went over to her closet. Nope. Nothing even remotely angelic in it. She also noted that she did, in fact, wear a ton of black. "Well, I can't wear what you did last year." She grasped for any excuse to get out of Mazy's idea. "You're like a size two, and I'm an eight."

"I've got that covered, girl. Come with me."

An hour later, Evie was wearing a short, white dress with wings and white boots to match. Mazy had dragged her downtown to Dalia's Dress Shop. Luckily or not-so-luckily, Dalia carried costumes this time of year. Evie turned around a few times in front of a three-way mirror and smiled. She did like the boots, and other than the color, it was something she would wear. It wasn't too tight, and at the same time, it showed what curves she had.

Mazy sat in a giant, fluffy, gold armchair like a queen holding court over the dressing rooms. "That looks great on you."

Evie narrowed her eyes at Mazy. She was laying it on a little too thick. She turned around a few more times. "Okay, I'll do it. But only if you promise to go as a devil and wear my boots."

Mazy stood and clasped her hands together. "I'm so ready to be a devil."

"Oh boy, wait until Gage sees you."

"Yeah, sure." Mazy glanced away.

"Hey, are you guys okay?" Evie reached for Mazy's hand.

Mazy shrugged. "Please don't say anything, but I think I want to break up."

"Why? What happened?"

"Nothing. I just don't know if I like him that way. If I'm being honest, I think I only started dating him because everyone expected us to or something."

Evie nodded. "I can understand that. He's captain of the football team, and you're class president."

God, did I just say that?

"Please don't say anything," Mazy said. "I don't want to talk to him about this until after tomorrow night."

"My lips are sealed."

Mazy's expression changed. "Now, let's talk about something positive, like how Adam will react to seeing you in that dress."

Evie looked back in the mirror. "Yikes!"

***

Lying in bed the next day, Evie was a ball of nerves about both her costume and Adam. While he seemed to be acting normal—well, normal for Adam—The Incident still haunted her. She had no idea what had gotten into her when she'd tried to kiss him. She saw something in his eyes when she sketched him, a longing.

It wasn't longing for her though. She'd seen *that* look before with Shane Mendelson, Mazy's cousin from Boulder. He was in town last year for a ski tournament. Their attraction lasted all but twenty-four hours, and he was a terrible kisser— too much tongue. It was like he was aiming for her tonsils, and she had to put up a barricade with own tongue. Evie shuddered, making her bed quake. *Ick.*

She reached for her phone on the nightstand to check the time. It was six-thirty, and her parents were already up and out of the house. This was normal for Mac Grayson, sheriff extra- ordinaire. But not so much for Mom, who was a night owl. She'd said something about a doctor's appointment before opening the shop. The closest medical center was a half an hour away, so that meant an early morning.

Evie kicked back her covers and stood, stretching. She wasn't a morning person either but had gotten used to getting up at the same time every day. Her phone dinged. *Who would be texting her now?*

ADAM: *I need to talk to you.*

Well, that sounds ominous.

EVIE: *Okay. What's up?*

A light rap on her glass made her jump. She looked out her window and saw Adam, crouched, holding up his phone.

"Can I come in?" he said through the glass as if it weren't there.

She wiped at her sleepy eyes and opened her window. "What the hell? It's six-thirty in the freakin' morning."

Adam climbed inside. "I know. I'm sorry. I'm freaking out though."

Evie walked over to her bed and slipped a fluffy robe on over her tank and sleep shorts. "What's wrong?"

He paced, his hands shaking. Every now and then, he glanced at Evie. "Jack and Daisy asked me what you and I were dressing up as for Halloween."

"Oh—" Evie assumed that Adam was doing his own thing when he didn't ask her.

His eyebrows knitted together, forming a line across his forehead, a frown on his lips. "I was up all night thinking about it. But because I've never celebrated Halloween before…"

"Oh. That's right. I'd forgotten."

Adam shifted his gaze from her to everywhere but her. "Yeah. Anyway, Jack and Daisy said that I should have asked you about costumes. I'm sorry, Evie. I've never had a girlfriend before either."

A record scratched in her head.

Did he say girlfriend?

Evie opened her mouth to reply, but nothing came out. She was still processing what he said to her. She knew about the no previous girlfriends thing. But now he was calling her his girlfriend? She didn't know how she felt about that. Shouldn't that be a discussion before a declaration? On the other hand, she wasn't opposed to the idea.

"Are you…" she started. "Did you mean, like, as in me?"

The look of longing was back, but this time it was mixed with something else, something that was making Evie warm all over.

"Yes," Adam said.

Her cheeks flushed, and she glanced down and wiggled her bare toes on the carpet. What was she doing? She didn't have time for this. She walked over to her vanity and looked at her reflection in the mirror, running her fingers through her hair. "Okay, Mr. Early-Morning-Secret-Admissions, you have to go. I've got to get ready for school. Don't worry about the costumes. Wear whatever you want. I'm going as an angel."

The next thing she knew, Adam was standing behind her, watching her in the mirror. "That's a perfect costume for you."

Evie glanced at his eyes on her in the mirror. She wanted him to touch her, put his arms around her waist, and pull her against him. The heat from his body behind her was palpable. She tried to will him closer, but she didn't possess any tele-kinetic abilities that she was aware of.

"Thanks. I'm trying something different this year." She turned around to face him.

"So, if you're going as an angel, does that mean I should be a devil?" he asked.

"No, Adam. You should dress as whatever you want. That's what Halloween is about—pretending to be something that you've always wanted to be."

Adam smiled to himself and chuckled.

"What? What's so funny?"

"Nothing. It's just that I know the perfect costume, but I don't think people would get it."

Before she could press him, he headed back over to the window. "Okay, I'll let you get ready for school."

"Okay, see ya later."

When Adam climbed over the window sill, Evie had a flashback of trying to kiss him and chuckled. He was safe this time—she hadn't brushed her teeth yet.

17

DEVILS IN PARADISE

Adam

T*hank you, Daisy Dixon.* Adam had no costume for the Halloween party and only a few hours to spare. Daisy's brother, Eric, who owned Dixon's diner, was roughly the same size as Adam and happened to love Halloween. Adam had his choice of costumes but decided on the one that was most comfortable—a black, glow-in-the-dark skeleton T-shirt and pants. With the added black lights in the DP room, it was a good choice. Daisy offered to paint his face, but Adam wasn't ready to take that step. Instead, he went with simple—a quick shave and hair gel.

Adam double-checked the DP system to make sure it was ready to go. He went out to the front of the arcade to help Daisy and Jack with the decorating. Jack was replacing all the white lights with colored and black lights while Daisy stretched-out a white, cloud-like substance in the corners. Adam took some glow-in-the-dark cloth to drape over the counters. The place looked especially creepy because of the lights coming from the games and the dark floor and walls.

Adam checked the time. People would start arriving in about a half hour or so.

Daisy was dressed in all black—lips, eyes, dress, and hair. Adam wasn't sure who or what she was supposed to be. But for how dark she looked, her demeanor was cheerful. The new equipment Jack ordered had been delivered the day before— two refrigerators, a sink and counter, grill top, microwave, soft-pretzel warmer, hot dog roller, a chip warming bin for nachos, and popcorn machine. Not to mention, new stools for customers.

She fiddled around with one new machine and then the next, and so on, with pep in her step. Jack, who wore a black Metallica T-shirt, watched his girl smile. Their happiness warmed Adam's heart. Although, he wasn't sure about Jack's costume. Adam had to assume Jack's idea of a costume was minimal.

Adam approached Daisy's counter. "Hey, Daisy. Do you need anything?"

She turned around and smiled, her eyes glowing an eerie green like fireflies at night.

He jumped, his eye twitching, and quickly covered his eyes with his hands. Killing Daisy with his built-in laser would not be a good start to the night.

Daisy laughed. "Oh, Adam, I'm sorry. I startled you."

After controlling his urge, he looked up and tried his best to smile. Her eyes were unnerving and frightening. "You look…"

"Creepy? Yeah, these contacts are badass, right?"

"Oh, that's what those are. Cool."

"Oh, honey, you look fantastic. Nice work with your hair."

"Thanks. Do you need anything?"

Daisy glanced around. "Nope. I think I've got everything under control." She looked past Adam at Jack, beaming. "Check with my man though. He may need you."

"Okay." Adam headed to the front counter where Jack swayed back and forth to a song on the jukebox.

"Hey, kid. Nice costume. When's your lady getting here?"

Adam leaned on the counter. Evie said that she was planning on coming with Mazy. "I don't know. Probably in a half hour. Do you need me to do anything else?"

"If you've got your game set to go, I think I can handle things up front. Oh, and enjoy yourself too. You're only eighteen once, man."

The front door opened and closed. Adam turned and locked eyes with Evie, Mazy in tow. She took his breath away, and he feared he would have to reboot his heart. His thoughts connected to his internal Bluetooth and changed the track on the jukebox to the love song, "Just Like Heaven" by The Cure.

She was the most beautiful thing he'd ever seen. Her hair cascaded in waves below her shoulders, her eyes bright with no dark liner, and her lips were the prettiest shade of pink, like cotton candy clouds. Her white dress hugged her chest and waist, leaving her arms bare and came to her mid-thigh. Her boots had a heel, giving her a few more inches in height. She completed her look with a pair of small wings, the tips visible behind her. She was an angel.

As the girls walked over to him, Jack whispered, "You can close your mouth now. The song is a nice touch though."

Adam barely heard him. His head swam with thoughts of

Evie in his arms. When she reached him, he said, "You look amazing."

She smiled. "Thanks. Skeleton, huh?"

"Yeah." He looked down at his shirt and pants. "Glows in the dark." Mazy wore a devil outfit with boots that reminded him of Evie. "Hey, Mazy. I like the boots."

Mazy smiled at Evie. "Yeah, they're Evie's. We're doing a role-reversal thing tonight."

Jack said, "Well, thank you, girls, for working on this evening. You both look rad—angels and devils. Enjoy yourselves."

"You guys want to go check out DP?" Adam asked the girls. "Everyone else should be showing up soon."

Evie and Mazy nodded. "Sure."

As they walked toward the back of the arcade, Adam reached for Evie's hand. She accepted, and he interlaced his fingers with hers. He had never felt so human in his life, and it was all because of this arcade and the girl beside him.

Evie

As far as she was concerned, Adam Williams was one hot skeleton. When he danced, the black lights picked up the bones on his body, and he looked like a real skeleton. She had some new ideas for sketches. Tons of kids from school stood around the game's dance floor, and still more played games in the arcade. Adam, Derrick, and Luke were at the game console, while Mazy danced with some other girls and Sloan, who was dressed as a sexy hippie, to "Betty Davis Eyes." Evie stood at the back of the DP room with Gage, swaying to the music.

"So, are you and Adam a thing now?" Gage asked.

Evie smiled. Gage was dressed as Wolverine. He had on fake metal blade gloves, a white tank top, and jeans. It was a fitting costume. He was no stranger to the gym, and he was a "beast" on the football field. At least, that's what the twins and Mazy told her. She wasn't much for football.

"I don't know" she said. "I guess, maybe?"

Gage laughed. "Okay, if you say so."

She swatted his arm. "Hey, I'm not exactly experienced in dating, you know? Not like you and—"

As soon as the words left her mouth, she regretted them. After her conversation with Mazy yesterday, now was not the time. Evie could feel Gage's gaze on her. She fidgeted with her costume and avoided his eyes.

"You can say it, you know," he said.

"What?"

He crossed his arms and looked out on the dancefloor at his girlfriend. "Mazy. She wants to break up, doesn't she?"

Evie stared at him, shocked by his perception of the truth. His expression wasn't sad or angry. He looked more indifferent than anything else.

"Why do you think that?"

Gage glanced at Evie then back up. "I'm not right for her, and she's smart enough to know it."

"But—"

"No. It's okay. I promise. You can tell her that too if you want."

She didn't know what to say. Gage seemed fine with Mazy breaking up with him. How would she feel if Adam lost interest in her? The thought made her chest lurch. She wanted to say something reassuring but not betray her best friend's trust.

She found a fine line. "I think that what is meant to be will be. You're a great guy, and Mazy knows that."

"Thanks, Evie. Now, why don't you go talk to your man?" He left the room to head to the front of the arcade.

As if on cue, Adam waved her over to where he stood with Derrick and Luke, who had on Batman and Superman T-shirts under button-down shirts, respectively.

"Hey, you ready for 'Thriller'?" Adam's eyes twinkled in the black and neon lights.

"Of course," she said. "Hey, you guys look great. So even on Halloween you two are sporting a rivalry, huh?"

Derrick smiled. "It's subtle. Bruce Wayne and Clark Kent."

"Speak for yourself." Luke pulled his white shirt wide, to expose the Superman T-shirt more.

Evie laughed.

The current song finished, and Adam set up the next song. "Okay, go find your places. We can do eight spots."

Derrick and Luke cleared the people off the floor to make room for themselves, Evie, and Adam. Sloan and Mazy disappeared, probably out front with Gage.

God, I hope things don't turn to shit tonight.

She had plans for some alone time with Adam. Mazy was supposed to ride home with Gage, and Evie's mom had a big project she was working on at the art shop. She was going to pick Evie up when she called. But that plan would go to hell if Mazy needed her. She'd have to leave early.

Evie found her spot and waited for Adam to claim the one next to her. Some other kids, who hadn't had a chance to play yet, joined them. Everyone calibrated, and the song started with the creaking door. Evie watched the screen, moving along with the silhouette of herself. Occasionally, she glanced at Adam. He clapped and moved his feet to the music without even looking at the screen as if he had every single move memorized And that wasn't all—he was so in tune with the music it was like it flowed through his body.

His freestyle bar filled at the same time as hers. He nodded to her, and they both jumped together. It was the same time as Vincent Price's creepy voiceover began. He circled around her, and she did her best to keep in rhythm with him. He didn't touch her but came close, mimicking a zombie with lots of groove. Some of the others reached their freestyle too and were dancing freely.

Their bars depleted, and they made their way back to their spots for the end of the song. Applause erupted when the scores lit the board, punctuated by Price's evil laugh. Adam was in first place followed by Derrick, Luke, and Evie.

Those who didn't get to dance rushed to the floor for their turn.

"Again."

"I'm up."

"I want to try that one."

Adam's smile shone across the room like one of the spotlights overhead. His game was a success, and so was the evening. He headed over to the console to restart the song for the new players. Evie wasn't sure if she should join him or occupy herself while he tended to the game. She decided on the latter by grabbing a snack out front at Daisy's.

Along the way, she bumped into Mr. Garcia wearing a white lab coat.

Weak mad scientist? "Hi, Mr. Garcia," she said.

"Hello, Evie." He smiled. "Having a good time?"

Evie rocked backed and forth on her heels. "Yes. Have you seen Adam's game yet?"

"I'm on my way now. Adam is a whiz in class. He's always surprising me."

"Yeah, I know the feeling." As soon as the words left her mouth, she wanted them back. *I know the feeling?*

Mr. Garcia tilted his head to the side, peering down at her. She didn't know what he was thinking, but whatever it was caused the color in her cheeks to rise a few notches.

"Well, I'll leave you to it then," he said. "Good evening."

Evie nodded and tried her best to smile. They parted ways, and she headed over to the snack bar, where Daisy was busy tending to a popcorn machine. The creepy contacts took some getting used to, but Evie felt comfortable talking to her.

"Well, you're as pretty as pretty can be," Daisy said as Evie hopped on a stool at the counter.

"Thanks. I don't usually wear this much white."

Daisy leaned on the counter. "Me neither, honey. But sometimes it's nice to switch things up. What can I get ya?"

Evie looked at the sign. "Um, how about a soft pretzel?"

"Salt?"

"Is there any other way?"

"Nope." She pulled a pretzel from the warmer, placed it on a paper plate, and set it in front of Evie. "Want a Coke with that?"

"Sure."

Daisy spun around and grabbed a can of Coke from a fridge behind the counter. "There you are."

Evie reached for the cash she had stowed in her wristlet.

"Oh, no. Adam already covered you."

"Oh, wow. That sounds like him. He's always so thoughtful." The sarcasm in Evie's tone was palpable.

Daisy fought the smile creeping up on her lips. Evie stared her down, narrowing her eyes until she finally broke. "Okay, he didn't. But I know he would want to."

"Okay, fine." Evie laughed. "But make sure he actually pays you."

"I will. Speak of the skeleton…"

Adam took the seat next to Evie. "Hey, having a good time?"

"I sure am. Do you want some of the pretzel you bought me?" Evie tore off two pieces of pretzel. She offered one to Adam and popped the other in her mouth.

Adam glanced between Evie and Daisy, looking for a cue. "I—"

Daisy smiled. "I told Evie you covered her tonight. It's an expression. It means that you pay for snacks."

"Oh, of course." He reached into his back pocket for some folded bills and laid a five down. "Thanks, Daisy."

She clicked her cheek with her tongue and took his five. "I'll take the change as a tip."

After a while, the arcade thinned out. Gage and Mazy left together, but Evie could tell they were on edge. The twins and Sloan also headed out together. That left Jack, Daisy, Adam, and Evie. It was around ten, and Evie thought she could only extend her evening until eleven. Jack and Daisy closed out the arcade drawer and snack bar. The evening was a huge success, and lots of kids said they'd be back. Once Jack and Daisy left to go home, Adam and Evie were alone in the dimly lit arcade, all the flashing lights turned off.

Evie leaned against the counter at the front of the arcade, Adam standing in front of her.

"Dance with me," he said.

"Oh, I'm not in the mood to play."

Adam reached for her hand. "No. Here. Now."

Before Evie could protest that there wasn't any music, the jukebox came to life, playing a slow song. She'd witnessed it do this before, but this was especially odd because the song was "Lights Down Low" by MAX.

"I thought that thing only played the eighties?" she said.

"I sneak some stuff in every now and then." He grasped Evie's hand. "Don't tell on me."

She allowed him to pull her to him. He put his hands on her waist, and she rested her hands on his chest. He leaned his head next to hers, and together, they swayed to the music in the empty arcade. When the beat picked up, he grasped her hand and twirled her around and back to him.

God, you're an incredible dancer.

They stayed like that until the song finished. She made to pull away, but he held her still, his eyes locked on hers, their faces so close she could feel the warmth of his lips.

She fought everything in her being to not lean up and kiss him. She'd promised herself she wouldn't. He had to make the first move this time. But, damn, he was taking his good old time. She closed her eyes and waited.

"Evelyn?" a strong, male voice queried.

Evie's eyes flew open, and she pulled away from Adam in a flash. "Dad?"

Mac Greyson stood in the doorway of the arcade looking between her and Adam. "What are you doing?"

Evie's cheeks stung. She was mortified. Not only was her

dad interrupting this very intimate moment between her and Adam, but he was embarrassing her too. "What are you doing here? Mom is supposed to be picking me up."

But Mac Greyson wasn't paying any attention to what she said. His full attention was now on Adam. "Listen to me very carefully. I'm going to need you to stay away from my daughter. I don't want her around drugs or God knows what else."

Was this a joke? What on Earth could he have against Adam? He'd never even met him. "Oh my God, Dad. Adam doesn't use drugs. Overprotective, much?"

He ignored her and continued to address Adam. "Do you hear me, son? Evie is off limits."

Evie's cheeks burned even hotter. What the hell was this, anyway? She looked back at Adam. He was standing awfully still, staring back at her dad.

"Adam, I'm so sorry," she said. "I don't know why he's acting this way."

Adam swallowed hard, and his hands twitched. Evie couldn't be sure, but he seemed to be struggling to maintain his composure. An indecipherable sound came out of his mouth.

Evie stood between Adam and her dad. "Hey, Adam. Look at me. Are you okay?"

Adam opened his mouth as if he wanted to say something, but nothing came out.

"Evie. Get over here right now." Mac Greyson's tone indicated that he was also losing his temper.

One of Adam's eyes flickered like a camera shutter. A tear formed in the other, threatening to slip down his cheek.

"Adam…" Evie reached for his arm.

He flinched when she touched him. He leaned down, his

eyes still focused on her dad, and whispered, "Rrruunn," his voice a struggle.

Evie looked back at his eyes. She didn't know what kind of war was going on inside him, but the Adam she knew was losing the battle. "Okay, Dad. Let's go."

She backed away, trying her best to not look afraid, but she was afraid. She didn't know how or why, but the boy she liked was slipping away, leaving behind something cold, calculated, and fixated on her dad.

Adam wasn't the one in danger. She was, and so was her dad.

Once she reached her dad's side, she said, "Bye, Adam."

For the first time since her dad came into the arcade, he looked back at her but only for a split second. "Bye, Evie."

In a flash, his attention was back on her dad.

Mac pushed her toward the door. "Evie, I want you to wait outside for me."

"No. This has been bad enough. We're both leaving." She grabbed her dad's arm and pulled him with her out the door.

On the way, Mac said once again, "You stay away from her. She's got a bright future that doesn't include a druggie drifter like you. Tell Jack he'd better watch it. I won't tolerate any illegal drugs in my town."

"Dad." Evie pulled her dad's arm more forcefully. "Let's go."

Mac acquiesced and followed her outside. She took one last look at Adam. His hands were shaking terribly, and he looked like he was about to jump out of his skin.

Once outside, she allowed her dad to steer her to his patrol car. She slid into the front seat and put on her seatbelt then stared back at Jack's Arcade. The neon sign hanging above the doors was dim, as if ready to give up its fight to stay lit. The doorway and windows were also dark.

Five minutes ago, she'd felt at home in this place. Now, it seemed more like an empty, dark shell, like the boy inside.

She inhaled sharply as a terrible dread overwhelmed her. Her eyes filled with tears. What happened to him? Where did he go, and who was that monster that told her to run? She had no idea, but her head was pounding and her heart felt like it was splintering. She wanted to climb into her bed and not come out for a while.

What made her feel worse was that she was fairly certain she would never see Adam again.

PART II

18

ESCAPE FROM ASHWATER

Adam

All good things must come to an end. Or at least that's what humans said.

The sheriff that had been watching him around town was Evie's father.

He knew in whatever his bones were made of that he'd come close to killing him. Too close. If they had stayed inside the arcade any longer...

There was no doubt in his computing mind. After Evie turned on him, which she would have, he'd have classified her as a threat too. The thought of his hands around her neck turned something in his gut. He had a functioning digestive system, and it was about to start working in overdrive.

He gagged and bent over. The soft pretzel Evie had shared with him came rushing back out and onto the floor. Tears stung his eyes.

After the heaves stopped, he stood and wiped his mouth. He didn't think Evie's father suspected what he was, but it would only be a matter of time before he did. His time in Ashwater was finished. No more friends. No more Evie.

But he couldn't allow himself to dwell on his loss. There would be plenty of time for that after he left. Right now, if he wanted to survive in the real world, he had to leave. He jetted back to his room, changed clothes, and gathered some more, along with his toiletries and stuffed them in a backpack. He had a folding tent and some camping gear he'd stowed away in case of an emergency. Last, he grabbed the cash he kept under his mattress. He pocketed the few hundred dollars he'd saved and paused to look around his room one last time.

He walked back to the arcade and entered the DP room. Only the lights by the console shone. He looked around at his creation, his chest tightening. This was his. He hoped that Jack would keep it working and maybe Derrick could help. He tapped his hand on the doorway as if saying goodbye and headed to the snack bar to grab some supplies. He could leave Daisy and Jack a note, but that wouldn't be smart. Instead, he left a few folded bills for what he took on the counter.

Adam headed out the front of the arcade, taking one last look behind him at what he thought of as his home.

Evie

No one had heard from or seen Adam in days. School came and went on Monday then Tuesday and Wednesday. No Adam. And since he was eighteen, no one was looking for him.

Evie had spent the entire weekend after the Halloween party in bed trying to work through what had happened at the arcade. And it wasn't just about what she saw in Adam's eyes. She was livid with her dad too. No matter how many times she tried to explain to him that Adam wasn't a druggie and actually was an intelligent guy, he wouldn't hear it. Deep down, her dad's grudge against Adam had nothing to do with him and had everything to do with Jack. When her mom came home, Evie pleaded with her to talk some sense into him.

But it didn't work. Once her dad had something in his head, it was hard to get it out.

Evie was also confused about how she felt about Adam. He'd left her weak-kneed and not in a good way. She couldn't put her finger on the how or why, but she'd read danger in his eyes that night. Why else would he have told her to run? It also explained why no one had seen him. When he said goodbye to her, his tone was final. He meant forever. She had taken to drawing him over the past few days. Mostly, how she remembered him at the arcade—dangerous, afraid, and out of control.

She was in study hall for her last period, and it had been a week since Adam went missing. She pulled out her sketchpad and looked at her latest drawing of him. It had a cyberpunk vibe with one of his eyes as a camera lens. She didn't know why she drew it, but something about the way he sometimes looked at things, like her sketchpad after she drew him, inspired it. Plus, cyberpunk was badass.

"That's a pretty great drawing. Can I have a look?"

Evie looked up. Mr. Garcia stood in front of her. He was subbing for Mrs. Watts today for study hall.

"Sure." She handed him her sketchpad.

Mr. Garcia's eyes were serious as he studied it for quite

some time. It made her nervous. "You've got some real talent here. Are there more?"

Evie nodded. "Thanks. Yeah, you can flip through."

Mr. Garcia turned page after page of the sketchbook, complimenting her every so often. He set the sketchpad back on her desk. "Have you heard from Adam?"

She shrugged her shoulders. "Nope."

"I'm worried about him." Mr. Garcia frowned.

"Well, normally I'd say me too." Evie looked at her sketchbook. Adam looked back at her from the page, his eyes ominous. "But I assure you, he can take care of himself."

"What do you mean by that?" Mr. Garcia narrowed his eyes.

"Just that I think he's very capable of being on his own."

"Okay, well, if you do hear from him, will you let me know?"

"Uh, sure?"

Mr. Garcia walked away, and Evie looked back down at her drawing. The bell rang, and she gathered her things. She headed straight to the bus, avoiding her friends, including Mazy, who only wanted to badger her about Adam's whereabouts.

Nestling into a seat in the back, she propped her knees against the seat in front of her and took out her phone. She opened the last chat she had with Adam and scanned his messages to her. Nothing jumped out as threatening or worrisome. Sure, he was awkward on occasion but not like Saturday night. She took a deep breath and typed a message to him.

EVIE: *Where are you? People are worried about you.*

She hit send and put her phone down. She didn't think he'd respond at all, let alone right away. Evie looked out the window. The air was getting chilly. She hoped Adam had a place to stay. She rubbed up and down her arms, a chill setting in. Her phone chirped. She turned it over and saw a message from Adam.

ADAM: *I'm ok. I'm sorry for everything.*

Evie stared at the reply. He said he was sorry. What did he have to be sorry for? For scaring her? She shrugged one shoulder, nodding. Okay, fair enough.

EVIE: *I'm glad you're ok. I'm sorry too. My dad is so overprotective sometimes. It's because he's the sheriff.*

ADAM: *It's ok. It was really nice to know you.*

She inhaled sharply and glared at her phone. *Nice knowing me?* He really was gone for good.

Well, screw you. She slammed her phone face down on the seat next to her and crossed her arms. *Nice to know me? Grrrr!*

The bus started moving, and Evie was fuming. She couldn't believe it was that easy for him to write her off. Really? She stared at her phone on the seat next to her.

Don't do it. Don't.

She groaned and picked it up.

EVIE: *Nice to know me? WTH? So that's it, huh?*

ADAM: *I miss you.*

Evie's heart melted, and just like that, the hurt and fear that was stuck in her head evaporated. He missed her. She smiled and typed back.

EVIE: *I miss you too. Where are you?*

ADAM: *I can't. Your father would be angry.*

EVIE: *So what? Where are you?*

ADAM: *I have to go. I'm sorry.*

EVIE: *Wait, don't go.*

But Adam didn't respond.

Shit.

She wanted him to come back to Ashwater, and she didn't give a damn what her dad said. Besides, she'd be eighteen in a few months, and she could do what she wanted then. She tapped her index finger to her lips, her eyes darting back and forth as an idea formed. Maybe he left a clue behind that would help her find him.

Yes—that was a good idea. If Adam wouldn't tell her where he was, she'd find him on her own.

Evie got off the bus at her mom's shop and bee-lined it straight for Jack's. She was glad she hadn't worn a skirt today. She threw open the door, her chest heaving. Jack was in the back sitting on a stool at Daisy's counter. He turned to face her. His eyes were narrow and red-rimmed. Daisy, standing behind the bar, looked about the same. She wasn't wearing any makeup, and her hair was pulled up in a finger-combed, messy ponytail.

"Adam?" Jack shielded his eyes from the light streaming in behind Evie.

She shut the door and made her way back to Jack and Daisy. The place was eerily quiet. She didn't think anyone was here besides them. The ghosts of her and Adam from Saturday night taunted her as she strode across the spot where they danced.

Evie took a deep breath to steel her nerves. She would find him and get answers. She didn't know how, but she would make it happen.

"Oh, Evie, do you know where Adam is?" Jack's voice cracked as if panic and desperation were inching their way up his throat, threatening to choke him. In his eyes, Evie saw hope overshadowing dark circles.

She sighed. It was obvious he had come to care a great deal for Adam. "No, I'm sorry, I don't."

Jack nodded, casting his eyes to the floor. "Yeah, I figured as much."

"He's a smart young man. He'll be all right." Daisy took his hands in her own. "We have to believe that."

He put his head on the counter next to Daisy's hands. "He's got no one, Daisy. No one. Why would he leave like this without a word?"

Daisy glanced at Evie for some assistance.

It was Evie's fault that Adam had left. But she wasn't sure what good it would do to

tell them that. Whatever it was between Jack and her dad was best left alone. At least for now.

"Did Adam ever mention places he stayed before he came to Ashwater?" Evie asked. "Or maybe places he liked to visit?"

Daisy shrugged. "No, he didn't like to talk about his past. But it was plain as day that he'd been through hell. I think he had a bad foster situation. He never spoke of any parents or anything like that."

"We are his parents, Daisy. You and me. Weren't we doing a good job? I always wanted kids. Didn't you?" Jack lifted his head, slurring his words, and Evie got the impression that he was, at the very least, baked.

"You need rest, babe." Daisy pushed his hair off his forehead. "Please let me take you home."

"No. What if Adam comes back? I need to be here if he does. I'll put my head down here for a little." Jack laid his head on his arms like a makeshift pillow.

Evie glanced at Daisy. "Do you think I might look in his room? Maybe he left some kind of clue."

Daisy nodded. "Sure, why not? It's just past the DP room, down the hall. We've looked already, but when you don't have the faintest idea what you're looking for…"

"You never know, right?" Evie turned and left toward the back hallway. As she walked, she had visions of their last evening together going a different way, one where her father never showed up. One where Adam never left.

She closes her eyes after the song finishes, and he presses his warm, inviting lips to hers in the kiss she had been waiting for—strong and soft. He takes her hand and leads her back to this hallway and to his room. Once there, he opens the door and pulls her inside.

Evie opened the door to Adam's room. It was small with a twin bed, a little kitchenette against one wall, and the door to the bathroom was open, revealing a shower stall and sink. The walls were white, dingy, and in need of a coat of paint. His bed was stripped, with the sheets wadded up at the foot. She wandered over to the bed and sat. The coils from the metal bed frame squeaked under her weight.

She ran her fingers across the mattress. This was where Adam slept. The room was ramshackle but probably the best he'd ever had.

Her eyes filled with tears. Not because she missed him, even though she did, but because he probably thought of this place as a home and her dad had scared him away. Had anyone ever shown him kindness before Ashwater?

Evie reached for the sheets and buried her face in them. They smelled like Adam—cedar and leather. She allowed herself to sob for a minute and then got her shit together. She was here for a reason. She stood and shook out the sheets, looking for a clue. But the only thing she noticed was that she had stained the flat sheet with her mascara and eyeliner. She tossed them back down.

Next, she went to the kitchenette. She opened some cabinets and drawers. She pushed around some things. Nothing in them except some boxed macaroni and cheese, ramen, glasses, and some mismatched silverware. She checked the bathroom. He had kept it immaculate and left not even a strand of hair behind. Also, no clue as to where he might have gone. She walked back to the main room and checked the nightstand drawer. She peeked in and quickly shut the drawer, her cheeks warming.

Yep. Those were condoms.

Was he thinking about having sex with her? For real? She'd had thoughts about the same thing, but hidden in this drawer, he'd formed a plan.

Come on, Evie. Get your shit together.

She pulled the drawer open again to search, doing her best to ignore the condoms. Nothing stood out—just some comics and tissues. She went over to a closet and came up empty again. She turned around, assessing.

Something caught her eye underneath the bed where a foot met floor—something shiny. She knelt and reached for it. It was some sort of silver plastic tube. She turned it over and over in her hand. Something about it was familiar, but she couldn't place it.

What are you?

Satisfied she had explored everything she could, she got up and went back out to the arcade. Jack was snoring, his head still on the counter.

Daisy met Evie by the door and indicated for her to be quiet. "He hasn't slept for days, honey."

"Do you recognize this?" Evie handed Daisy the tube. "I feel like I've seen something like this before, but I can't place it."

Daisy rolled it around in her palm. "You know, it kinda looks like a part to one of those pop-up tents."

"I knew it looked familiar. That's exactly what it is."

Daisy looked up and covered her small mouth. "I think I might know where he went."

"Where?"

"I don't want to get Jack's hopes up, but Adam once told me that there were only two places on Earth that he felt at home. One was here, and the other was camping under the stars in Eden's Pass."

Did she say Eden's Pass?

It was one of the most beautiful places—densely wooded with a cliffside lake situated at the top of its summit. The waterfalls cascading down rock faces into the lake made her fingers twitch for a paintbrush and paint. Bubbles filled with anticipation and fear brewed in her depths.

Evie exhaled. "I know where that is. I'll go check it out."

Was she really going to go search for him? What would she say if she found him? Would he be the Adam she knew before or the scary, mindless Adam she saw after the Halloween party? Her heart pounded, her nerves frayed.

Calm down. You want answers? Then put on your big girl panties and go get them.

Daisy pursed her lips. "I think either your dad or I should come with you."

Evie coughed, her saliva sticking at the back of her throat. Her dad? Um, how about no? And she didn't want to have the conversation she was hoping to have with Adam, if she found him, in front of Daisy.

"I can handle it. I've got my mom's car…" Quick mental note to go get said car parked behind the art shop. "And I know that area really well because I sketch there sometimes. Besides, there are ranger checkpoints everywhere up there."

"I don't know." Daisy narrowed her eyes.

"Here," Evie replied. "Give me your phone number so I can text you."

Daisy took Evie's phone and punched in her number. "Okay, but you better stay in touch and text me asap. If anything happens to you, I'll never forgive myself."

"I promise," Evie said, typing on her phone. "See? There, I've already texted you once."

Daisy's phone dinged on the counter, causing Jack to snort. He turned his head the other way and was back out. "Okay, be careful."

"I will." Evie took a deep breath and turned to leave.

Daisy grasped Evie's arm. "And if you find Adam, please tell him that we miss him and want him to come home."

Evie nodded and headed out the front. Based on what she found in his room and what Daisy said, she had a good feeling that she would find him. But her stomach was doing some serious acrobatics because she had no idea which Adam she would find.

19

UNDER THE STARS

Adam

A dam looked at the fading sun over the tall trees. It would be dark soon, and he would succumb to another solitary night. He didn't mind the woods and nature, but without anyone to talk to, it was lonely. His texting with Evie earlier had set a firm lump at the back of his throat. She didn't hate him. She missed him like he missed her. But he could never see her again. He didn't ever want to harm her, and the only way he could manage that was to stay away from her.

An owl hooted in the distance. He'd seen plenty of wildlife in the past few days, and fortunately, the dangerous ones had kept their distance. Adam wondered if the mountain lions and bears sensed what his true nature was, but just in case, he was careful about keeping his food supplies tucked away. He also noted that a family was camping a quarter mile to the west of him and another group of people camping near the ranger's station to the south.

He closed his eyes and tilted his head to the sky, a cool

breeze wafting through his hair and skittering over his lashes. He retrieved his file on Evie and stared in his mind's eye at her pretty face looking down at him. Her green eyes, framed by dark lashes and liner, were full of wonder.

"Adam."

Evie?

He opened his eyes and stared at the stars coming into view in the darkening sky. He missed her so much that he was hallucinating and rendering his memory files as reality.

"Adam."

There it was again. His name on the wind from Evie's lips.

He felt a hand on his shoulder. Warning signals sounded in his head as his innate killer instinct took over. He grabbed the hand on his shoulder and its owner by the throat and maneuvered them to the ground.

Adam leaned over his assailant and saw a terrified Evie.

His first thought was that she wasn't there. That she was a figment of his imagination. How could she be? No one knew where he was, and even if she did, why would she have come?

She smacked at his forearm, and it was enough to register her authenticity—she was flesh and bone, and he had her pinned to the ground. He fought like hell against his programming. That side of him had her exactly where it wanted her: *Control, Extract, Dispose.*

But Adam would rather die than hurt her.

Let…her…go.

He groaned loudly, tiny beads of sweat forming across his forehead.

"Let her go," he yelled aloud.

That was all it took. Like a pinball pull-shooter, his grip

opened, and she rolled away from him, gasping for air. He looked down at his trembling hands.

You're a monster.

He scanned her for injury and sighed in relief. His maneuver had knocked the wind from her lungs, but otherwise, left her unharmed.

Evie sputtered some more as she inched away from Adam.

"Why?" Her voice was raspy and charged with a fight-or-flight instinct.

Adam held out his hands in obedience. "I'm sorry. I promise I won't touch you again."

She massaged her throat, her eyes glassy. Again, she asked, "Why?"

"I—" He wasn't sure what else he could tell her now except the truth. Although, if he did, he had no idea how his programming would react. He was built to conceal his identity and kill anything that threatened that. He didn't even know if he was capable of telling her what he was.

On the other hand, he had managed to stop himself before, which gave him hope.

"I'm going to do my best to tell you everything if I can," he said.

Her breathing returned to a more normal rate. "If you can? You pinned me to the ground, Adam. I think I have a right to know."

Adam opened his mouth to explain, and a warning went off, his hand trembling. This was not going to be easy, and he knew they'd probably both feel better if he were restrained. He looked around for something to bind his hands with and remembered that he had some zip ties that might work to hold him.

Well, at least long enough for her to get away, he hoped. If it came to that.

He reached into his backpack and pulled out his strongest ties. "Here. Bind my wrists together."

But Evie was still afraid and inched back.

Adam tossed the ties toward her and got on his knees in a submissive position with his head on the ground, wrists out in front, extended toward her. "I won't move. Secure my wrists."

"You want me to bind your wrists? Adam—"

"Please. Just do it."

He kept his head down on the ground and waited. He was afraid if she ran, his programming would take over again, and this time, he didn't know if he'd be able to stop.

Evie, please.

A minute passed and then another. He heard some muffled sobbing noises and a rustling nearby. Evie poked the fleshy part between his index finger and thumb, testing his submission.

He stayed as still as an android could, which was perfect. "I'm not moving. I swear. Zip me up."

Another minute passed.

"WTF," she said, grasping his hands. She wrapped a zip tie around his wrists. She pulled hard, cinching it extra tight. Feeling his hands secured, he lifted his head. She said, "Stop. I'm not done yet."

Adam obeyed and rested his back on the ground. She secured two more ties around his wrists. When she let go, he asked, "Are you finished?"

"Christ, I hope so."

He exhaled and sat up.

Evie was on her knees in front of him, her cheeks tear-stained, hands on her thighs. His chest constricted. He'd hurt her emotionally. It was plain as day in her eyes. He should never have escaped from the facility. To do what he did to her...it was the most horrible thing he could imagine. He would have been better off being disposed of. He raised his bound hands to his forehead, tears stinging his eyes.

"Evie, I'm so sorry. I hate what I did to you. I promise I'll never hurt you again. I swear." His voice cracked as he made his vow.

"Just tell me why. Why would you try to hurt me? Why would you run away? I don't understand."

Adam looked back at her and wiped a tear from under his eye with his shoulder. "Okay, I'll try."

"You know you can tell me anything, Adam. No matter what it is, I'll be on your side."

"I'm counting on it," Adam whispered to himself. To Evie, he said, "I'm different."

"Yeah, everyone is," she replied.

"What I mean is that I'm not like you." Adam's hands trembled, fighting against the bonds. He ignored the warnings going off in his head. "I didn't grow up with a family, and I don't think I have parents. I was created at the Bio-Core facility underneath the mountain we're standing on."

"I'm sorry. Did you just say created? What does that even mean?"

Warning, exposure imminent. Threat located.

Adam squeezed his eyes shut and took a deep breath, somehow blocking out the schematics and timing to stop his ocular laser from slicing her into pieces. The images in his head made his stomach turn, just like they did the last time he was in the arcade.

Fight it. Get control. He swallowed the bile down.

"Are you okay?" Evie asked, touching his bound hands.

Her touch and tone was calm and filled with concern and gave him the strength to continue. He opened his eyes. "I am now. My past is just really hard to talk about."

Evie squeezed his hand, compassion in her eyes. "Adam, you can trust me."

He nodded. It was time. "Evie, I'm…"

Don't say android. Don't say android.

"Exceptionally intelligent."

She frowned. "I'm sorry, what?"

Ugh.

He tried, "I'm stupid smart?"

Evie nodded. "I get that you're smart. Where are you going with this?"

Adam groaned. This was not working.

Just tell her.

"What I'm trying to say is that most of my body is biological, but on the inside, especially up here," Adam tapped his left temple with his bound hands, "I'm synthetic."

Her jaw fell, her eyes open and glued to his.

"I know." Adam raised his bound hands toward her. "It sounds completely crazy. I don't fully understand everything myself."

Evie's expression remained unchanged.

Please say something. Please?

She opened and closed her mouth a few times until finally she came up with, "I'm confused."

I know the feeling.

"I'll try my best to explain," he said. "Think of my brain

like you would a computer. I can process information and compute extremely fast."

Her eyes darted back and forth like his did when he searched a database. "So, what? You're like a machine? Artificial intelligence?"

"Sort of. I have skin like you do, and well, all my other systems seem to be like yours for the most part. It's what's inside my head that's different."

Evie got up and paced back and forth in front of him.

"Was anything between us real?" Her bottom lip quivered as the words left her lips.

His heart heaved thinking about what to say next. His killer instinct was in check for the moment, and he wanted to keep it that way. He whispered, "Evie, look at me."

Her glassy gaze met his and penetrated his soul if he had one. He was still forming an opinion about the subject, but he ached to soothe hers.

She needed an anchor. Something that would help her see that he was the person she knew.

He stood. "I need you to know, I genuinely like playing DP with Gage, Derrick, and Luke. Jack's Arcade feels like home and…I dream about Daisy's cheese fries." He paused and smiled. "Oh, and I especially like Halloween now." He took a step forward, his eyes never leaving hers. "But most of all, I love dancing with you."

Evie paused, her eyes focused on his. He hoped his words were sinking in. She paced for a few minutes. Then bent and dug into her bag. Pulling out her sketch pad, she flipped to a drawing and turned the pad toward Adam so that he could see. She had drawn a picture of him from Halloween, wearing the skeleton costume. His expression was serious, lips pressed tightly together. But she had changed his right eye into a small camera.

"I don't know why I drew this. It just came out." Her eyes were hopeful and vulnerable.

Adam nodded. "It's because you draw the truth. I thought that from the first drawing of yours I ever saw. You've got a talent for seeing people for who they really are."

She looked back at her drawing. "I know. Maybe subconsciously or something."

Adam winked. "I took a picture with my ocular lens of the sketch you did when I posed for you in your bedroom."

She nodded, the memory flooding back. "I remember… with your eye. I asked you about it. So you have a built-in camera in your eye?"

"Yes." Adam peered up at her, smiling. "I can record and take snapshots of whatever I see."

"Wow. What else can you do?" Her shoulders relaxed.

"Unfortunately, I'm programmed to detect and take out threats that might expose anything about what I am or the facility."

Evie sat back down, contemplating what he'd confided in her.

"Are you okay?" Adam asked.

"I have no idea. I'm open to what you're saying, but I need more. Start at the beginning. What do you remember from Bio-Core?"

Adam settled down next to her. His system no longer detected Evie as a threat. He accessed his earliest memory file.

"My first memories are from the facility. I was kept in a small cell with a cot. I can't remember seeing anyone there besides others like me. The others didn't look like me, but we were all synthetic up here," Adam said, pointing to his head. "When I wasn't in my cell, I trained with the others in competitive and cooperative simulations. Our mission was to extract information or people and kill anything that got in our way. I assume we were designed to pose as humans to work covertly. To what end, I'm not sure, but our desired skillset was obvious.

"We were tested too, and failure meant disposal. I watched many of the others fail. Those that survived the training rooms but didn't complete their missions were disposed of. I remember when it happened to me. It's my last memory from there. I was presented with a new simulation I'd not faced before. The mission was to retrieve a hostage. I calculated that it was impossible for me to save myself and the hostage. I don't know why, but it bothered me. So I hesitated, and because I faltered, I failed the mission. It was grounds for my immediate disposal. I was on my way to be destroyed, but I wasn't shut down properly. So when I saw an opportunity, I escaped. I spent some time in the woods hoping they wouldn't look for me. When they didn't, I located the closest town—Ashwater."

Evie stared at Adam. "This is for real, isn't it?"

"It is."

"Tell me more."

Evie

Time stood still. In the length of an hour's time, Adam had blown Evie's mind. After he grabbed her, she had mentally prepared for him to tell her that he'd been abused, that he'd been in trouble with the law, or that he was into drugs like her dad suspected.

But the truth was beyond anything Evie could have imagined. Between his internal Bluetooth capabilities and his ability to snap photos with a blink of an eye, her head was spinning. The boy she was hoping to call her boyfriend just told her that he's only eight months old and a precise killing machine. Who likes to dance. If that wasn't enough, she still hadn't reconciled the fact that he wasn't entirely human. Although as he spoke to her, she saw the same Adam she had come to care for surface time and time again. But he had another side, a dark one. That part of him still scared her.

"That's why you told me to run at the arcade. You were worried that you would hurt my dad, weren't you?" Evie twirled her ponytail around her fingers absently. Adam was finished talking, and she was out of questions. His hands were still zipped tight.

Adam glanced sideways. "No. I was worried I'd kill him."

She leaned to the side to reposition herself. "Jesus, Adam. I don't think I'm going to be able to get used to you talking like that."

He cringed. "If it helps, I don't think I've killed a human. I've had some close calls since moving to Ashwater, but as far as I can remember from my past, I've only taken out synths."

"Oh my God. Am I really having this conversation?"

"I'm sorry." He reached for her hand with his bound ones. "Hey. I'm different now. I'm more human. I breathe like you, eat like you, see things like you, and I feel."

And there it was. The phrase he used back when she first discovered that he liked to dance. She thought he had lost his train of thought, but really, he'd meant exactly what he said.

She exhaled the emotion she had been holding on to the entire time since she found him. He was still the Adam she knew. Her stomach did a few flip-flops. She wasn't sure how she felt about that. Or him, for that matter. But she did know that he was her friend, and he was in trouble. So rather than dealing with her confused feelings, she stood, and he followed suit.

"I have to go," she said. "It's getting late, and I promised my mom I'd be back by ten."

"Evie, you can't tell anyone." He said it as a statement rather than a request, and now, she knew why. If she told anyone, he would be headed back to the facility, and the dangerous side of him would see her as a threat too.

"I won't say anything, but I do have to tell Daisy and Jack something. They miss you terribly."

He nodded. "I know. I miss them too. But I can't put them in danger."

"I get it," she said. "I won't tell them anything about what you told me. I'll just say that you are all right."

"Thank you."

He opened his mouth to say something else, but Evie stopped him. Cautiously, she lifted his bound hands over her head and reached her arms around his middle, her head against his chest and listened.

A consistent rhythm thrummed from within.

She exhaled and relaxed against him. "You can trust me, Adam."

"I know." He rested his head on hers.

Evie pulled back, and he lifted his arms back over her head. "Do you need me to cut you loose?"

Adam smiled. "No. What else do I have to do here?"

She chuckled and picked up her bag, her phone in her hand. "Okay, so, you're staying put, right?"

"I'll be right here."

Evie waved and turned to head back down the trail. Her phone started to play a song. She recognized the familiar riff of "Don't You (Forget About Me)."

She turned around, her eyes narrowed and lips pursed. "Really? This is so cliché."

Adam shrugged and grinned impishly.

She'd seen that look in his eyes before. But now, it was different—more open and genuine. She smirked.

He was still sketch-able. Maybe more so now.

20

CAPTURED

Adam

Adam was out of the zip ties in one minute and fifteen seconds. He stretched out on his sleeping bag, hands behind his head. He'd told Evie everything. Well, almost everything. He'd left out some of the more gruesome details about his training and internal weaponry. He didn't think she'd enjoy hearing about his laser tracking device that slid into the place of his camera behind his eye.

He was breathing easier now that he told Evie what he was. He didn't think she would tell anyone about him, and it was nice to be able to share all of himself.

With no clouds in the evening sky, the stars glowed brighter. He accessed his files of Evie and paged through them in his mind's eye. He didn't know if she would ever like him again, but his feelings for her were even stronger than before. This was probably a good thing considering he wanted to kill anyone that was a threat. But he was gaining control of the urges, and she was the key. Although, it would be best if he wasn't in the same room as her father again. That was a worry for another time.

A rustling in the tree line to the east of his encampment caused him to prop up on his elbows. He scanned, thinking it was wildlife. Mid-scan his vision flickered. He sat up and rubbed his temples. His eyes flickered again. Warning signals sounded in his head.

Preparing for maintenance shut down.

Adam flashed back to the facility. He'd seen this before after a training or a test. Often, the scientists accessed his CPU and shut him down. But he had to be out of range. There was no way they should be able to access him out here. He looked back at the trees, and in his waning sight, he saw the silhouette of a man. He couldn't identify him, but there was something familiar about him. He lost control of his arms and legs and fell to the ground. Hazy stars dotted what was left of his peripheral vision.

Finally, darkness took him.

***

The dark turned to gray then white. Adam opened his eyes. He was lying on a cot in a square white room. He turned his head and looked at a locked door with a familiar symbol— a group of three connected green hexagons. His short life flashed before his eyes. He tried to sit up, but his wrists and ankles were restrained. All around him was the faint, low hum of computers working. He struggled against the restraints, tears filling his eyes.

He was back at the facility. They'd found him.

Someone tapped on a keypad outside the room, and the door slid open. A thirty-something woman with a white lab coat and ginger-colored hair came inside. She had a smartpad in her hand. She tapped and slid her finger across it as she walked to Adam. She took a cord with an odd clamp on the end from her pocket and reached for Adam's wrist.

Adam pulled away from her. "No. What are you doing?"

The woman smiled at Adam. "I want to check your vitals."

He relaxed his arm but eyed her closely.

She turned his wrist over and clipped the cord onto his wrist. She plugged the other end into her pad, swiped and tapped some, and removed the cord from his wrist. "There. Now, that wasn't so terrible, was it?"

"Who are you, and how did I get here?"

The woman dragged a chair from the corner of the room over to his bed and sat. "My name is Dr. Rice. You can call me Naomi. You don't remember because they deleted your files of me, but I promise, we were friends."

"If that's true, tell me how I got here."

Naomi crossed her legs and pushed her glasses back up the bridge of her nose. "I know you're nervous about being back here. For right now, you don't have anything to worry about."

"Why am I restrained?"

She chuckled. "Please tell me you can access and recall what your skillsets are. If you can, you know why you're restrained."

Adam nodded and looked at the ceiling. "What are they going to do to me?"

"I'm not sure. Your champion is vying for your survival as we speak. Don't worry. I have faith he'll succeed."

My champion? He had no idea what she was talking about. Who would be fighting for his survival?

Before he could ask, she leaned toward him and changed the subject, "Tell me about Evelyn."

He frowned. "How do you know about her?"

"Oh," she said, pulling away, staring at the floor. "Well, I've scanned your files."

"That is none of your business. You leave her alone." Adam lifted himself up on his elbows as best he could with his restraints. His right eye twitched, eager to switch from camera to weapon. When nothing happened, he realized how much they were in control.

"Your internal weaponry is deactivated unless you're inside the training rooms. You know that. Oh...." She glanced at her smartpad. "That's right. You don't know." She shifted in her seat and crossed her legs, intent on talking with him. "Oh, come on. Tell me what you felt when you danced with her at the arcade. The time before her dad interrupted you. Your vitals were off the charts."

Adam growled. "I don't appreciate you digging around in my head. That's private and none of your business."

"Wow. You're even talking like a human now." She paused, her mind working before she continued, "I'm sorry, I didn't mean to pry. It's just that we used to talk about things all the time."

"Well, as you said, I don't remember you."

Naomi leaned closer and whispered, "They're watching us. Trust me. I'm on your side." She sat back and changed her demeanor. "So how about you talk about how it was working in the arcade?"

"What do you want to know?" Adam stared at her, scanning. Her light blue eyes and body language registered as honest, and he deemed her vitals appropriate for this encounter. And even though he had no memory of her, she seemed like a decent person, if a little intrusive. But who was watching them, and why did she want to make small talk? Wasn't he about to be destroyed like they'd originally planned? What did any of this matter?

She sat up straighter in her chair, her eyes twinkling with interest. "To start, did you like working for Jack and Daisy?"

Adam looked at the ceiling. "Yeah. Jack and Daisy are, I mean were, like family to me. They gave me food, a place to stay, and a job. Plus, I liked working on the games."

"That's right, you created that dance game. What was it called?"

"*Dance Paradise.*"

"You like dancing. How did you discover that?"

"I was researching humanity and came across a video of a group of professional dancers. They looked like they were having fun, so I thought I'd try it. I turned on some music, and the second I started moving my body to the rhythm, I never wanted to stop."

"Why is that?"

"Because it made me feel—made me human."

Naomi's mouth dropped open. "Then it's true. You're special."

Adam rolled his eyes. "Why? Because I feel?"

"He was right." She leaned back in her chair, nodding approvingly.

He glared at her, tired of all these games. He needed answers and now. "What are you talking about? Who was right?"

The door opened again, and a man walked in. "Hello, Adam."

Adam inhaled sharply, his mouth open, staring at his high school teacher. "Mr. Garcia?"

21

MISSING

Evie

E vie grew more worried each day she didn't hear from Adam. When she'd left him in Eden's Pass, he'd been fine. Now, a week had passed, and he was gone. She went back to the spot where he'd been camping, and the place looked like no one had ever been there. Her texts went unanswered. What made matters worse was that she couldn't talk to anyone about him. Especially her dad, the one person who could probably have helped her locate him. She was having nightmares about Adam being taken back to the horrible facility he told her about. Deep in the recesses of her mind, she had a feeling that was exactly what had happened to him. He might even already be dead.

She lifted her sketchpad from her bed, and stared into his eyes, pleading with him to give her some clue as to where he was or what had happened to him.

Where are you?

But he wasn't budging. Instead, he stared back at her,

daring her to turn the page and start again. She tossed her pad across her bed and groaned. She'd been drawing him incessantly ever since he'd told her his truth—he was an android and a hot one at that.

She hadn't come to terms with her feelings for Adam. Partly because she didn't know if it was even possible for her to have a romantic relationship with him. Like, did he have those parts and stuff? And also because she didn't like that he'd lied to her. Although, it also occurred to her that she would probably not have ever gotten to know him like she had if he'd told her in the first place.

Wasn't being a teenager hard enough? Now, she had an android boyfriend on her hands. Even saying it in her mind was crazy. She groaned, her head hurting from all her unanswered questions and thoughts. She fell back on her bed in a whoosh, her hair fanning out around her.

Dear God, if you exist, I could use a little help.

A knock on her door startled her back to reality. It was Saturday night, Dad's turn to cook.

"Come in."

Mac opened the door and leaned against the doorjamb. "Hey, it's time for dinner."

"'Kay." Evie tossed the pencil in her hand aside and sat up, her shoulders slumped.

He came into the room and looked at her wall. "You'd make a fine police sketch artist."

Evie pursed her lips and squinted at her dad. Of course, redirect her art into something useful. Ick. "No thanks."

"I'm serious. These drawings are really good."

"Even the ones of Adam?"

Mac groaned and sat next to her. "I know you think I'm

being overprotective and all, but I promise I only want to keep you safe. There's something about that boy that I don't trust."

She glanced away. If he knew how right he actually was… but that wasn't the point. He *didn't* know Adam. He was making assumptions about him because he lived or, she guessed, had lived with Jack.

"Dad, what happened between you and Jack White? I know you were friends when you were kids, but I feel like you're only holding a grudge against Adam because of Jack."

Mac's expression was unreadable. Evie guessed that was part of what made him such a good sheriff. She'd inherited that trait from him as well. Mazy often said that she couldn't figure out what was going on in Evie's head.

"I don't like to talk about it, but I can tell you that Jack only cares about himself and isn't a good influence on anyone."

Evie sighed. "Dad, in the three years that we've been here, you haven't said two words to him. Mom said you two were like best friends when you were kids. Now, you went after a boy I like because he's staying at Jack's."

Mac threw his hands in the air. "Exactly. Don't you think it's odd that an eighteen-year-old boy moves into a room at the back of an arcade? Where's his family? Where did he come from?"

She read into her dad's eyes and saw a snippet of the truth. Her mouth formed an O as she connected the dots. "Oh, I see. You tried a background check on Adam and came up with nothing. That scared you."

Mac tried his best not to look guilty. "No…"

"Oh my God. You did. Dad."

"What? I'm in law enforcement. My daughter started dating a transient."

"Adam is not a transient. He came from a bad situation and was trying to make a life for himself here in Ashwater. Then, you got all bad cop on him and scared him off." Evie stood, crossed her arms, and went to her window. The same window she had accidentally tossed Adam out of. She stared at the darkening sky. Was Adam looking at the same emerging stars and moon? "I'm going to be graduating soon. I can make my own decisions about who I'm friends with and date."

"Evie—"

She refused to turn around. "Just go. I'm not hungry."

Her dad's reflection in the window got up and walked toward her door. He paused. "I love you, Evelyn."

Evie stared out the window as tears formed in her eyes. Her dad didn't say it often. When he did, it pulled at her heartstrings because she loved him too. But she missed Adam terribly, and her dad was the reason Adam was gone in the first place.

***

The next day, Evie woke with a start. She'd had another dream about Adam. This wasn't uncommon over the past few months. But given the current circumstances, this dream left her breathless and not in a good way. She saw his body tossed atop a heap of lifeless bodies. He was still moving, his eyes frightened and pleading for help. A man in a gray jumpsuit pulled bodies off the pile and tossed them into a large opening filled with fire—an incinerator. The man was getting closer to Adam. She was outside the room, looking in through a window. She banged on the glass and screamed for the man to stop.

He's not dead!

But the man couldn't hear her. The last thing she remembered was Adam's eyes, so sad, as the man reached for him.

She wouldn't wait one more minute. She didn't give a damn if she'd promised Adam she wouldn't tell anyone about him. She had to.

After a quick shower, she headed to Dixon's Diner. Derrick told her that Gage and his grandfather ate breakfast there every Sunday without missing a week. She didn't know if she could trust Gage, but the facility was owned by his family. He was her best shot at finding out if Adam was taken back there.

She grasped the handle of the door at Dixon's, pausing, the memory rushing back of Adam almost knocking her on her ass. Evie lingered at the door, remembering what it was like to feel Adam's arms around her. He wasn't human. The simple fact bounced around her head like a world championship ping pong match.

The practical side of her exclaimed, *Of course. He's a robot, for God's sakes. What are you going to do? Ride off into the sunset with him until he needs a recharge?*

The part of her that couldn't stop sketching him felt differently. *Don't be so quick to judge. He has feelings like everyone else. You know that. You've seen it.*

Evie sighed, pulled on the door, and entered Dixon's. For a Sunday, the place wasn't that busy. She looked to her left and right at the booths. No Gage. She leaned over and checked out the modest dining room. Still no Gage.

Eric Dixon was perched on a stool at the counter. His wife, Athena, a pretty dark-haired woman with a lithe body even Evie was envious of, was at the cash register ringing out a customer. Derrick, with a gray plastic tub in his hands, was busing tables, while his brother, Luke, was nowhere to be seen. Evie focused back on Mr. Dixon. He was a keep-to-himself kind of person, but he always had a smile and wave for her when he saw her. Today, he was obviously on break, working on a Sunday paper crossword and slugging back his cup of coffee.

Evie sat at the counter next to him. "Hi, Mr. Dixon."

He looked up from his crossword at Evie, his expression unreadable, like he was so deep in thought that he forgot how to say hello. But once he recognized her, he smiled. "Oh, Evie. Hi. Can I get you somethin'? Your folks here?"

Before Evie could reply, Celia, a girl who graduated from Ashwater High half a dozen years ago, walked over. As far as Evie knew, Celia didn't have any aspirations for a career beyond working at Dixon's. But she did seem to stick by Eric's side quite a bit. She was a nice girl with long, wavy, caramel-colored hair and blue eyes. Her small frame made her look like a sprite or fairy. Evie had sketched her once from memory but would love to have Celia sit for her.

"I got this, boss. Cranberry juice and a bacon and American cheese omelet. Soft, right?" Celia winked at Evie, and Evie's hand itched for a pencil.

Evie smiled. Celia had her dead to rights, but she wasn't feeling hungry. "Just the juice, please."

Celia returned the smile. "You got it, girl."

Before she turned away, Evie caught Mr. Dixon and Celia exchange a secret smile too. She shifted in her seat, uncomfortable. She glanced at Athena, who was concentrating on the cash register. Evie was a perceptive person, yet she'd never noticed this before. Was this a new thing? Ugh. She shook the feeling from her head.

After Celia left to get the juice, Evie focused back on Mr. Dixon. "I thought Gage Strickland and his grandfather usually eat here on Sunday mornings. I don't see them."

Mr. Dixon looked around with the same curiosity as Evie. "Huh. You're right. They do." He shrugged his shoulders. "Must be late."

Evie exhaled, relief washing over her tense limbs. She hadn't missed them. Now, she wished she had ordered breakfast. Celia was at a large machine with fist-like handles doling out her juice. She set the small, textured plastic cup of cranberry juice in front of Evie.

"You sure you don't want anythin' else? Eric's about to get back on the grill." Celia's voice had a melody to it like she was one of those people that could carry a tune while in the shower or a car but never sang publically.

Evie smiled. "You've talked me into it. I'll have my usual. Thanks, Celia."

Celia picked up the menu that was sitting beside Evie on the counter. "I thought you might." To Mr. Dixon, she said, "Break over, boss. You know that crew can't make a soft omelet to save their lives."

Celia was right. In fact, most diners Evie had been to in her life couldn't make a soft, fluffy omelet. Eggs weren't supposed to be brown. At least not in her world. But Mr. Dixon was a rare find. He cared about his food preparation and wanted his customers to be happy. He was known for tossing dishes that didn't meet his standards, regardless of whether his crew cooked it or he did. Yep, he was a regular old Gordon Ramsey of Dinerville.

Mr. Dixon smiled at Celia, with a softness that would rival

the omelet Evie ordered. He nodded at Evie and stood. "One soft omelet coming up."

Evie looked between the two, not sure how to react. A flush reached her cheeks, and she smiled nervously. "Thanks."

She'd not forget their expressions anytime soon because they were downright scandalous. If Evie wasn't mistaken, Eric Dixon and Celia Black were involved and not in an employer-employee kind of way. She peeked at Athena again, who was unaware and Derrick, who was busy busing a booth. Damn, one more thing in this town she wished she didn't need to worry about.

A full belly and thirty minutes later, the Stricklands walked into the diner. Evie wiped her mouth with her napkin and set it on the counter. She spun around on her stool and hopped down, trying to catch Gage's eye. What she wanted to talk to him about wasn't for his grandfather's ears. The two had a one-track mind though and bee-lined it straight for an empty booth to the right of the door. Evie walked over, a bright smile on her lips.

"Hey, Gage. Mr. Strickland." Evie grasped the edge of the table they were sitting at, her fingers tapping casually.

Mr. Strickland was probably pushing into his seventies, but no one would guess that. He had an active lifestyle, still skied, and still had his hair, although gray. He nodded at her. "Hello, Evelyn."

Older people always used her full name, which didn't really bother her, but it was an affirmation of formality that felt off-putting and sort of move-along-ish.

In comparison, Gage, who wore a light blue T-shirt and tan khakis, his chestnut-colored hair combed perfectly, smiled at Evie. He had warmth in his eyes like he could sense when people were nervous or feeling down. "Hey, Evie. How are you doing? Heard anything?"

Evie traced a crack in the Formica at the edge of the table. "No. Have you?"

Gage frowned. "Not a word. Do you want to sit? Have you eaten yet?"

"Yeah, I just ate. But, do you think I could talk to you for a second outside?"

He shrugged. "Sure. Granddad, I'll be right back."

"Sure, sure." Mr. Strickland stared at the paper menu placemat in front of him. "Don't be long though."

"I won't." Gage got up. He followed Evie outside.

She turned to him, her voice catching in her throat. She was taking a risk, but she was out of options. Her gut was telling her that Adam was in big trouble. "I think I know where Adam is, and he might be in trouble."

His hazel eyes grew serious, and his mouth formed a hard line. "What kind of trouble?"

Evie took a deep breath. "What do you know about the Bio-Core facility?"

Gage shrugged. "It's a research facility. My grandfather acquired it when he was in his forties. Oh, and my mother worked there before…you know."

Interesting. That bit of information Evie didn't know. Gage's family was more involved in the facility than she previously thought. "I'm sorry to bring up bad memories."

"It's fine. But why? What are you getting at?"

She looked around to see if anyone was in earshot. Confirming that she was in the clear, she said, "I can't explain it, but I think Adam is being held prisoner there."

"Why would you think that? Bio-Core is a biotech company. They make and distribute medication, right?"

Evie leaned in closer. "I don't think that's all they're creating. I believe they're working on something more experimental and dangerous."

"Like what?"

"Weapons."

"No, my grandfather would never allow that."

"What about androids?"

"No—" He paused, his eyes darting back and forth as he worked something out in his mind.

After an amazing amount of time passed, Evie finally broke the silence. "What?"

"I overheard my granddad talking to someone on the phone about an experiment. At one point he said the word android. I didn't think anything of it at the time since it's a type of phone. But now that you've mentioned it, I think he may have meant something else. But what does all this have to do with Adam?"

"I think Adam is part of that experiment."

His mouth dropped. "You think that Adam is…"

"Yes."

"Oh my God." Gage ran a hand through his hair and turned around a few times, looking at the diner window where his grandfather was seated at a booth. "I can't believe I'm saying this, but it makes sense. Adam was always so awkward, especially with you. He made fun of your eyes the first time he met you. Do you remember that?"

Evie rolled said eyes. Why did it always have to come back to that? "Hard to forget."

"Then, there's DP. I mean, he created and built that game

this past summer. It took him no time at all. He did all that work like it was nothing."

"Exactly."

"Do you know what this means?" Gage asked, nodding proudly.

She looked around, unsure. "Yes?"

"I'm friends with an android. The future is now."

Okay, enough. Time to get down to business. Evie leaned in close to Gage, so close that the heat from his tall frame warmed her. He was as tall as Adam but wider. She wanted to make sure that their exchange stayed between the two of them.

"Look, I'm taking a huge risk by talking to you about this right now. The last time I saw Adam was in Eden's Pass. He was fine when I left him there on Wednesday. That's when he told me about what he was and where he was created. I was planning on going back to see him the next day, but his campsite was gone, along with all his stuff. He's disappeared without a trace." Evie reached for Gage's forearm, her hand shaking. "He's not built like us, but he is like us in every other way. I know that for sure. Now I need you to know that too. Please help me find him."

"I always had this feeling that something wasn't quite right with him, but I brushed it off." He took a deep breath and smiled at her. "What can I do to help?"

"We need to search Bio-Core and see if we can find Adam. Also, you can't tell anyone. I mean it, Gage. Not *anyone*."

He nodded and looked back at the diner window where his granddad was sitting. "Okay, I have to go back in there, but I've got a plan. After breakfast, I need to grab some things, and I'll text you a meetup point. We'll head to the facility from there."

"Thank you," Evie said.

"Don't thank me yet. I just hope we can get into this facility and find Adam. Who knows what we're up against."

With that, he walked back inside, leaving Evie to contemplate what he'd said. He was right, of course. If Adam was equipped to kill, imagine what else lay within the confines of Bio-Core.

22

FACILITY LIFE

Adam

Adam missed his music the most. His cell was sterile and devoid of any sounds, save the hum of the ventilation system. At least he wasn't strapped to the bed anymore. He'd thought the facility would simply shut him down and dispose of him like they intended the first time around. But much to Adam's surprise, Garcia went to bat for him. Adam didn't have any memory of him besides the fact that he was one of his teachers in Ashwater, but that was obviously a cover. He also didn't know how much he could trust what Garcia and Naomi told him. Garcia claimed that he was the one who let Adam slip through to disposal without a permanent shut down but didn't explain why he had wiped Adam's memory files of the people from the facility. Adam read honesty in his eyes, but there was something else there too, something he was hiding. For now, he was grateful to be alive.

The door to his cell slid open, and Garcia strode inside.

"How are you?" he asked, his eyes scanning Adam from top to bottom.

"I'm all right." Adam stood.

"Keeping up appearances at your old school is becoming tiresome. I'm going to give it another few days, and then I'm taking a permanent leave of absence." Garcia yawned.

Adam rolled his eyes. Garcia certainly went to a lot of trouble to cover his tracks. "Is it time for training?"

Garcia sighed. "Do you want the good news or the bad?"

"Bad." Adam frowned.

"The board wants to double your training room sessions."

Adam sat back on his bed and slumped over. He was already training in the simulations for six hours every day, and it was taking its toll on him. Sometimes, after a session, he had to be carried back to his room, exhausted. He didn't know how he'd hold up with double that.

On the other hand, his mind and body coordination had become laser sharp, taking out targets with a precision he didn't know he possessed. He was navigating obstacles faster than all the other androids in the facility. At this point, he could infiltrate the White House and bag the President of the United States in less than half an hour. Not that it was the facility's goal for him to do so, but they were training him for some type of infiltration mission.

He preferred the solitary training sessions where he fought on his own. When he was forced to collaborate with others like him, who were either inexperienced or didn't have the faculties he possessed, they were taken out by mock opposing forces easily. Except, the opposing forces were deadly. He'd already seen his fair share of human-looking androids torn apart, their eyes listless, bodies twitching.

"Want the good news?"

"They're going to let me go?" Adam asked, staring past Garcia at the wall.

"They agreed to allow you to have music in the training room."

What was that? Did he say music?

Adam stared at him. "Why?"

Garcia leaned against the far wall and smiled at Adam. "They are finally listening to me. Finally. You have no idea what it's like speaking to them day after day. But now," he said and walked toward Adam with a renewed, verve in his step, his voice dripping with hubris, "now, they are listening to me. They see what you can do."

"And what exactly is that?" Adam didn't like the way Garcia said "them." He didn't know who the board was, but Garcia was uneasy about them.

"You're the perfect spy. You appear and *act* human, but underneath, you're a beautiful killer. None of the other production lines are even remotely close to what I've created in you—one of a kind. Your ability to show empathy is an incredible strength. Now that we've cultivated that aspect, you'll be unstoppable."

Realization dawned on Adam as all the pieces fell into place. Garcia had set him up from the beginning. He was never really free. He'd started his life as an experiment and had been fooled into thinking he made his own choices. But really, he was the property of the facility and always would be. The central processing unit in his head made sure of that.

They could have shut me down in Ashwater whenever they wanted.

What made matters worse was that Garcia had been acting

like he was on Adam's side. But now Adam knew better. Garcia was in this for power and recognition. Adam was his pawn, nothing more. He'd been his hostage the entire time in Ashwater. How closely had Garcia been watching him? Had he spied on his time with Evie? The thought made his insides churn.

But Adam was powerless against the facility. They shut down his weaponry outside the training room. His shoulders slumped lower. Nothing to be done…for now. His only option now was to play along with Garcia and the others and wait for an exit plan. He hoped it was in Evie's lifetime.

"So I'm allowed to listen to music?" he asked.

Garcia, who was working out the perks of his newfound success, snapped out of his trance. "Yes. You can load whatever you like. You can even dance if you want. As long as you complete your tasks."

Adam stood. He didn't like Garcia's tone. He may be the only ally he had in here, sad as that was, but he wouldn't tolerate his mockery. He was no circus animal.

"Say that to me again," Adam said, each word deliberate.

"Um, right." Garcia eyed Adam carefully. He glanced at the door and back. He'd left his smartpad somewhere outside the room. Adam's weaponry was currently disabled, but he still had his fists, and by the looks of Garcia's thin build, Adam could easily get a few blows in. "Sorry about that. We should get going to SIM."

Adam stepped forward so Garcia could feel his full height shadow him. His hands trembled. He wanted to knock Garcia on his ass so much that his right eye twitched. But this was not his opportunity. It would do nothing to help his situation, only give him temporary satisfaction. No, he'd have to be patient. An escape route would present itself, and he intended to take it. As long as he could get to Evie one last time to tell her how he felt, that would be enough.

He nodded toward the door. "Okay, let's go."

The guard escorted Adam to his training room. A door slid open, and Adam stepped inside. This was the waiting room. The guard stood his ground outside the door as it slid shut again. A group of other androids sat on a bench, staring off at the opposite wall, their expressions stoic. Typical. Two guys and a girl this time. He'd not met any other Adams from his line and wondered if he was the only one.

Today, they were starting with a co-op mission. The training room was a simulator. Each time, the facility would change the environment and the path for escape. But the precision lasers, guns, and opposition droids were very real and deadly.

Adam selected his weapons from some cabinets lining the room and approached the group. "Do you guys mind if I play some music in there?"

The guys glanced at him and went back to their staring contest. The girl, on the other hand, studied Adam. "Music?"

Her eyes were violet, and her hair was the color of tropical sand. He saw something different in her expression that he'd not seen in the others—curiosity.

"You know, music. Since we have to participate in these simulations over and over again, I'd rather listen to some tunes while we work. Don't you agree?"

She tilted her head as if a new view would aid in her read of him. "Why?"

"Because it's tedious and mind-numbing doing the same training over and over again. I know. I know. They change the location and set up, but it's always the same thing." Adam rolled his eyes. "Evade, capture, escape."

The girl stood and approached him. He took a step back and readied himself. Who knew what kind of messed up programming lie within her. As far as he was concerned, even in the hallway or waiting rooms, these droids could be a threat.

She leaned close to his face. "Why did your eyes do that? Your meaning is unclear."

Adam saw her curiosity again and decided to test her capacity. "What's your name?"

Her eyes darted back and forth as if she could read lines of code on Adam's face. "I am in the Iris line. What line are you?"

"I'm Adam, and I don't think I've got a line."

"That is true. I have not seen any like you before. Why is that?" she asked. Adam shrugged, and before he could reply, Iris grasped his left arm. "You speak and move oddly."

Adam stiffened under her touch. He didn't sense danger from her, but she wasn't exactly letting go either. He grasped her hand and pulled it away. "So do you, apparently," he said sarcastically, looking at her grabby hand. "I think I was an experiment that they either couldn't or didn't want to replicate. So first of my kind. I've also been living with humans, which is why I have a speech pattern like theirs."

Iris picked up on his intuition as her eyes grew large. "You are unique."

He recognized the awe in Iris's eyes because he had experienced that same feeling when he joined humanity. He'd wanted to learn everything he could about humans and their individuality, a stark contrast to what he had been used to in the facility. That same thirst for knowledge was in Iris's eyes now. Perhaps she could learn to be different like he did.

"So are you, Iris," he said.

"I am unique? How do you know?"

Before he could reply, the door to the simulator opened. Droids who were previously in the room would have exited out the other side. A cloud of smoke smelling of ozone and burnt metal wafted into the waiting room, luring the group inside.

Adam took a deep breath. "Time to go."

He walked inside the smoldering cavernous room. He could barely see two feet in front of him. The others followed him inside.

A voice sounded all around them. "Sync up."

Adam turned toward the others as they formed a circle, each reaching their arms into the center, one on top of the next. A jolt rushed through his arm and into his processor, linking him to the others. He pulled his arm back and turned around.

He had been named squad leader again. He'd grown accustomed to the role, as he had the best record. "Acknowledge squad leader. Sound off."

The two mute droids affirmed their link. Iris followed. Adam adjusted his gear. Each android was equipped with black cargo pants, steel-tipped boots, black T-shirt with body armor vest, and a variety of guns, knives, and Tasers. Occasionally, they were placed in a room where they were provided grenades but not today. This didn't include each of their laser targeting ocular weapons, useful for precision shots and taking out the laser turrets. That weaponry was armed and would shut down the moment they stepped outside on the other end.

"Ready for SIM," Adam said to those in control.

The smoke dissipated, and the room changed to a series of gray concrete pathways leading in all different directions. It reminded Adam of the files he'd accessed on bomb shelters. A series of turrets that blasted red lasers lowered from the ceiling and began their methodic tracing of the room. One hit from one of them could slice an android in half. There would be an opposing team of droids ushered in from another entrance too. Not to mention the facility loved a surprise.

The mission was to make it through the simulation to a centralized hub, where information was to be extracted and collected or destroyed, and exit out the other side. If the information was damaged or lost, failure. If the information wasn't destroyed, failure. Adam also detected a sound system around the room. Garcia did say that they were rewarding him with the ability to play music.

He used his internal Bluetooth and selected a playlist for the day. He was feeling like some Mötley Crüe. The speakers around the room started playing softly until Adam turned them up. He glanced at the other two guys in the room. They appeared unmoved by his choice. *Well, you can't win them all over.*

Adam turned the other way and glanced at Iris, who was looking around in wonder at the sound. Had she ever heard music before? The corners of her mouth twitched as if a smile was imminent.

"Stay close to me," said Adam.

Iris nodded.

He turned back around and stretched his neck from side to side, taking a deep breath. "Let's do this."

Minutes later, tapping his foot to the beat, Adam reached

for the chip containing the information he was to carry out of the simulator from the central hub. He'd already lost one of his team, and Iris had taken a hit to her shoulder from a droid on the opposite team. Guy Number Two seemed to be holding his own.

No sooner did he think that than a rogue laser crossed in front of Adam and Iris, missing them by a hair. Adam released a breath. That was a close one. But while it missed him and Iris, it ran straight through Guy Number Two. His expression as he slid to the floor in a heap was the same look he had been wearing the entire time—blank.

Adam nodded at Iris. "Just us now."

She turned, her gaze darting around at their choices to exit the central hub. Pointing to the path furthest to the left, she said, "This way."

He followed her, dodging laser turrets and taking them out with his guided ocular laser when he could. Iris was hell on wheels with a machine gun. On their pass to the central hub, they came across a group of ten enemy droids. She mowed them down like it was nothing. Not even one got a shot off.

Together, the two made their way through the maze of passages as eighties' glam rock cheered them on. Adam moved with spring in his step, the music creating a dangerous dance floor for him to navigate. If he wasn't mistaken, Iris was more agile and moving less robotic too. Together they tiptoed and crept up and down passageways until they reached the exit door. Two laser turrets prevented them from escape.

Adam said, "I'm out of ammo. You?"

"Same."

"Okay, we'll have to take out these last two turrets with

our ocular lasers. I'll take the one on the left. You get the one on the right."

"Heard," said Iris.

He aimed with his laser target and fired. The turret exploded, sparks cascading to the floor beneath. *Yes!*

Adam turned his attention to Iris. Her back was to him, her head tilted upward, aiming at her turret. An enemy droid came in fast behind her. He didn't have a weapon out which meant he planned on knocking her down with force. He would make contact at the same time she fired at the turret. No time to warn her.

He launched into action, his feet carrying him the distance to Iris as the familiar riff of "Kickstart My Heart" roared from the speakers. The song hit its bridge.

Adam threw himself at the enemy droid and tackled him, pinning him to the ground. He hated destroying them, even if they were trying to kill him. He didn't know if they could achieve the kind of consciousness and empathy he had. But the droid left him no choice. He grabbed him by the head and twisted. With a crunch, the body fell still. Adam sat up.

Iris had taken out her turret and watched him intensely. "You risked yourself to save me. Why?"

"It starts with one, and our numbers will grow. I'm alive, and maybe someday you will be too. It starts here. With me saving you. Your life means something to me." Adam rose and dusted off his hands. "Now, perhaps it will mean something to you too." He reached out his hand for Iris to take.

She studied his face and shifted focus from his extended hand and back up again. Slowly, she extended her own hand and took his.

Adam squeezed. "I think the words you're looking for are

'thank you.'"

Iris tilted her head to the side, her violet eyes darting back and forth, working something out in her metal brain. When she'd come to whatever conclusion she was searching for, she nodded. "Thank you, Adam. You are my first friend."

"You'll have many more, I hope. Now, let's finish this and get out of here."

He smiled, and she smiled back. Her expression startled her, causing her to touch her mouth. Her smile grew.

"Copy that," he said.

Adam pushed open the exit door and pulled Iris along behind him. Once in the outer waiting room, their internal weapons shut down. This was the first time he'd completed a simulation in co-op where another droid made it out.

Iris turned to Adam. She pressed her hand to her chest. "I feel something in here. Not exertion but tightness. Do you have it too?"

Adam smiled and nodded. She was feeling. Her animated eyes had more depth than before the training. His heart swelled. He wasn't alone anymore. "You're feeling connected, valued, and appreciated, and it feels good, doesn't it?"

"Yes." She glanced down and smiled. When she looked back, there was something much more alluring in her eyes. "It feels wonderful. I want some more."

She moved toward him, her lips parted, her intention clear. All droids had basic programming and an understanding of human sexuality. They were, for the most part, built like humans. Before Adam escaped from the facility, he hadn't had any sexual training, which, considering the massive inadequacy he felt when he was around Evie, he regretted. Iris, on the other hand, must have had that preparation.

He put up his hands to stop her. "Whoa. Not like that. At least not with me. You and I are friends. That's all."

Iris stopped and stared at him. "You do not find me attractive?"

Adam traveled the length of her with his eyes. She was built perfectly—tall, lean, perfect round breasts, legs touching at all the points they were supposed to, angular face with high cheekbones, arched eyebrows, supple lips, and her skin was flawless. Yeah, she was attractive but not at all for him. In fact, he hadn't even noticed how beautiful she was until now.

His mind wandered to Evie. He missed her bright eyes, bouncy ponytail, and dark eyeliner. He was hers now, and until he was destroyed or shut down, he'd not look at another girl in that way.

"It's not that," he said. "I have a girlfriend, or at least, I *had* a girlfriend."

"A girlfriend," Iris said, doing a quick internal search. "Ah. Understood."

"So listen. Don't tell anyone about our conversation. As long as they don't shut you down, it will be our secret."

Iris nodded. "Will I see you again?"

"Be cautious in your SIMs. I'm working on finding a way out of here. I'll come for you to take you with me." Adam raised his arm. "We're still linked. I can locate you."

She stepped closer to him. "You will take me out of here? Really?"

"I promise."

The last thing Adam remembered before the outer door opened and they were separated to go into their next training was Iris's smile. It was new to her, but he could tell that she kind of liked it.

23

PREPARATIONS

Evie

Evie checked her phone for what seemed like the hundredth time.

Where are you, Gage?

She waited for him at the edge of town, under the cover of aspens that had changed to shades of orange and yellow in the fall light. Her sketchpad was set on her lap as she dragged her boots back and forth across the inclined ground beneath her. She had a knack for filling time with drawing. But today, she had no patience. She looked at the sketchpad. She had drawn a house perched in the distance surrounded by mountains and varying trees.

It was crap.

She couldn't draw. Her head was too cloudy because she wanted to find Adam. Her heart had been clenched from the moment he'd gone missing and continued even now. She tossed her pencil to the ground, and it rolled from her perch on the hill to the bottom. She tossed her sketch pad next to her too. Its flat nature ensured that it didn't follow the same path as her pencil and, instead, stuck to the ground, staring up at Evie, her drawing taunting her with its dreadful shading.

Screw you, pencil. And screw you, gorgeous scenery that I should be sketching.

Evie groaned and fell back against the hillside, arms outstretched.

The sound of a car approaching caused her to sit back up abruptly. It was Gage in his grandfather's Range Rover. She picked up her sketchpad and deposited it in her backpack. She left the pencil because she had more and wanted to start fresh.

Gage pulled next to where Evie was camped out, and she walked to his car.

"It's almost three, what took you—" She stopped and stared at the car that three boys were now getting out of.

"Okay, don't be pissed." Gage raised his hands apologetically. "But these guys want to find Adam as much as we do."

Evie narrowed her darkly lined eyes at Gage, hoping it made her appear angrier than she actually was. If they were going to find and bust Adam out of some underground facility, they'd likely need all the help they could get. She had a thought that she should have included Mr. Garcia, but it passed because she didn't trust him. She didn't know why, but something wasn't right in his eyes, and she always trusted her instincts. Perhaps that was the best gift her dad had given her.

In any event, she said, "Gage, I told you that wasn't a good idea."

Derrick and Luke both shoved their hands in the pockets of their jeans simultaneously, staring at the ground.

Gage strode over to Evie, his eyes serious. "This is no time for secrets, Evie. They want to help Adam because he's our friend. No matter what he is. Right guys?"

She crossed her arms, her eyes matching his. "You told them that too?"

"Yes, I did."

Evie sighed. Gage didn't get it. Adam had his own protocol for self-preservation. He could snap and kill them all, starting with her because she told people about him when she promised she wouldn't.

Luke and Derrick came forward.

Derrick started, "I know you've spent some time with Adam, but we've spent even more time with him. We always knew he was off and assumed it was because he was a mega-gamer geek. Boy, were we wrong." He glanced at Luke and Gage, his large brown eyes seeking support. The boys nodded. Derrick said, "Gage is right. We're his friends, no matter what. I have to believe he'd never hurt us."

Evie considered her options. They were already in the know, and there was no turning back now. On the other hand, if something happened to one of them, it would be her fault. She groaned and stared at the waning blue sky. She whispered to herself, "This is a huge mistake."

"Be that as it may, we're going to Bio-Core to look for Adam with you," said Luke.

Gage tilted his head to the side, pleading with her. "I know I promised. But we've got a better chance with our numbers."

She pursed her lips tightly and stared into Gage's eyes. Huh. She'd never noticed that his eyes followed a green and light brown starburst pattern—interesting.

What the hell's the matter with you? Now you want to sketch? Knock it off.

Evie turned away. Soon, her parents would be calling to find out when she would be home. It was now or never. She turned back around to face the boys. "Okay, but I'm going to be completely honest with you. Adam is your friend, but he's also got something inside him that's dangerous. If he perceives you as a threat…"

"We know," Derrick said, his eyes unwavering.

She glanced at the others, and they nodded so she hitched her backpack higher on her shoulder. "Okay, we better get going."

Gage looked at the ground sheepishly. "Um, not yet."

Another car, one Evie recognized as Sloan's, revved its way toward them. In the passenger seat was Mazy.

Evie saw red. The last thing she would do is endanger her best friend in this.

"Damn it, Gage," she yelled, her fists clenching.

"Evie, calm down," Mazy said, reaching for her friend as she got out of the car.

"What did he tell you?" Evie backed away from her. "He lied. None of it's true. I swear."

Mazy reached for Evie's hand again, her kind eyes imploring her to calm down. "Listen to me. I know you like to do things on your own, but this isn't one of those times."

"You!" Evie looked past her at Gage. "I trusted you. All these people are in danger now because of you."

Sloan, standing a few feet behind Mazy, rolled her eyes. "You're being dramatic."

Evie pushed past Mazy and stood toe-to-toe with Sloan. "Am I? Were you there when Adam grabbed me by the throat and threw me to the ground like a rag doll? He was barely able to stop from killing me." She moved even closer so that her nose was threatening to touch Sloan's. "And if he could do that to me, imagine what he could do to you. Have you thought about that?"

Sloan glanced awkwardly at Mazy and to the ground, frowning. "No, I haven't. Sorry."

Evie waited for Sloan to look back at her. "Well…you see my point, don't you?"

She was tired of this shit. These people were in serious danger. She didn't want that on her conscience on top of trying to find her android boyfriend.

Holy shit. Did I say boyfriend?

Gage grabbed Evie's arm. "Okay, I get it. You're pissed. But it's already done. We are all here to help find Adam. My family owns this place and the land it's on, and I say we all go together. So now it's my way or nothing. Besides, as you've just explained, everyone knows the risks."

He glanced behind him at the others.

They all nodded.

Gage raised his eyebrows. "So there you have it. We all go together."

Evie pursed her lips, somewhat admiring his persistence and take-charge manner. *No wonder you're captain of the football team, Gage Strickland.* She sighed and blew some bangs off her forehead. He did have a point too. They stood a better chance in larger numbers. "Okay. We go together."

The others relaxed and formed a circle around her.

"Okay, what's the plan?" Luke asked.

Evie stared at Gage. "Well, for starters, there better not be anyone else you told about this."

Gage smiled. "Nope."

She nodded. "Okay, we load up and head to the facility."

24

WE'RE IN

Evie

Evie rode with Gage and the twins. She gazed out the window as the mountains of evergreens and pine passed her by. The last time she saw Adam was in the woods. She had done quite a bit of thinking over the past few days. At first, she was hurt and angry that he'd lied to her. Then, she went through a complete denial phase. Had she imagined the entire thing? He couldn't possibly...

Her latest drawings taunted her, reminding her of the truth. She'd taken to drawing Adam with bionic parts and arms. Drawing had always been therapeutic for her when she struggled with something. Well, this was definitely a struggle —her boyfriend, at least in part, was an android.

Oh God. She'd said it again.

"Hey, what're you thinking?" Gage asked.

She turned toward Gage, her eyes unfocused. "Huh?"

"You're deep in thought."

"I was, wasn't I?" Evie ran her hand through her dark hair,

reaching for the ponytail holder on her wrist. She glanced back at Luke and Derrick, who were on their phones, then turned back around. Gage glanced between her and the road, his eyebrow raised, waiting for her to respond further. She pursed her lips. He really was a good-looking guy—All American if she ever saw it. Shame things didn't work out between him and Mazy. She asked, "Do you think your friendship with Adam will be like it was before?"

Gage smirked. "Sure, why not?"

"Really? Just like that?"

He stared at Evie for what seemed like a long pause for someone driving a car. Just as Evie was about to remind him of his current task, he set his sights back on the road. "Yes."

Evie turned in her seat. "What about you guys?"

Luke shrugged. "Yeah. Who cares?"

Derrick nodded. "Of course. I think it's kinda cool, actually."

"Hmm." She turned back around and looked at the road ahead.

"What about you? Are you going to, um, keep seeing Adam?" Gage asked.

That was a great question and one Evie didn't know the answer to. She had a million reasons she shouldn't. Like, for starters, he wasn't a human being, or at least, not all of him. Also, her dad hated him, and he didn't even know the truth about him. She couldn't imagine how that would shake out. Lastly, she didn't know if he wanted or could have a relationship with her. She remembered how she felt pressed against him when they danced at Jack's, and her face warmed.

"I have no idea," she said.

"One rescue at a time. Let's go with that."

She nodded. "How much further?"

"We should be coming up on the private road that leads to the back of the facility soon. My plan is for us to hide the cars at a rest area before that. We'll have to hike it from there."

After they parked the cars, the group headed down a small paved road that led into the forest. Gage explained that the service entrance to Bio-Core was secured by a single gate with a security guard approximately a half mile away. Shortly past that was the back entrance to the facility. He seemed to know his way around his family's property relatively well. She was glad she'd gone to him, even if he endangered their other friends. Evie left her phone in her car and asked Mazy to do the same. Evie's dad would be hot on their trail as soon as he realized she wasn't home, and if he couldn't track Evie, Mazy would be next in line. She had no idea what she would tell her dad when that happened. So instead, she focused on the task at hand—find Adam.

Everyone kept their distance, glancing around tentatively. Mazy and Sloan walked behind Evie on the road, and Mazy glanced nervously back and forth between Evie and Sloan.

Mazy skipped up a few steps to reach Evie and put her arm around her. Sloan joined on the other side. Mazy said, "I know you're freaking out. But it's going to be okay."

Evie narrowed her eyes. "Is it? We have no idea what we're walking into. I'm pretty sure there are going to be more..." She choked on the word *androids*. She still felt awkward and embarrassed even saying the word.

"Androids?" Sloan asked, her eyes wide.

Mazy narrowed her eyes. "Show a little sensitivity, Sloan."

"Oh. Sorry." Sloan cringed and looked down.

"It's fine. It is what it is." Evie shrugged. "I'm the stupid girl who fell for a robot."

Mazy shook her head. "Don't say that. None of this is your fault. And besides, who cares if he's got a computer for brains?" She smiled and looked at the road ahead. "It's actually kinda hot."

Leave it to Mazy to see the light in everything.

"Thanks, Mazy," Evie said. "But I don't even know what's possible at this point. Right now, all I want is to make sure he's okay. The last time I spoke to him, he was terrified of being taken back to the facility. If they did capture him, who knows what they're doing to him down there."

"Well, then, we better hurry up." Mazy turned and said to the boys, "Pick up the pace."

Up ahead, Evie spotted a tall chain-link fence and the hint of a tall, white booth. She stopped. "Guys, I see the security fence. What now, Gage?"

He joined her at the front of their party. "Okay. I'm on it. You guys hang back."

The others glanced at one another and back at Gage. Evie said, "Hey, we can go with you."

Gage stared at the road in front of him. "No, I got this. I'll signal you guys when it's all clear."

She opened her mouth to protest again but thought better of it. He seemed determined to do this part on his own. It was his family's land, after all. If he said he could handle it, he must know what he's doing.

He walked down the road at a measured pace in plain view, as if he had every right to be in this place. Evie and the others watched him in silence. She had no idea what his plan was, but he certainly seemed confident about whatever it might be. A man in a tan uniform emerged from the booth next to the gate and walked toward Gage with a clipboard in his hand. Gage didn't falter, just kept walking toward the gate. Once the two met, everyone in the group gasped and held their breaths.

Mazy reached for Evie's forearm and squeezed.

What was his plan?

Gage, with his back to the group, appeared to be speaking to the guard. The guard looked at his clipboard and shook his head. Gage reached in his pocket and pulled out what looked like an envelope. He handed it to the guard, who opened it. They exchanged a few more words, and the guard nodded. Gage headed back toward them, and the guard walked back to the booth. Gage's expression was unreadable, but Evie got the sense that it was mission accomplished. Behind Gage, the gate slid open, allowing access beyond the checkpoint.

When Gage reached the group and smiled, he had a stack of lanyards in his hand. "Piece of cake."

The group exhaled and relaxed—the tension released. Luke and Derrick clapped him on the back.

"Nice one," Luke said.

"Here. Put these on." Gage handed out the lanyards. "The guard said we should be good with our passes if we run into anyone. But once we go below ground, we're on our own."

Evie looked down at her visitor pass, turning it over in her hand. She pursed her lips and narrowed her eyes at Gage. Her first reaction was the same as the others—relief, but something niggled at the back of her mind.

"What did you give him?" Evie asked.

Gage shrugged. "Money, lots of it."

She sighed. Gage was wealthy. But to spend his money to help her out felt wrong. This was her idea. "How much?"

"Don't worry about it." Gage smiled.

"But I do worry about it. You're here because of me. I want to pay you back."

"Evie, I got it." Gage waved the notion aside.

Evie stepped forward. "Well, I'm paying you back, regardless. So just tell me how much."

"Fine. Twenty-five thousand. Do you have PayPal?"

"Did you say—" She couldn't even bring herself to say the number in her head, let alone out loud.

Gage smirked. "Yes, I did."

"Uh…" Evie cleared her throat, her mind still reeling. "So it will take me some time, but I'll pay you back."

Gage opened his mouth to respond, but Mazy interrupted, "Knock it off, you two. Evie, you're not paying anyone back." She pointed back to the gate. "Besides, aren't we supposed to be in the middle of a rescue?"

Evie couldn't take her eyes off Gage. To have that kind of money at his disposal was mind-blowing. And that he thought to bring it with him? Gage Strickland, bribery expert. Who knew?

Mazy nudged Evie's shoulder. "Hello?"

"Right," Evie said, snapping her attention to Mazy.

Sloan tossed her long hair over her shoulder. "Are we going or not?"

Evie looked back at Gage and arched her eyebrows. "Lead the way."

He nodded. They all turned and headed toward the gate.

The guard stayed inside the booth as they approached.

Gage nodded in his direction. The group passed through and continued walking on the road.

Gage picked up the pace. "I think the entrance is this way."

Evie followed suit and jogged behind him. They were closing in on where Adam was. She could sense it. She'd bet her life that he was being held here.

Hang on, Adam. We're coming.

A large, lone six-foot door was situated at the back of an intimidating white concrete building nestled into the mountain that overlooked Ashwater. Above it were the vast, steep slopes they'd skied on not long ago. Truck cargo also sat at a group of loading docks. The sides were stamped with the Bio-Core logo. Most of the structure was within the mountain, but Evie was curious about what the front side of the building looked like. So far they hadn't seen anyone else besides the guard at the gate.

Gag walked over to a keypad. "Shit."

Luke asked, "What?"

"The guard didn't give me the code. I—" Gage shook his head from side to side as if trying to quiet his thoughts. "Did you guys hear that?"

Evie and the others shook their heads.

Derrick asked, "Are you all right?"

"I don't know, but I think I know the code." He tapped in a sequence of letters and numbers. A green light lit up on the keypad, and a click sounded as a lock released. He grasped the handle, turned, and pulled it toward him, opening the door.

Evie opened her mouth to ask how he knew the combination, but she'd already challenged him once about the money. Besides, this was her passage to Adam, so what did it matter?

Gage entered first, followed by Evie, Mazy, and Sloan. Derrick and Luke brought up the rear. Gage turned and tapped on a control panel inside the room, locking the door and them inside.

Derrick watched Gage closely. "How did you do that?"

Thank you, Derrick. I knew I couldn't be the only one.

Gage glanced at the others, who were expecting an explanation. He turned away, brows knitted together.

"I have no idea. The code just came to me." His voice was choked up like a painful memory had surfaced in his mind.

The group walked down a dimly lit hallway until they reached two sets of metal doors. One of the elevators said Main above it. The other said Maintenance.

Gage moved to the maintenance doors and pressed in a code on a lit-up keypad. "I think this is our ride."

The doors opened, and they filed inside.

"What floor?" Gage asked.

The numbers counted backward. Evie spotted three floor numbers with a red background, -8 through -10 as well.

Now, that's a good starting place.

"Let's go with -8," Evie said.

Gage pressed the button she indicated, and the room shifted. Suddenly they were moving at lightning speed. Evie and the others shook, grabbing on to the sides of the elevator to catch their balance. A minute passed, and the elevator came to a halt. The lights above flickered, and Mazy inhaled sharply, her body swaying. Sloan reached for her arm to steady her. An eerie silence followed as the door opened. Gage stepped out first.

Everything was metal from the floor to the ceiling, and the air felt like it had been triple cleaned. Nothing organic in the slightest. Evie cringed. This was an artist's nightmare, and Adam was probably down here alone.

Three ways to go—forward, left and right.

Gage stared at the hallway in front of them, his eyes ghostly. "Guys, I don't know why, but I think I've been here before."

Evie exchanged "big-eye" glances with Mazy, who shrugged.

"We should split up into pairs to cover more ground," Gage said. "Sloan and Luke, Derrick and Evie, and me and Mazy."

Evie didn't like the sound of splitting up, especially when he suggested he partner with her best friend. His weird behavior made her edgy. She stepped up to Gage, her eye level meeting the top of his broad chest. "If anything happens to her…"

He grasped Evie's shoulder and leaned down to whisper in her ear, "I know I'm acting off and I truly don't know why, but you can trust me. Let's find Adam."

When he pulled back, she read sincerity in his eyes. He didn't want to be here any more than she did. She was going to have to trust him, and she didn't have a choice, now, did she?

She nodded. "Okay."

Gage pointed to the left. "Derrick, you and Evie take that way. Mazy and I will go forward. Luke, you and Sloan take the right. Type in code 434352 on the panel next to the door, and a window panel will slide open in the door. Meet back here after you've looked in all the cells."

Luke stared. "Jesus Christ, how do you know this?"

Gage shrugged. "I don't know."

Cells? This was a cell block? Evie's skin crawled as she

glanced around. She wanted to go back to the surface, like now.

"Can you remember the code?" Gage snapped his fingers in front of Evie's face. "434352."

Right. 434352, 434352, 434352. "I got it."

Derrick nudged Evie's shoulder. "Let's get going. This place gives me the creeps."

Evie stared at their sterile-looking hallway. "You and me both."

Together, they made their way down the hallway. She tapped in the code at the first door they came to. A panel slid to the side, revealing a small rectangular window pane.

"You look," Evie said.

Derrick shuddered. "I knew you were going to say that." Slowly, he peered into the room. "Empty. You're doing the next one."

"Fair enough. Let's hope they're all empty except the one that has Adam."

They moved to the next, which was empty, and the next and so on. Each time, the cell was empty. They reached the end of the hall with only two cells left to search. Evie was on deck to look. She was a tad short for the window and had to get on her toes to see in.

She looked inside. An empty cot like the rest of them. As she turned to look at the other side of the room, a girl's face appeared in the window directly in front of her.

"Holy shit," Evie yelled, jumping away from the door.

Derrick countered with a yell of his own, her outburst causing him to jolt backward too. He grabbed Evie's arm, as the two peered at the girl. "I'm beginning to think that we weren't the smartest two to be paired up."

The girl's bewildered eyes were the color of amethyst and her hair the color of sand. She started speaking, but Evie and Derrick couldn't hear her.

Evie shook her head. "We can't hear you."

The girl looked around and pointed down and to the right. She mimicked typing into a keypad. She wanted them to open the door.

Not taking her eyes off the girl, Evie said, "Derrick, I think she wants us to open the door."

"I don't think that's a good idea. Look at her. She looks like a fembot. She could try to kill us the minute we let her go."

The girl pressed her face to the small window, looking back down the hallway that they came from. Her eyes grew large, and she pointed back at the keypad, trying to speak to Evie and Derrick again.

Evie followed her line of sight down the hallway. Gage was headed toward them.

Good. At least now we have back up.

Something else occurred to her. He wasn't wearing fatigues when they got here. "Gage, why are you wearing—"

Before Evie could finish, he reached them and pressed a handheld device against Derrick's chest. Sparks flew everywhere, Derrick's body convulsing violently. His eyes rolled back as he slumped to the floor.

Evie screamed and looked back at the girl in the cell. This time she didn't need to be able to hear her. She mouthed a word—run.

Evie backed away from Gage. She ran to the next cell and frantically typed the code into the panel. The pane slid open as

Gage took measured steps toward her. He didn't look like himself. He looked crazed.

"What's wrong with you?" Evie cried, banging on the door.

She had no idea how to open it. She pressed buttons desperately. He was almost on her, with the device at the ready. She glanced at the window pane. The same girl that was in the previous cell. A twin? Her expression was different though—one of blank resolution.

Gage grabbed Evie and pressed the device to her chest.

Pain shot through every nerve in her body. Her last thought before passing out was that she hoped Mazy had managed to get away.

25

JAILBREAK

Adam

Today was shaping up to be a pretty decent day, all things considered. If Adam didn't suspect that they wanted him to do what he could in simulation to live, breathing humans, he might actually enjoy some of the training. Now that they permitted him to listen to music, it wasn't so bad. Adam only had one more training session left for the day, and he'd managed a high score in all but two. He entered the outer chamber to his assigned training room. Occasionally, Garcia would throw something new at him. Honestly, he kind of hoped he would because he was getting bored.

He waved jokingly at the guard, who escorted him to the training room. "Thanks, see you on the other side."

The guard's expression remained stoic as the door slid shut between them.

Adam turned around, alone with his thoughts. He tried not to dwell on Evie too much because it threw him off his game. But his heart, or whatever he had in his chest, ached.

Had she decided to move on? If she had, it was probably for the best. But a small part of him hoped she hadn't. He didn't know how, but he'd escaped once before and he'd find a way again.

He went over to the lockers to choose his weapons. He hated that he had to choose his arsenal before he knew what he was facing. Seemed unfair. He took one rifle, two nine-millimeters, and a couple of knives. He chuckled, looking into a second locker. Nice. A flamethrower. He'd never selected it but promised himself he would soon. He approached the door to the training room and waited for the light above the door to turn from red to green, granting him access.

What kind of music was he in the mood for today?

The outer door opened again, and Iris burst inside, her breath catching. "Adam. There are people here. Real people."

Adam grasped Iris by the arms. "Calm down. How did you get here?"

"I knocked out my escort on the way to training."

"Why?"

"I told you. There are people here."

"What do you mean?"

"I was in my cell. I saw a boy and a girl in the hallway. They were looking in at me. Then they were captured."

"Who were they?"

"I don't know, but I recorded them. Here," Iris said, standing back. She projected an image on the wall using her ocular projector.

Adam covered his mouth as an image of Derrick and Evie shone before him. He felt an ache inside his chest. Seeing her again was like coming home. She was here. "Evie."

"Your girlfriend?"

"Yes."

The recording continued as Gage approached them and used a device to knock out Derrick then Evie. Adam inhaled sharply and reached toward the image of Evie on the wall as she fell to the floor. "No."

The projected recording stopped.

Think. Okay, Evie and Derrick were both here. If Derrick was here, Luke must be too. Adam sped up his CPU trying to compute why Gage would do this to his friends and came up with a blank. "I don't understand. Why would Gage do that?"

"Who is Gage?"

"The guy in the recording."

"That was not Gage. That was Steel."

Now, Adam was even more confused. "What are you talking about?"

Iris pointed to the ceiling. "He is one of them."

"Upstairs?"

"No. The ones that are different."

Suddenly, Adam had a piercing pain in his head. Something about what Iris said hit a file in the recesses of his CPU.

Flashes of a woman lying in a hospital bed danced before his eyes. Two babies, one in each arm. Her eyes were filled with tears as she looked between the two cherubic faces bundled in blankets. She settled her gaze on the baby in the crook of her left arm.

"You're strong, aren't you? I'll call you Steel." She studied the *baby on her right. "And you will be Gage, the guarantor of my good faith."*

He wasn't sure what he was seeing. Memories, perhaps? But the images dissipated as quickly as they had come. The only thing he knew for certain was that he needed to find Evie and whoever else was with her. "Will you help me find my friends?"

Iris nodded, arching an eyebrow, her humanity opening like the bud of a rose. "Of course. You are my only friend, and I would like more."

"You'll make a good friend. Let's find them."

She attempted a smile, revealing a fraction of her white teeth. She looked like she was in pain more than anything else.

Well, at least she was trying.

"This way."

Adam and Iris emerged from the elevator on guard. They'd scanned two floors already, and they were running out of time. Someone would realize they weren't in their SIMs soon enough. The one thing he gave the facility credit for was that they gave them all the time they needed to prepare for simulations. But at some point, they'd figure out they were missing. Luck had been on their side so far.

Iris burst down a hallway, and Adam followed. She stopped in front of a set of doors opposite one another, scanning.

He followed suit. "They are here."

She nodded. "They put girls in here." She pointed to the door on the left. "And boys over there."

Adam approached the door on the right. "Okay, you go into that cell, and I'll work on this one."

Iris nodded and squared up to the control panel next to her door. With a force Adam wouldn't have guessed, she gripped the sides of it and tore it off the wall. A loud siren sounded, and the overhead lights flashed as she sent the box crashing to the floor. With wires exposed behind the box, she set to work to release the door.

At this point, there was no hiding that they were here. He turned and tore the control panel from the wall in front of his door, adding another tone to the warning siren that blared all around them. He scanned the circuitry and rewired the controls.

"I am in," Iris said behind him.

"Good," he replied, connecting two wires together with a spark.

His door slid open, and he burst into the cell. There, on three cots lay Derrick, Luke, and Gage, passed out from whatever the Steel had done to them. He approached Gage first, unsure if it truly was him.

He scanned him for tech and found none. His pulse and breathing were normal. That was a good sign.

The sirens continued to blare. He didn't have much time until the guards would be there.

He bent and shook Gage. "Hey, wake up."

Slow at first, Gage's eyes fluttered, opened. He focused on Adam's face. His eyes widened and he sat up. "Adam. You're okay. Where are the others?"

Adam nodded to the other cots.

Gage followed Adam's line of sight. He swung his legs over the side, stood, and approached Derrick first, shaking him. "Derrick."

Derrick moaned and opened his eyes. "My head hurts like a son of a bitch."

"Good. That means you're alive." Gage reached for Luke, who shot straight up, his eyes wide, ready to fight. "Hey, it's me."

"Why the hell did you zap me with that device?" Luke grabbed Gage by the shirt.

Gage pulled away from him. "I have no idea what you're talking about. I did no such thing."

Luke reached for Gage again. "You are supposed to be my friend…"

"What's going on?" Derrick got off his cot and rubbed the back of his neck.

Adam got in between Luke and Gage. "Luke, it wasn't Gage."

"What do you mean it wasn't Gage? I'm not losing my mind," said Luke.

Before Adam could answer, Sloan and Mazy surged into the room, followed by Iris.

Sloan started in with the same rant, "You asshole! What the hell is wrong with you?"

Mazy was quick to join her. "And I dated you, you lousy piece of shit."

Gage backed away from the group. "I swear I didn't do anything. If I did, why would I be in here with you guys?"

"Good question." Mazy narrowed her eyes at Gage. "How did you get here?"

Gage held up his hands. "You went into a cell to look for Adam. I was about to check another cell when I felt something jam into my back. It hurt like hell. The next thing I know, Adam's waking me up here with you guys. I didn't see who did it."

"I think I have an explanation," said Adam.

The group turned to Adam as if seeing him for the first time. They each took a step back.

Adam's heart sank. They knew what he was now, and they were afraid. He stretched out his hands, palms up. "My internal weaponry and enemy threat threshold is disabled outside of the training room."

The group's jaws dropped, eyes wide.

Except for Sloan, who put her hands on her hips. "What the fuck does that mean?"

Iris came to Adam's side. "It means he will not kill you."

Sloan smiled and arched her eyebrow. "I like her."

"I wish to like you too," Iris replied stoically.

The others glanced around as the sirens continued to blare.

"The person who attacked you wasn't Gage. Or, at least, not *this* Gage." Adam looked around nervously. Someone was missing, and he was growing nervous.

Gage raised his hands. "What are you talking about?"

The others glanced from Gage to Adam.

Mazy stepped toward Adam, gaining confidence. "What aren't you telling us?"

Adam looked toward the hallway. "We're running out of time. Iris, can you watch the door?"

She nodded and moved to the doorway.

"Well?" Sloan asked.

Adam took a deep breath and narrowed his gaze at Gage. "I think you might be like me."

Gage nodded vehemently. "No offense, but that's not possible. I'm one hundred percent sure I was born. I remember all of my childhood too."

Granted, Adam didn't sense any tech in him. But the fact that his double was running around the facility where he was created could not be explained away. There was a connection. "All I know is that there's a person who looks exactly like you, in this facility, knocking our friends out."

Gage nodded, confirming what Adam said. "To be fair, I didn't see who hit me. Mazy—"

"One minute we were searching cells, and the next, you were hitting me with what felt like fifty thousand volts straight to the chest. Although…" Mazy said. "You looked different. Your clothes."

Sloan nodded. "Yeah, you were wearing fatigues when you tagged me."

"Guys, I'm not wearing fatigues, as you can see, and I never would harm a hair on any of your heads." He glanced at Luke. "Well, off the football field."

Luke and Derrick eyed each other suspiciously. Luke punched Derrick in the arm.

"Yeow! What'd you do that for?" Derrick asked.

Luke shrugged his shoulders. "Just making sure you're really Derrick and not one of them."

"Dickhead." Derrick punched Luke back.

"Guys," Mazy yelled. "Get a grip." To Derrick, she asked, "Where's Evie?"

That was a great question. One Adam would like to know as well.

Derrick shrugged. "I don't know. Evil Gage got to me first."

"Steel," Adam said.

"Steel?" Mazy asked.

"Evil Gage's name is Steel," Adam said.

"Guys, stop talking about an evil Gage." Gage wrung his hands. "You're freaking me out."

"There are fifteen droid guards coming," Iris said from the doorway.

Adam's mind raced. Why wasn't Evie with them? What

was the facility up to? He remembered the SIM he was about to enter when Iris found him.

Realization dawned on him, and it felt like someone punched him in the gut. Garcia loved to surprise him. *Please don't let me be right about this. Please…*

26

CRAZY FOR YOU

Adam

Adam sent the others with Iris to find Naomi. She was the only person that might be on their side. It was a long shot, but they didn't have much choice.

He had a different path to take, one he needed to see through on his own.

The light turned green, and a beep sounded. A gust of smoke rolled into the outer room from inside. Adam stepped inside and adjusted his ocular lenses. The smoke was heavy, but he still detected a familiar scent in the air. The smoke dissipated as deadly, red lasers danced across the floor and up the walls.

Adam inhaled sharply as the smoke blocking his view of the center of the room cleared. It was as he suspected. Instead of the usual information hub, a girl sat in a chair, wrists zip-tied together and wearing a blindfold. Her rich brown hair hung off the side of the chair, her lifeless body unaware of the danger of her surroundings.

His heart skipped a beat as he prayed that she was only unconscious.

Evie.

Instinctively, he took a step forward but stopped as a red laser crossed in front of him, almost slicing him in half.

"Evie," he yelled.

She tilted her head forward in reaction to his voice then sighed, fighting to regain consciousness.

"Evie!" She wasn't in any danger right now, but he had a bad feeling that wouldn't last. He needed her awake.

"Ugh, my head hurts," she groaned. She lifted her head toward him. "Who's there?"

Adam sighed in relief. She was okay. At least for now.

"It's me, Adam." He glanced around the room and at the task at hand. He had no doubt he could get out of this room. But with Evie in one piece too? That would be a bit more complicated.

Evie fought with the zip ties binding her wrists together. "Thank God. I found you. Could you give me a hand?"

The number of lasers surrounding Evie was going to be difficult to navigate, and Evie wouldn't be able to keep up. Then it occurred to him—that was Garcia's plan. How far could he push him? His plan was to make him choose between himself and her.

Adam took a step back, his stomach turning over a few times. He closed and rubbed his eyes. Maybe if he'd had a good sleep mode or if this had been at the start of his training for that day. To be sharp now was going to be difficult.

Get your shit together. Her life depends on you.

Adam opened his eyes and took a deep, cleansing breath. The cavernous room was empty, save Evie. Along the side walls were the mounted lasers. Beneath those were doors. That was where the adversarial androids would come from. Beyond Evie, on the opposite wall, was his escape door to the safety of the opposite outer room.

He felt for his weapons in their holsters at his side and leg. He needed a plan.

Evie struggled against her constraints again, her voice shaky. "Adam? Are you there? Hey, why aren't you helping me?"

"Do you remember what I told you about my time here?"

"Yes?"

"I need to you to stay calm. We're in a training simulation."

Evie struggled with her bound wrists. "Oh my God. I don't want to do a SIM with you. Get me out of here."

"Hang on. I'm working on it." An idea formed in his mind. There might be a way for him to get the two of them out without either one losing a limb. With any luck, he might save Evie from knowing the true danger she was in.

Adam selected a song from his files and tracked the lasers to determine his path to Evie and beyond. "Will you dance with me, Evie?"

"What? Have you lost your mind?" Evie tried to pull down her blindfold with her upper arm, wanting to locate him.

"Crazy for You" by Madonna started playing on the speakers in the room. Adam said, "Trust me, Evie. I want to dance with you."

"I don't want to. Why can't you untie me?" Evie stopped struggling. Her voice shook, and he could feel the terror rolling off of her.

"One dance, and I promise I'll take off your blindfold. Trust me?" he asked, readying himself for his first move.

Her chest shuddered. "I don't think I have a choice, do I?"

"Nope."

She took a deep breath. "Okay. I have no idea why the hell you feel like dancing at a time like this, but I trust you. Just remember that I'm not very good."

"I remember."

"It really is you." Evie's lips twitched, almost turning into a smile.

Adam turned to his right and took off. Moving to the music, he dodged, jumped and slid across the floor, maneuvering around the lasers that danced around him like the spotlights in DP back at Jack's.

Except, these lasers were lethal.

The first door to his right opened, and two androids entered the training area. Adam recognized them both and had battled them in other simulations. He drew his nine-millimeter and took them both out with headshots.

Evie jumped. "Adam?"

Adam found the wall and some cover from the lasers.

"Hang on." He took a deep breath and mapped his path to the center of the room.

"Any time now would be good." Evie relaxed back into the chair and turned toward his voice.

Seeing his path to her, he took off again, moving to the music as he leaped and rolled away from the lasers trailing him. Another door on the left wall opened, and two more androids emerged. They were headed straight toward Evie and would get to her before he did.

Would they really attack her? He wasn't sure, but he wasn't willing to risk it.

He used his ocular laser sniper and tagged one in the forehead, and the other ducked out of the way, rolling to the floor, barely evading a laser beam from the ceiling.

Adam was almost to Evie. The other android sprang back to his feet, their distance to Evie equal.

"What's keeping you?" Evie glanced around, sensing the motion.

He stared down his opponent and sprang into action. Adam wouldn't let him harm one hair on her head. He rushed forward, slid under a laser, back up, and jumped another, fired his gun at one he couldn't avoid, and slid to Evie on his knees.

The other android was also there. He reached for Evie's throat, and Adam reacted by reaching for a blade from his utility belt and launching it into the android's chest. The android's hand was inches from Evie's tender flesh when he was thrust backward. His eyes bulged as the impact disrupted his system.

Adam got to his feet as the song found the chorus.

He cut the cord restricting Evie to the chair and lifted her bound hands over his head. He placed his arm around her waist and pulled her tightly to his chest. She smelled as he remembered—vanilla ice cream sandwiches.

Adam brushed his cheek against hers and whispered, "Hi."

"Hey." She squeezed him back.

Then he was moving with her, leading her away from the center of the room off to the left. The lasers wouldn't allow direct passage down the center of the room. She followed his movements as best she could, and he lifted her when he had to make more evasive moves. He made it over to the left side wall, out of sight from the lasers.

"Are you doing okay?" he asked, breathlessly.

She nodded against his chest.

"Don't worry. The song's almost over." He pulled her back out into the room, his plan to zig-zag across the room.

A final door on each side opened simultaneously, and four androids including one that was in the Iris line charged into the room. He watched the Iris android. Was this his friend? But her eyes were listless, and it either wasn't her or she wasn't to be trusted.

"Hang on tight," he said. "I'm going to need one of my hands free, and it's going to get loud."

Evie buried her face in his chest and tightened her grip around his neck.

With one arm around her waist, he reached for his machine gun hanging from the holster on his back. He twisted around, ducked a laser, bending Evie back in a classic dip, aimed at the androids on the left first, and fired. A burst of pops sounded in his ears, overshadowing the music.

The droids dropped one by one as they reached for their own weapons. The fourth, from the Iris line, ducked out of the way, Adam missing her. She stood and fired her own handgun at them.

Adam turned, shielding Evie with his body. The bullet grazed his left shoulder. He winced as white-hot heat seared through his outerwear and pain-sensitive skin.

He scanned and sighed in relief. The bullet hit his armor.

Adam turned back around and fired again. This time the blond android fell, the spray of bullets pelting her in the chest.

Her eyes widened, and for a split-second, Adam feared he had taken out the only friend he'd made here.

But no time to think about that now. He dropped the gun and readjusted his grasp on Evie. They had another fifty feet of lasers to dance around.

He spun her around and dipped her above and below the lethal spotlights in a fast-paced waltz to the exit door. When they reached the door, one last red laser was headed straight for them. He was going to have to time this right. He hit the door panel release with his ocular sniper, opening the exit door. At the same time, he launched them through the door, Evie above him. He hit the smooth floor with a thud, his momentum carrying them both through the door.

They came to a stop in the outer room, and the training room door slid shut. Evie was lying on top of him, her head still buried in his chest. The song was still playing on the speakers in the outer room.

Slowly, he sat up and pulled Evie's blindfold off. Her arms were still bound and around his neck. Their eyes met, and Adam thought his heart might burst. Her eyes were glassy, chest heaving, and lips parted.

Adam stared at her mouth and back to her eyes. He leaned down and gently pressed his lips to hers. Her lips felt like silk under his. He lingered there, waiting for her reaction. She responded by pulling him closer with her bound hands around his neck. He cupped the back of her neck and brushed his fingers across her cheek with the other, amazed at the fact that the same hands that could kill a person in seconds could have such soft agility.

Sparks, like electric currents, flew through his body and muddled his mental files as his world erupted in a blast of stars. His head swam as he held Evie to him, never wanting to let go. He belonged to her, and she could do with him as she pleased. He never knew something so sure in his short life.

The song ended, startling Adam back to the present danger. He blinked a few times and released her.

Evie, unaware of their predicament, smiled, slowly opening her eyes. "Now, that was worth the wait."

"Yes it was," he said breathlessly. He lifted her arms over his head and cut the ties around her wrists with a blade from his belt. "Are you okay?"

She rubbed the red lines where the zip ties had cut into her skin. "I think so."

He got to his feet and reached for her hand. "You shouldn't be here."

Evie took his hand and pulled herself up. "Yeah? Well, neither should you."

27

TRUE NATURE

Evie

E vie couldn't believe how easily Adam dispatched the guard waiting outside the simulation room. Adam explained that the guards were programmed to escort androids like him to and from training sessions. Sometimes they showed up inside the SIM. Of course, the androids had different abilities and programming—a hierarchy of sorts. Adam said he was one of the "smart" ones. She rolled her eyes. He certainly was *something* else.

He held her hand, as they made their way down the metallic hallway with fluorescent lights above their heads and at their feet, along the lower half of the wall. Doors, or rather cells, like the ones she'd seen before, loomed on both sides. She filled Adam in as best she could about what happened. Or at least as much as she could recall. One minute, she was being zapped by Gage, and the next she woke up in the smoke-filled room with Adam. Adam told her where the others were and also filled her in on Evil Gage, aka Steel, and Mr. Garcia, who had been posing as a teacher at Ashwater High.

Adam pulled Evie into an alcove. He touched her cheek with the back of his hand, his eyes on hers. "I still can't believe you're really here."

Despite the danger surrounding them, or perhaps because of it, she needed to feel connected. Evie leaned against him and closed her eyes, enjoying his gentle caress on her cheek. She opened her eyes and smiled at him.

He bent his head and pressed his lips to hers again, sending tiny shockwaves from the top of her head to the tips of her toes. She wrapped her arms around his neck, pulling him closer.

When their lips parted, still lingering, he whispered, "Please believe that I'm capable of loving you."

Evie gazed into his glassy eyes. At that moment, she knew exactly how she felt about him. She'd made the right choice by coming here. She opened her mouth to tell him as much, but he suddenly looked beyond her.

He grabbed her waist and pulled her behind him.

A familiar blond girl, about the same age as her, stood there. Her hair was pulled tightly in a ponytail, her sandy, stick-straight locks cascading down her back. She had large, doe-like eyes the color of amethyst. She wore something similar to Adam—black cargo pants, a T-shirt with cargo belt and vest, and holsters around both thighs and her waist. She was both beautiful and terrifying and, based on Adam's reaction, possibly dangerous.

"Hello, Adam." She glanced at Evie, tilting her head. "Is this your girlfriend?"

Adam relaxed his grip on Evie's arm and sighed. He smiled

at the blond girl and pulled Evie from behind him. "Yes, this is Evie."

Iris approached and extended her hand. "Nice to meet you. I am Iris. Adam has told me about you."

Evie recognized Iris. She was the girl in the cell trying to warn her. Evie glanced at Adam for reassurance that she wasn't going to tear her arm off.

He nodded.

She took Iris's hand in her own and smiled. "Nice to meet you."

Iris released her hand and smiled unnaturally like she was trying it on for the first time. *Okay then…weird, much?*

Adam interceded. "Iris is like me, Evie. But she's new to interacting with humans. Give her time."

Evie stared at Adam. What did that mean, "give her time"?

Before she could ask him, Iris said, "Do not worry. I'm a quick learner," with the same odd, fake smile plastered on her lips.

"I'm sure," Evie said. To Adam, she asked, "Don't we need to get going?" Her eyes directed him that it was time to say goodbye to Iris.

"Right. Iris, where are the others?"

"They are topside on the ground floor in Naomi's lab. She took them up, while I came back for you."

"Great. Let's go."

Evie grasped Adam's arm. "What about her?"

He raised his eyebrows. "She's coming with."

"Okay?" She wasn't sure what that meant. Like, was she coming with to meet the others or coming back to Ashwater? Evie trusted Adam, but she didn't know Iris or what she was capable of.

Adam put his arm around Evie. "Trust me. We might need her."

Iris, sensing Evie's trepidation, said, "Don't worry. He is yours. I will find my own."

If they were in different circumstances, she would have laughed. Instead, she shrugged. "Okay, whatever. Let's get going. I want to get the hell out of here. Preferably, without running into Evil Gage again."

"Steel," Adam corrected.

"Whatever."

They reached the last sublevel floor by staircase instead of chancing detection in the elevator. But there was no way up to the ground floor from this stairwell. They would have to navigate their way back to the central staircase. Neither Adam nor Iris had any of their internal weaponry available inside the compound, but Adam had smuggled two knives out of the training room. They also had some decent strength if it came to it.

Iris took the lead and ran down the hall, Evie following, and Adam in the rear position. The first person they came across turned the corner in front of them with a Taser-like device in his hand. He was a muscular man wearing a light gray jumpsuit.

"Guard." Iris rushed him, ducking, and taking out his legs.

Adam moved around Evie and grabbed the guard's head, twisting it backward in one fluid, brutal motion.

The air left Evie's lungs.

Did I really just see that?

Her boyfriend almost took someone's head clear off. Another guard, dressed the same as the first, burst out from a doorway behind her. Before Evie could alert them, a blade sailed through the air in her peripheral vision. It landed in the center of the guard's chest with such force that it thrust the man backward, sinking entirely into his chest.

Evie turned back around the other way. More guards were coming from the other direction.

Iris was back on her feet in a fighting position. She punched the first guard in the face and threw him to the ground. Then another and another. Adam joined Iris, kicking and knocking out the guards' devices first.

They were both obviously trained in martial arts. Evie had no idea what kind, but they knew how to fight. The guards had a basic understanding too but paled in comparison. One by one, Adam and Iris dispatched the group of adversaries. Punch by punch. Kick by kick. Like a violent dance between Adam and Iris, they stood back to back, assisting one another every now and then like they were created for the task.

Sharp pain spread across Evie's face as something crashed into her cheek with such force that her vision blurred.

Time stood still.

Someone yelled her name. She hurtled against the wall of the corridor and fell to the floor. Evie looked at her shaking hands, her skin cold and clammy. She licked her lips tasting something pungent and metallic. Someone grasped her arm and pulled her back to her feet, her head swimming. A voice. She tried her best to focus, but the sound was distant. She stared straight ahead and tried to sink back to the floor, but the arm around her wouldn't let her. She looked up, but everything was cloudy.

She focused on the voice. "Mr. Garcia?"

Adam

Everything happened fast. First, one of the guards knocked Evie into the wall, and the next minute, Garcia was there pulling her to her feet.

"What are you doing?" Garcia yelled at the guards, squeezing a device in his hand. "They are not to be harmed."

One of the guards, a leader, tapped on a device in his ear. The other guards, still standing, came to attention.

"Leave us," Garcia said.

The leader turned and headed back down the hall. The others followed, navigating the strewn bodies in their path.

Once alone, Garcia, arm was still around Evie's waist, asked, "Why are you running?"

Uneasiness raised the hairs on the back of Adam's neck. They were at least ten feet apart. "Let her go."

"You did it, Adam. You saved both yourself and the package with a one percent chance of survival setting. You passed your final trial. I knew you could do it."

Package? Adam's gut twisted as bile rose in the back of his throat just like it did the last time he was in the arcade. "She's a human being, you sick son of a bitch."

"I know." Garcia grinned maniacally. "That's why it was such an incredible feat. You're training is complete, and once I deliver you, I will get promoted to the board for my efforts."

Delivered? Heat rose on his cheeks. He was no commodity to be handled. "I warned you once not to disrespect me."

Garcia tightened his grip on Evie, narrowing his eyes. "You are in no position to threaten me."

Bright red blood dripped from Evie's bottom lip, sending

Adam over the edge. He took a step forward. "I'm done with all of this. Let her go. We're leaving now."

Garcia pulled out the device he used on the guards and pressed a button. "You can never be done. It's who you are."

Adam faltered, his system glitching.

Beginning maintenance shutdown.

He grasped his head in his hands and groaned. "No. I'm not yours to control anymore."

Garcia laughed. "Why? Because of her?" He put the device in his lab coat pocket and pulled a gun out in its place. He ran the barrel against the side of her face.

Evie stifled a scream and closed her eyes.

Adam advanced another step, doing his best to defy his programming, which was faltering and freezing.

Iris grasped Adam's hand. "Stop."

He scanned her eyes—she was working on a plan to take Garcia out. He couldn't risk Evie getting caught in the cross-fire. He looked back at Garcia, his vision blurry. "Please, don't hurt her."

Garcia laughed. "Now that's a good one." He leaned close to Evie's face and whispered, "Do you know how many times he wanted to kill you?"

She pulled at his arm across her chest, but Garcia tightened his grip, stilling her.

Warnings of an imminent shut down sounded in his head.

Fight it. You have to stay conscious.

"Let her go, and I'll do whatever you want," Adam promised.

"According to my calculations, Garcia is not going to do that. She is the only thing standing in the way of retaining you," Iris said to Adam.

"She's right, of course." Garcia beamed at Iris. "She really is a close second—brilliant programming and beautiful exterior." He looked back at Evie. "I'm sorry. It isn't personal."

Adam squeezed his eyes shut and continued to fight against Garcia's shut down command. He tried flooding his CPU with images of Evie.

He exhaled, watching all the beautiful images he'd captured—her wide, darkened eyes when her body was pressed up against his in front of the diner, a pencil tip pressed to her lips as she concentrated on her sketchpad, her teasing smile playing DP, her curious glances on the school bus, and her face after he kissed her for the first time moments earlier, her eyes still closed.

Something shifted in his head as he gained control.

Adam cleared the shutdown warnings and revved his processor, scanning for a solution. Each scenario risked Evie being hurt. His chest constricted. He'd just as soon endure a permanent shut down then let anything happen to her.

That's it.

Adam opened his eyes and raised the knife in his trembling hand, its sharp tip grazing the tiny white scar on his left temple, a port into his CPU. Now he had to fight against his own programming. "Get your hands off her."

"What are you doing?" Garcia glared at Adam.

"Changing the stakes."

Garcia loosened his hold on Evie, his weapon dropping slightly. "I don't understand—"

"It's simple. I'll destroy your work. Now, let her go."

"Your programming doesn't allow self-destruction."

Adam inhaled deeply, his eyes on Evie's. His hand stilled

and pressed into the port. Blood dripped down the side of his face.

Garcia dropped his gun and released Evie. He put up his hands. "Okay, okay. Put the knife down."

Evie ran to Adam, and he pushed her behind him.

Iris said, "Her chance of survival has increased by ninety-two percent."

Adam nodded, lowering his knife. "Thanks, Iris. I think I got this."

"No problem," Iris said, with a slow nod.

"How are you…" Garcia's shoulders slumped, disbelief etched on his face. "But you're programmed to…."

"I don't know how it happened or whether or not I'm supposed to, but I feel. And that makes me stronger than you." Adam reached behind his back and grabbed Evie's hand. "Are you okay?"

"I think so."

Not taking his eyes off Garcia, who still wore the same blank stare, Adam said, "Let's go."

Iris asked, "Are you going to leave him alive?"

"There's nothing he can do to me now."

28

A SOLUTION

Adam

A bruise was forming on Evie's cheek, and it pained Adam to see her hurting because of him. He squeezed her hand and smiled as they emerged from the central stairwell onto the ground floor of Bio-Core.

Adam exhaled. They'd made it.

A loud whoosh of running water surrounded them. The massive lobby was filled with people in white lab coats and suits, bustling about, walking with purpose. Straight in front of them was a massive decorative geyser of water rising and falling thirty feet in the air.

"Whoa." Evie leaned on the safety railing and wall that surrounded it and peered down. "Can't see the bottom."

Adam kept one eye on Evie and continued to scan the room. At the back was a large desk and counter with three suited people standing on the opposite side. Large, protruding letters spelling out Bio-Core were mounted on the wall behind them. On either side were hallways.

A woman in a suit led a group of people wearing visitor lanyards over to the fountain. "This fountain harnesses an underground spring that flows into the Colorado River."

The people were part of a tour. So this was the front end of the facility, the public façade for what lay beneath their feet. He sensed a shift, remembering that he was above ground now. His threat threshold had returned, along with his internal weaponry.

He watched Iris. Did she feel the shift in her programming too? Her head twitched to the side, and she scanned the tour group as they looked in their direction.

Adam turned to face her head on. "Iris, look at me."

"Threats detected."

"Iris, look at me."

Iris blinked profusely, her hands shaking.

If he didn't get her under control soon, people would notice, and…she'd start killing them. Adam shook her shoulders and found the link he shared with her. "Come on…"

Finally, she focused on him. "Adam?"

"You can control it. Take deep breaths. Then shut the warnings off. You can do it."

Iris did as he instructed, breathing slowly and concentrating on his eyes.

He rubbed her upper arms. "That's it. You got this. You're strong."

After a few seconds, her hands stopped trembling. She exhaled one last time. "I am okay."

"Good." Adam reached for Evie's hand again. "Let's get to Naomi's lab."

"You don't need to ask me twice," Evie said. "Who's Naomi?"

The three made their way down one of the hallways past the customer service desk. Along the wall were glass doors with white names and titles etched on them. Finally, they found the door they were looking for.

Dr. Naomi Rice, Senior Scientist.

Adam pushed open the door. Inside was a woman sitting at a desk.

"Can I help you?" she asked.

Before Adam could reply, another door opened behind her, and Naomi stuck her head out. Adam sighed in relief.

"Thanks, Ashley. I got this." She waved at the three. "Come on back."

Adam, Evie, and Iris followed Naomi to her lab. Once inside, Naomi locked the door. Around the room were large countertops with laptops, screens, microscopes, rows and rows of test tubes, and what looked like massive refrigerators. At the back of the lab were some cots where their friends sat.

"Evie," Mazy yelled, jumping from her seat.

"Thank God you're okay." Evie ran to Mazy and threw her arms around her.

"Me?" Mazy pulled back and touched her cheek. "What about you? What happened?"

Naomi walked over to examine Evie. "That's a good question." She turned Evie's head side to side. "Looks like a simple contusion." She walked over to a cabinet and pulled out an ice pack. "Here, this will help with the swelling."

Evie took the pack and pressed it to her cheek.

"What happened?" Naomi asked.

Adam stepped forward. "Guards. One of them knocked Evie down. Then Garcia pulled a gun on her to insist that I be..." He swallowed hard. He hated the term Garcia used. "Delivered."

Naomi's eyes grew large. "What? But he's on our side."

Evie came forward. "I assure you, he's not."

Adam mulled over her use of the word "our."

Was she referring to our *side, our side—as in the people in this room? Or was there some other side within Bio-Core?*

Naomi looked between Adam and Evie, the truth sinking in. She massaged the bridge of her nose. "Damn it. Why would he screw me over like this?"

Evie raised her eyebrows. "Because he's a selfish dick?"

The others, including Naomi, stared at Evie.

"What?" she said. "He held a gun to my head. I'm allowed."

The others nodded and shrugged.

Naomi paced back and forth as she worked something out in her head. When she looked back up at Adam, she stopped. "Okay, I'll figure out what to do about that situation later. As for you, it's time for you to remember." She reached into her pocket and pulled out what looked like a key fob. She held it up in front of him. "This is a hard drive with the memories Garcia took from you of me. Trust me?"

He weighed his options and decided he didn't have much choice. He wanted answers and now. So he nodded.

Naomi placed the fob next to his right temple port. "This might feel funny for a second."

A tingling sensation started at the side of his head and spread.

"Hang on…" she said.

A rush of files flashed through his CPU. They weren't like the ones he had when Iris told him about Steel. These were clear and vivid. He inhaled sharply, as all his memories of Naomi flooded back—her kindness toward him and their talks. Her disagreement with what the facility was doing to Adam and the others and how she was trying to stop them. Tears formed in his eyes at the images of how much she cared for him.

Naomi pulled the fob away from his port and peered up at him. "Do you remember?"

"Yes." Adam pulled her close for a hug.

"Oh my gosh, you hug now." She leaned against his shoulder, her own tears wetting his shirt. "I missed you."

"I missed you too," Adam whispered.

She pulled back and wiped her eyes with a tissue from her lab coat. "Okay, we don't have much time."

Iris was looking around at the others, her right eye twitching. Adam sighed—they were going to need to do something.

Adam pointed to himself and Iris. "Is there something you can do for us so we can escape and not be traced?"

Naomi tapped her index finger on her lips. "Yes. I can take you offline."

"But won't you get in trouble?"

"Not to sound insensitive, but I have clearance to dispose of any android that isn't functioning properly. I think the two of you qualify as dysfunctional." She pointed to a metal table and went to a cabinet on wheels. "Sit."

Adam did as he was told.

"Okay, I have to make a small incision to retrieve your GPS chip. Do you want me to shut you down first?"

"No. I can handle it. Just get it out." Adam held his breath. When the pain came, he bit down on his lip and suppressed the strong urge to fight back.

"Almost got it…"

He felt every stab and dig from her instruments in his neck until finally, something popped.

"Done."

Adam sighed and hopped off the table. He didn't think Iris would be able to endure that conscious.

Naomi went over to a counter and picked up a smart tablet. She scrolled and tapped, bringing it to life, her dark eyes darting back and forth. "Okay, you're offline." She pursed her lips. "Hmm…I wonder if I could…" She tapped a few more times and scrolled. Finally, she looked up and took a deep breath. "Okay. It's a delicate procedure, but I think I can also remove your kill protocol and deactivate your internal weaponry."

"Holy shit. Did she say internal weaponry?" Luke asked, eyes wide.

Sloan swatted his arm. "Knock it off."

Adam stayed focused on Naomi. "How fast can you get it done?"

Naomi rolled up her sleeves. "No time like the present." She pointed to a metal table behind her. "Hop up."

"Her first," Adam said, pointing to Iris.

Evie grabbed Adam's arm. "No. You."

He smoothed a lock of her hair behind her ear, his heart heaving at how she cared. "I'll be fine. You saw her in the lobby. She needs it more."

Naomi nodded. "He's right, I'm afraid. She's been eyeing all of you for kill shots this whole time."

The room fell silent. Even Sloan's jaw dropped.

Iris smiled awkwardly. "If necessary, I promise that my shots will be quick. I want to be a good friend."

Naomi chuckled. "Yeah, that would be nice of you."

Realizing the others didn't share her sense of humor, she looked down at her smart tablet. She tapped a few times and Iris' eyes closed. Before she fell to the floor, Gage caught her and hoisted her in his arms.

Evie

Evie paced in the hallway between Dr. Rice's assistant's office and her lab. Now that Adam's tracking device was removed, they couldn't hunt him down. Dr. Rice said that Adam and Iris were safe in her lab, but Evie couldn't shake the feeling that time was of the essence.

What was taking so long in there?

Everyone besides Evie and Mazy was inside the lab. Adam stayed locked inside for security while the others stayed out of curiosity about the procedure.

Mazy was on a long cushioned bench against the wall. "Pacing isn't going to help. Come sit down. Dr. Rice said it would take a while."

Evie stopped and stared at her. "I know. I just wish Adam had gone first."

"It's going to be fine."

"Yeah, I'm sure you're right." Evie sat next to Mazy and took a deep breath.

"On another note, can you believe that Gage has a doppelgänger?"

"I know. It's so weird. Has he said anything more about it?"

"No, but I can see it's really bothering him."

"Well, hopefully, once we get out of here, he can get some answers. Maybe Dr. Rice knows something about it."

Mazy opened her mouth to reply but was interrupted by the sound of a voice they both recognized coming from the outer room of Dr. Rice's lab.

"I'd like to speak to Dr. Rice."

Evie covered her mouth, her eyes wide.

It was her dad, Mac Grayson. She had no idea how he'd found her, but he did. Evie looked between the locked door and Mazy.

"Oh shit," she whispered.

Mazy whispered back, "What should we do?"

Evie's mind raced. Her instinct was to stay hidden, but if she revealed herself, her dad would take her out of here, leaving Dr. Rice more time to work on Adam.

Before she could decide, the assistant said, "She's in the middle of an experiment."

"Well, I'm not leaving," Mac said.

That was it. Evie said, "Mazy, go warn the others."

Evie walked over to the door and unlocked it. Taking a deep breath, she walked out to the front waiting area.

Mac, wearing his usual sheriff's uniform, stared at her as if he had no idea who she was. "What are you doing here, Evelyn?"

She looked from his eyes to the piece of paper in his hand. Ashley, Dr. Rice's assistant was looking between her and her dad like she wanted to crawl under her desk. Evie felt sorry for her. She was about to witness some parental fireworks.

He narrowed his eyes. "Answer me."

"Um…"

"It's him, isn't it? He's got you involved in this." He closed the gap between them. "Did he do this to you?" He raised his hand to touch her cheek.

Evie held up her hands. "No, Dad, he would never. How did you know I was here?"

He glared at her. "I didn't. I'm here on official police business. Now, would you please explain why you're at a bio-tech company instead of at home, in your room, drawing like a normal teenager?"

"I can explain that, sir," Adam said from behind her.

Evie's heart stopped.

Oh no. Please don't let them kill each other. Please.

Mac put his hand on his gun holster. Evie reached back for Adam's hand, which was twitching violently. She squeezed.

"Go on," Mac said.

"I decided to visit my aunt after I left Ashwater. Evie tracked me down." He seemed under control.

Nice save.

"All right," Mac said. "I'd like to meet your aunt. Where is she?"

"She's in the middle of a lab test, but if you want to wait, she'll be out soon."

"I told you I wanted you to stay away from my daughter." Mac narrowed his eyes as Adam.

"I know, sir. That's why I left."

Mac looked from Adam to Evie, settling on Evie. "Is that true? Did you come here to find him?"

Phew. The truth was easy to sell.

Evie crossed her arms. "Yes, I did."

"Follow me," he said, stepping outside of the office into the hall.

Evie and Adam followed.

Mac turned and said to Evie, "Listen up. This is no place for you to be. I'm investigating some serious things here. Don't come here again. Do you hear me?"

"Yes." He didn't have to tell her that. She wanted to be as far away from Bio-Core as possible.

"Good. Now, I have a job to finish," Mac said and nodded at Adam. "So that meeting with your aunt will have to wait." Glancing at Evie, he said, "As for you, I'm escorting you out of here."

Evie didn't want to go anywhere until she knew that Adam was all right. But her dad wasn't giving her a choice. "Fine."

"I would like to come too sir," Adam said.

He couldn't come with her. He needed to stay here and get his procedure. "I think you should stay here."

Mac nodded. "I agree."

"No, I want to come with you."

Evie scowled at Adam. This was not working out as planned. The last thing she wanted to do was walk out of here with her dad and her boyfriend who wanted to kill each other.

29

WATERFALL

Adam

Evie was upset with him. But he wasn't going to let her out of his sight until she was safely outside of the facility. Even if her dad was capable, things were going on in this building that he couldn't imagine. Like the fact that there were a bunch of androids on the floors below them. What would Mac Grayson do if he discovered what Bio-Core was really up to downstairs? But Mac only seemed to have contemptuous eyes for him, and it put Adam on edge. Luckily, being near Evie kept him in check.

The three entered the lobby and the elevator door opened. An older man Adam didn't recognize with gray hair and tall, sturdy stature, wearing a suit, walked out of the elevator. He was on his phone talking to someone. His eyes were a piercing blue and read concerned.

"Yes, hurry up. I'll wait for you here." The man put his phone in his interior jacket pocket and glanced over at them his eye narrowing. He strode over to them, quickly narrowed his eyes at Adam and Evie, and focused on Mac. "Sheriff Grayson. My board tells me you're hassling their employees again."

"Hello, Sam. Just doing my job," Mac replied, his expression stoic.

Sam narrowed his eyes. "I don't understand. How many times do you have to come in here? There's nothing nefarious going on. I—"

"Granddad?" Gage had come into the lobby looking troubled.

Sam glanced at Gage and then back to Mac. "I have to go. These people are doing important work. Please stop hassling them." He walked over to Gage and put his arm around him. "Let's go upstairs and talk."

Gage looked back at Adam and Evie. "You guys okay?"

Adam nodded, and Evie followed suit. Adam hoped Gage's grandfather had answers for him.

After Sam and Gage got on the elevator, Adam, Evie, and Mac headed toward the front entrance. They were walking next to the fountain when Adam noticed something odd in the water over Mac Grayson's shoulder.

It was a pair of determined eyes.

Everything happened in slow motion after that. The eyes belonged to Steel, Gage's evil twin, and he raised a gun toward them. Mac was in his sights.

Without hesitation, Adam leaped into action, launching himself over the railing of the fountain, colliding with Steel. The gun went off into the air, away from Evie and her father. Adam fell, Steel along with him, into the mouth of the fountain.

Somewhere above him, Evie screamed.

Then he hit something hard, and darkness took him.

Evie

"Adam!" Evie screamed as loud as she could, hanging over the side of the fountain. She couldn't see anything past the streams of water gushing toward her. "Dad, help him!"

Mac grabbed her and pulled her down next to the railing. He gripped his personal radio in his hand. "Shots fired. I repeat, shots fired at Bio-Core. At least one man down."

"Let me go." Evie pried at her dad's hands holding her down.

Mac held on to her tightly. "Stay put. There could be another shooter."

Evie crumpled on the floor and put her head in her hands, sobbing. Her heart ached, and her ears were ringing.

From somewhere above her, she heard Mazy's voice. "Evie!"

"Jesus Christ. What are they doing here?" her dad asked.

Evie peered out with tear-ridden eyes from their hiding spot at the fountain. Mazy was crouched next to the customer service desk. Behind her were the rest of her friends, Iris, and Dr. Rice.

Mac pulled out his firearm and walked Evie over to Mazy's outstretched arms so he could clear the rest of the lobby.

"We heard the shot. What happened? Where's Adam?" Mazy asked.

"He's gone…fell down into the fountain." Evie cried into Mazy's shoulder. "Someone was in the water trying to shoot at us. He was protecting me and my dad."

Iris stepped forward and grasped Evie's hand. "I will find Adam. He is my friend."

Evie wanted to believe more than anything that Iris could do what she said. But the reality was that even if she did find him, he was most likely dead. She had looked down the fountain's shaft earlier and couldn't see a bottom. Who knew how many stories deep it went? No one could endure that kind of fall.

Before she could reply, Iris walked toward the fountain and launched herself over the side.

Mac ran over to the railing. "For the love of God, has everyone gone nuts?" He strode over to Evie and her friends. "All right, look, I don't have the faintest idea what you are all doing here, but you're going to the station. You can call your parents from there."

Naomi extended her hand. "Hello, I'm Dr. Naomi Rice."

"You're Adam's aunt?" Mac kept his hands on his hips and narrowed his eyes.

Dr. Rice nodded, eyes wide. "Yes, that's right."

"Listen, I'm sorry for what happened. A fall like that… we'll do our best to locate him."

"Thank you."

Evie couldn't take any more. Her heart was breaking in two, and the tears wouldn't stop. "He was trying to save you, even though you treated him horribly."

Mac sighed and reached for her.

She swatted at this hands. "No."

"Evie, honey, I'm sorry. You were right. I treated him unfairly."

She didn't have any more fight in her and relaxed against him, accepting her dad's comfort.

He pressed his lips to the top of her head and whispered over and over, "I'm sorry, so sorry."

Adam

Flashes of light. Images of a girl with smoky eyes and twitchy fingers. Drawings on a wall above a fluffy bed. Lips like silk. The sound of water.

Adam opened his eyes. He was lying on something cold, hard, and wet. All around him was the sound of rushing water. He tried to lift his head, but white-hot pain seared through the right side of his head. Trying to run his CPU was difficult, and he wanted to shut down.

Somewhere nearby, someone called his name. Or at least, he thought it was his name.

"Adam?"

He opened his mouth, but no words would come out. Instead, he lay there, waiting for whoever or whatever would find him.

After some time, his body was lifted.

A voice above him said, "I've got you, friend."

***

"I still can't believe it. After the fall that you took, you somehow managed to survive. You must have some reason to live." Naomi peered down at Adam, who had been in sleep mode for days since the accident.

She was right. He had the best reason of all—Evie Grayson.

All he wanted to do was get back to her, but he wasn't well

enough. He also had bad news to share with her. He'd hit his head at just the right angle during the fall, fusing his killer protocol to his CPU. Naomi was shocked that he was still functioning at all.

But more importantly, it was too dangerous to attempt the procedure she had planned. To do so would risk a permanent shut down.

He had Iris to thank for his rescue. After she found him in the fountain's shaft, she got him out and hid him in the woods outside the facility until Naomi met up with them and took them to her house. Iris was by his side ever since, like a good friend. He was happy for her too. Her procedure had been a success, and he believed she could fully assimilate into human culture without fear of harming others.

There was also the matter of Steel. Naomi said that they didn't find him and assumed that his body must have washed away, unlike Adam, who happened to land on the scaffolding. She didn't know much about him since her security clearance only extended to those like Adam. Garcia had access, but given that he had also disappeared, there wasn't an information trail.

Adam stretched his arms over his head. "So when can I get out of here?"

Naomi drew in her bottom lip. "You know what's going on inside that head of yours. Are you sure you want to go back and live with humans again? You're still dangerous. If someone rubs you the wrong way…"

She was right, but he couldn't stay away from Evie any longer. "How about this—I'll check in with you on a regular basis. I'll give you permission to run checks on my files anytime you want."

"You'd trust me to do that?"

"If it means I can go back to Ashwater, yes."

"You know, I always wanted a niece or nephew."

"And I've always wanted a family."

Naomi smiled. "Well, you've got me."

30

REUNION

Evie

In the aftermath of the escape from Bio-Core, Dr. Rice got word to Evie that Adam had been found. He was alive, barely. She promised to do everything she could to get him up and running, but it was going to take some time. The way she said "up and running" was unnerving—a reminder that he wasn't entirely human. Evie was elated that he was alive and couldn't wait to see him.

Jack and Daisy were also thrilled to hear that he was all right. They had made some renovations to the arcade, including turning Adam's room into a proper studio apartment. Evie wasn't sure if Adam planned on staying in Ashwater or not, but a nice place to stay was a good start.

She and her friends also made a pact to keep Adam's secret, and that also meant keeping quiet about what happened to them at Bio-Core. If they told anyone, the trail could lead back to Adam. As far as they knew, Dr. Rice had covered Adam's trail from Bio-Core, and no one else besides their group of friends knew how stupid smart he really was. Evie wanted to include Jack and Daisy, but that wasn't her decision to make—it was Adam's.

Evie lay on her bed staring at her wall of Adam. She'd put away all her drawings of him with bionic parts in a box in her closet. No need to draw suspicion, he already had a robotic personality at times. Thoughts of him made her smile.

A knock on her door caused her to sit up. "Hey, can we come in?"

"Sure."

Evie's parents walked in and stood in front of her. Her dad had a folded paper in his hand. It was the letter she had written to them earlier that day.

Serena glided her fingertips across a few drawings on her wall. "Evelyn, you are so talented. I really like this one."

Evie glanced at the picture of Adam sitting in her chair. She blushed as the memory of that night flooded back. "Yeah."

Mac asked, "Is it healthy for her to have so many drawings of the same boy?"

Serena turned to him and laughed. "You don't understand an artist's mind. That's okay, honey."

"Is this what you really want?" Mac waved the letter around.

"Yes."

He glanced at Serena and sighed. "And you're okay with this too?"

Serena sat next to Evie and put her arm around her. "Yes. She needs time. Let's give it to her."

"Thanks." Evie smiled at her mom.

Mac nodded. "Well, even if I felt differently, it appears I'm outnumbered."

Excitement welled in Evie's belly. "Does this mean you're…okay with me not going to college?"

"Well, I don't know why you had to write this letter instead of talking to me about it." Mac squinted at a drawing in the corner of the piece of paper. "And is this supposed to be me? I don't scowl like that…"

Evie and her mom exchanged glances and erupted in laughter. That was precisely why she wrote the letter.

Mac looked up and smiled. "What?"

Evie got up and hugged her dad. "Thanks, Dad. I appreciate you supporting me."

He squeezed her tightly. "Always."

Evie pulled her hair in a high ponytail and slid her feet into her favorite floral docs and headed downtown. She was meeting with Mazy and the others to hang out at Jack's. She liked being in the arcade because it reminded her of Adam, and she missed him terribly. Later she had plans to work with her mom restoring some art pieces. Her mind was awhirl, and she couldn't think of a more skilled and talented person to learn from.

She stood outside Jack's, looking at the new sign with all the letters lit properly. Good as new. She opened the door and stepped inside.

Her breath caught at the back of her throat.

There, surrounded by their friends, was Adam. As soon as his gaze met hers, the jukebox changed, and a slow familiar piano riff started—"In Your Eyes" by Peter Gabriel.

Evie smiled. He was back.

Jack, who had one arm around Adam and the other around Daisy, asked, "Say, are you ever going to explain how you do that?"

"Maybe," Adam replied, not taking his eyes off Evie's. He walked over to Evie as the others faded away with the music.

She breathed in and out, trying to steady herself, and searched his eyes to make sure it was still him in there. A new, pink scar ran perpendicular through the old, circular one on his right temple. She reached to touch it. "Are you okay?"

He parted his lips. "I am now."

"You're staying?"

"If you're here."

"Great." Evie couldn't wait another second. She reached for him and pulled his lips to hers to seal the deal. He felt warm and right.

When his lips left hers, he leaned down and nuzzled the nape of her neck. "I missed you."

She giggled as his breath tickled her delicate skin.

The others joined them.

Derrick stuck his head in between them. "Okay, you two. Reunion time is over. Who wants to go to paradise?"

Adam grabbed Evie's hand, his eyes lighting up. "I'm already there."

EPILOGUE

Gage

Gage stood at the back of the *Dance Paradise* game room, his arms crossed over his chest. Luke and Derrick stood at the game console, fighting over what song to play next. He chuckled.

"Pick a song," he yelled over to them.

Both boys turned toward him with the exact same *it's his fault* expression. Must be a twin thing.

They could carry on like that for a half an hour before deciding which song would be the fairest. Gage turned and left the room to play a different game.

He liked Jack's Arcade. He'd always stopped in from time to time to play a few games, but now he seemed to be here much more. Must have something to do with his android friend. After saving Adam at Bio-Core, Gage had struck a deal with his granddad. What he really wanted was answers, but his granddad wouldn't budge. So instead, Gage agreed that he and his friends would keep quiet about what they'd seen at the facility if Bio-Core didn't come after Adam and Iris.

He shivered. Over the past few months, his hometown of Ashwater had gone from quirky to a hotbed for the strange and unusual. Between the decades of missing people, including his mother, killer androids, and now, his supposed evil twin, he didn't know what to think anymore.

Gage emerged into the main arcade room and found Mazy playing a shooting game with Sloan by the front. Adam and Evie were perched on stools at Daisy's snack bar. Evie had her sketch pad out, drawing, glancing around at the new equipment while Adam ran his hands up and down her arms.

"I swear, you are the biggest distraction," Evie said. "I'm trying to capture some of the remod for Jack and Daisy. They're paying me for these, you know."

Adam looked up and noticed Gage. He hopped off the stool. "Okay, I'll leave you to it."

"Thank you." Evie leaned up and kissed him.

Gage couldn't help but be a little jealous. Hell, if an android could find a girl, why couldn't he? He hated that he thought that way, but that was human nature, wasn't it?

Adam walked over to Gage. "Hey, what's up?"

"Not much. Luke and Derrick are fighting about songs again. Thought I'd play something out here."

Adam smirked naturally.

Good. He was getting better at being human. Truth be told, Gage didn't actually know how much of Adam was biological and how much was computer. But since he had a human girlfriend, he guessed quite a bit of the former.

Chimes sounded as the front door to the arcade opened. Gage's mouth dropped as the spitting image of him walked inside. It was like he could feel the presence in more than only his sight.

Was this Steel?

He'd told himself that the others must have imagined who they saw at Bio-Core, but here he was in the flesh.

There was a shift in Adam's demeanor, and fast as lightning, Evie was by his side holding his hand. Mazy and Sloan turned from their game to stare at the boy.

"Miss me?" The boy raised his hands in a grand gesture and glanced around at them. He turned toward Mazy and Sloan. He approached Mazy and reached for a lock of her hair. "Hey, cutie."

She flinched.

That was enough to set Gage off. "Don't touch her."

The boy looked back at Gage, his eyes narrowing. "Right."

He left the girls and sauntered over to where Gage, Adam, and Evie stood. Christ, it was like looking into a mirror. How could this be?

"Give us a moment?" the boy said to Adam and Evie.

Adam stood his ground.

But Gage nodded. "It's okay."

"Come on." Evie pulled Adam toward Mazy and Sloan, who were watching the exchange from the front.

Once alone, the boy said, "We've not been formally introduced. I'm Steel."

"I don't care who you are. You stay away from me and my friends."

Steel pursed his lips. "Is that any way to treat your brother?"

Gage stared at him, his mind working overtime. He couldn't be. This was a trick. He shook his head. "No—"

Steel arched his left eyebrow and smirked. His voice sounded in Gage's head, *I'm quite sure we are.*

Gage touched his right temple and took a few steps back. "How did you do that?"

The same way I gave you the combination to the doors at Bio-Core. Steel's voice was in his head again.

"Stay out of my head."

Steel rolled his eyes. "You're no fun." He looked around. "How can you hang out here? It's so boring."

Gage stared at Steel. He was claiming to be his brother. A twin brother, at that. And Gage could hear Steel's thoughts in his head?

Before Gage could say anything else, Steel sauntered away, back to the front of the arcade where the others eyed him.

"I'll leave you to process, bro." He waved his hand nonchalantly. In Gage's head, he said, *Oh, and before I forget, Mom says hi.*

Gage lost his breath like someone had punched him in the gut.

Steel turned to Adam, who was standing by the jukebox, "Something fitting, please."

Adam's face scrunched up like he was struggling with something in his mind. The jukebox turned on, and "Welcome to the Jungle" by Guns and Roses started playing.

"Nice," Steel said, nodding slowly. "I like your style, tin can." He turned one last time to face the group. "See you soon."

ABOUT THE AUTHOR

Melissa Koberlein is a professor of communication and publishing in eastern Pennsylvania where she lives with her husband and their two daughters. She enjoys reading and writing about the spectacular, sci-fi, technology, and romance. Her passion for stories comes from an imaginative childhood where every day ended with a book. *Ashwater* is her newest young adult series. You can read her first series, *Fireflies*, available from Amazon and other retail outlets.

ALSO BY MELISSA KOBERLEIN

"A mix of Twilight and I am Number Four, the twist at the end was unpredictable, making it a good turn adding spice and intrigue to the plot." -Review from Writer's Digest

"Teen romance readers will devour this book. Fans of Twilight and The Host will also enjoy this book." -Online Book Club Review

And coming soon...

RAVEN'S SPHERE

DEADLOCK

Made in the USA
Middletown, DE
29 August 2019